BLINDERS

Kristy Shelton

Publishing

Published by
Innovo Publishing, LLC
www.innovopublishing.com
1-888-546-2111

Publishing

Providing Full-Service Publishing Services for
Christian Authors, Artists & Organizations: Hardbacks, Paperbacks,
eBooks, Audiobooks, Music & Videos

BLINDERS

Scripture is taken from the King James Version of the Bible.

Except as noted by the author, the characters and events
in this novel are fictitious.

ISBN 13: 978-1-936076-65-9
ISBN 10: 1-936076-65-9

Cover Design & Interior Layout: Innovo Publishing, LLC

Printed in the United States of America
U.S. Printing History
First Edition: March 2011

In loving memory of Memaw
Blanche Gano Rollmann
April 28, 1909–August 9, 1989

Acknowledgments

I hold a great deal of gratitude in my heart for the special people who stood beside me as this book was being written. However, before I can thank any of them, I must give my total praise and honor to the One who made it possible. Without God's divine providence and faithfulness, I could not have completed a project of this magnitude while also teaching and coaching full time. I'm thankful that God gave me *the dream* along with an undying obsession to continue writing, despite my busy schedule. I pray that every word is just the way He wants it and that this book will bring honor to the name of Jesus.

I am blessed to have some very dear friends who took the time to read my first draft and gave me their honest feedback. My heart friend, Andrea Popham, along with fellow teachers Darcy Huber and Catrina Baldwin, were invaluable to me as I picked their brains for ideas of how to make this novel better. Each one of them had so many wonderful ideas, thoughts, and questions that were of vital importance for each rewrite. Their enthusiasm for the book is what kept me going, especially during the times that I doubted the story or my ability as a writer.

Thank you to my first editor, Tammy Hughes, one of our high-school English teachers. Tammy kept my manuscript for an entire month, working through it three times. If I had to pay her for every comma she inserted, she would be a very rich woman today!

I want to thank my mother, Norma Rollmann, who also read my first draft. I appreciate her prayers and encouragement so much. All I wanted to know was if she cried when she read it. She did. Success! Just remember, Mom, there are no regrets. You are an amazing mother—I am who I am today because of you.

A special thanks goes to Karen Cherry for her steady pushing and prodding for the past five years. There is no way to number how many times she asked in passing, "Have you started that book yet?" It was her wonderful Writer's Workshop in the summer of 2006 that helped me recapture the imagination I thought I had lost.

To my husband, Cliff—what can I say? So many times you wanted to talk to me while I was writing. You were such a good sport to find odd jobs around the house or wait patiently for me to finish a thought. Dinner was occasionally late and you often headed to bed without me during this journey, but you gave me so much encouragement to keep going. Thanks for being so understanding. God knew what He was doing when He put us together more than thirty years ago.

To my son, Ty, and daughter, Alex, I love you dearly. I hope you don't mind, but I'm glad you were away at college while I was writing!

Finally, I want to thank the folks at Innovo Publishing. For months I prayed that God would put my manuscript into the right hands and I believe He led me to Innovo. I am grateful to Bart Dahmer for making the decision to take a chance on a first-time author. I will never forget our first conversation on the phone and his unwavering spiritual focus. I am also grateful for the wonderful support I have received from Terry Bailey and Yvonne Parks, along with much appreciation for senior editor, Darya Crockett, whose encouraging words are imprinted on my heart.

Prologue

Fall 1910

Rachel Wyatt stood beside her husband's grave searching her heart for the right words. She glanced at her nine-year-old son as he climbed on a rock wall not far away. Rachel knew her son's life was about to change drastically, and she prayed that it would be for the better. When Eugene sat down on top of the wall, Rachel turned her attention back to her husband. For some strange reason, she was struggling to remember James' voice. It had been eight long years since his passing, but up until this moment she had always been able to hear his deep, southern voice echoing through her mind. Maybe it was a sign from God. Maybe she truly was making the right decision to marry again.

Eugene had never known his father. He was only ten months old when the accident happened that left Rachel a young widow. James Wyatt had been a handy man and well known in Winchester, Kentucky for his ability to fix anything. He had a reputation as a hard-working honest man, which brought him steady work six days a week. If your wagon broke down, James would fix it; if your roof needed repair, James could repair it; if your stovepipe cracked, James knew how to replace it; and if your horse needed shoeing, James Wyatt was your man. He took pride in the fact that he had a way with horses, even the ornery ones that wouldn't stand still for anyone else to shod.

As Rachel knelt on the grass, she quietly asked James to forgive her for the anger she had briefly carried after his death. He had left her to raise their son alone all because of his stubborn pride. James had always called it confidence, but whatever it was, it ultimately cost him his life.

Everyone in town knew that old Mr. Simpson owned the meanest horse this side of the Mississippi. James Wyatt had been so sure that he could nail shoes on Buck. Even a small crowd of locals had gathered to watch him do it. With three shoes already in place, James was working on the back right hoof when a bucket was inadvertently knocked off a bench by one of the bystanders. The noise startled Buck, and he kicked both hind legs with such force that James was knocked to the ground. Before he could roll out of the way, the horse had dealt a fatal blow to James' head. Two local men jumped the fence and pulled James away from the startled animal, but there was nothing anyone could do for him. As soon as old man Simpson heard one of the men pronounce James dead, he went into the house and emerged moments later with a shotgun. Without a single word, Mr. Simpson dropped Buck to the ground right next to James' body.

Rachel glanced over to the wall of the cemetery and realized Eugene was no longer there. She noticed he was exploring around some of the older gravesites. He seemed to be fascinated by the huge stone monument erected to the founder of Clark County. She had asked him not to wander out of her sight, so she knew he wouldn't go far.

Rachel breathed in the fresh, autumn air, trying to rid herself of that old feeling of shock and pain she had experienced eight years earlier. She tried to block the memory of walking to the doctor's office with a crying baby in her arms while the preacher and his wife held her steady. Preacher Holden's wife, Olivia, had gently taken Eugene from Rachel's arms and remained outside to try to stop his crying. For some reason, Rachel remembered how quiet it had been inside the doctor's office that day—deathly quiet. Her James was lying on the table with a cloth wrapped around his head. Rachel's first thought was how hard she would have to work to get the bloodstains out of her husband's work shirt. But when she touched his cold skin, she knew in her heart he was gone. It took much longer for her mind to catch up with her heart as she had asked the doctor repeatedly, "Is this real?"

Pulling herself back to the present, Rachel ran her hand through the grass on top of her husband's grave. "I'm going to get married next week." She paused as if there would be some response, but the only sound she heard was the rustling of the colorful leaves in the trees.

Rachel nervously continued, "James, you were my first love and for that reason you'll always be in my heart. You gave me the greatest treasure of all. You gave me Eugene. I wish you could see him now; he's so much like you."

As a matter of fact, nearly everything about Eugene reminded Rachel of James—his dark hair and eyes, the hint of a dimple in his chin, and his easy-going confident manner.

Eugene suddenly appeared at her side and dropped down cross-legged on the grass beside his mother. "Mama, have you told Daddy about Louis yet?"

"Yes, I told him," she said gently.

"Do you think he minds?" Eugene was searching his mother's face to make sure they weren't doing anything to hurt his daddy in some way.

"He won't mind, Eugene. Your daddy always wanted what was best for you and me."

Rachel rose to her feet and reached down for Eugene's hand.

Eugene hopped to his feet and put his hand in hers. "Will Louis be my daddy now?" he asked.

"He'll be your stepfather and . . ."

Eugene didn't give his mother a chance to finish her sentence before he asked, "What should I call Louis after you marry him?"

Rachel laughed softly and said, "You can call him Daddy or Papa if you like, or you could even call him Mr. Louis. It will take a little time for you both to get used to each other, but I think you'll know what to call him soon enough."

Mother and son walked hand in hand through the

cemetery toward their small house in the middle of town. Rachel had tried desperately for the last few months to hang on to the house she and James had bought when they first got married in the summer of 1899. But this past year had been a hard one. Old man Simpson passed away, and he had been one of the primary reasons Rachel had been able to hang onto the house. Every month since the accident, Mr. Simpson had faithfully paid money into an account for Rachel and Eugene. Adding Mr. Simpson's money to the small salary she brought in as a seamstress, Rachel was able to provide for her and Eugene the way James had. But it was quickly evident after Mr. Simpson's death that she could never bring in enough income on her own to make the necessary payments on the house.

Fortunately, Rachel had met Louis Tillman at a church social back in April, some five months ago. Louis was nothing like James, in fact, nearly the complete opposite. The only thing the two men had in common was their height—both of them approaching the six-foot mark. Any other similarities stopped there. Louis was now in his mid-thirties, five years Rachel's senior, and slightly balding with sandy brown hair. He was a quiet man, a little on the shy side, and had never been married before.

According to Louis, he had fallen in love with Rachel at first sight. During the social, he had watched her from across the crowded room for a long time before he got up enough nerve to speak to her. Rachel was struck by the kindness and warmth in Louis' blue eyes, and they spent the rest of that evening talking and enjoying each other's company.

During the last five months, Louis had taken Rachel out to dinner on several occasions, but he much preferred a quiet evening on her front porch talking. He was kind to Eugene and always brought him a small gift on the evenings he would be taking his mother out. Rachel had slowly fallen in love with Louis and easily accepted his proposal of marriage just one month ago.

Eugene let go of his mother's hand, and Rachel watched as he excitedly ran into their next-door neighbor's yard. His best friend, Robert, was outside playing on this sunny Saturday morning. Rachel smiled as the two boys raced into the backyard to play in the tree house that Robert's father had built. Her smile quickly faded as she realized Eugene would no longer be able to run outside and play with Robert whenever he felt like it. The only time Eugene would be able to see his best friend now would be at school.

As she walked into the house, Rachel felt a cold wave move over her despite the warmth of the October morning. She sat down in an armchair as the shiver went up her spine. The slightest apprehension passed through her mind, but Rachel quickly dismissed the feeling as she looked at the packing boxes scattered around her parlor. It was only natural for her to feel nervous about leaving the house she had lived in for over ten years. She only wished Louis didn't live so far outside of town.

Once again, Rachel hoped and prayed that this would be the start of a wonderful new life for her and Eugene. After all, Eugene would finally have the father he always wanted.

Chapter 1

Summer 1912

Eugene awoke with a start, instinctively covering his head in preparation for the next blow. Hearing Louis snore loudly in the next room greatly reduced the panic that had sent his heart racing. In the early morning gloom, he watched his belly rise and fall and felt his heart slow down from its galloping pace. Each breath brought a dull ache to his ribs, but Eugene was just thankful to wake up one more day, even if it meant facing the wrath of his stepfather Louis. He allowed himself to relax for a moment, and his thoughts began to wander to the only person he'd ever known who loved him. If it hadn't been for his mother, he would scarcely have known that love even existed. She had been tender and kind, and he longed to be back in her arms where he felt safe and secure. But ever since the sickness took her away last autumn, his life had been nothing short of miserable.

Eugene was jarred from his thoughts by the sudden silence. He quickly jumped to his feet from the pallet where he slept on the floor. If he were still lying there when Louis walked in the room, he would surely receive a swift kick to his side. He doubted whether his ribs could handle another assault. Eugene was so frightened of his stepfather that he was beginning to wonder if he would reach his twelfth birthday.

In the dark and musty back room of the house, Louis put his bare feet onto the wooden floor but didn't dare stand until the nausea passed. His head was pounding from a hard night of drinking, and his tongue seemed to be stuck to the roof of his mouth. He rubbed his hands through his thinning hair as the reality of his life washed over him anew. Every morning when he woke up, he was keenly aware that he did so alone.

When Eugene's mother Rachel died of pneumonia, Louis felt like his heart had been ripped right out of his chest. Any love or compassion that had ever existed in his life was now buried inside Rachel's coffin. To make matters worse, the distillery where he had worked for sixteen years had shut down only two weeks after Rachel's death. Now that his wife was gone, Louis had one less mouth to feed, but oh how he wished it was the boy lying underneath the Kentucky bluegrass and not his precious Rachel. That Louis felt a bit angry after Rachel's death was an understatement. He could barely control his raging emotions. It just seemed so much easier to drink the homemade whiskey to dull his senses and take his anger out on a boy who wasn't his own child to begin with. It made *him* feel better and never once did it enter his mind how Eugene might have felt after losing his mother.

"Boy, you better have my coffee ready." Louis walked into the front room of the house, secretly hoping Eugene was still lying on his pallet. No such luck. Eugene had a fire going in the pot-bellied stove and a kettle already steaming with hot coffee. The boy even had his eggs sliding off the skillet onto a plate, over-easy just the way he liked them. Something in the look on the boy's face reminded him of Rachel, and before Louis could rub the stiffness out of his neck, he was already filled with a rage he didn't know how to control. He pictured himself back-handing the boy across the face. If he didn't think he'd lose his precious eggs to the dog he would've done it. Instead, he snarled for Eugene to hurry it up and get outside to take care of the chores.

Eugene quickly started on his chores, yearning for the day that his stepfather would be satisfied with his work. No matter how many chores the boy got done, Louis never seemed to be content. Eugene had long ago given up on the hope that there might be a word of thanks at the end of the day. Now, the only thought that consumed him was avoiding Louis at all cost. On most days that was hard to do, seeing as how his stepfather rarely left the house to go into town.

As Eugene spread the feed along the ground for the chickens, he kept tugging down on the legs of his overalls. He'd outgrown most of his clothes last spring, but there was still one pair of overalls he could fit in as long as the straps were let all the way out. Even if he was allowed to venture into town, Eugene didn't have any money to buy new clothes, not even a penny to buy a piece of hard candy. He was embarrassed to think about starting school next fall without clothing that fit properly. Somehow he would have to muster up enough nerve to broach the subject with his stepfather. Just imagining how that conversation would go turned his stomach sour.

Eugene looked over the horizon as the summer sun began to fully appear. If he squinted just right, he could make the light into a perfect cross. He'd always loved Sunday mornings when it was just him and his mother. Bright and early they would set out for church from their small house in the middle of Winchester. While the buggies and wagons rolled into town, Rachel and Eugene would wave to the fellow churchgoers as they passed. Rachel was one of the few women in church who could sing harmony. Sometimes Eugene would find himself singing alto with his mother's strong clear voice, but most times he just sang the melody along with the rest of the congregation.

Occasionally, Rachel and her son would be invited to share dinner with one of the families from church. But on the Sundays when no one offered, they'd just walk back home hand in hand and eat their dinner together. Eugene remembered one such meal when his mother told him how special he must be to God. "He made sure you were born on the very first day of January 1901. That makes you a special *one* to me and to God." Since he had never known his real father, Eugene felt certain he was the only *one* in the world his mother truly loved, that is until Louis came along.

Eugene still enjoyed Sundays. Even though Louis stopped taking him to church after his mother died, Sunday was the day he got to go fishing down at the river. During the summer he could catch enough fish to last him and Louis most of the week. It wasn't hard finding worms along the banks of Howard Creek and by the time the sun had fully appeared, Eugene was already sitting in his favorite fishing spot. He'd found this spot only a couple of weeks earlier in the shade of a large sycamore tree where a small pool had formed along the bank. Fish loved to congregate in the shade underneath that tree.

Before noon, both of his tin buckets were filled with fish, and he leaned back against the huge sycamore to relax for just a few minutes before he had to carry his heavy load back to the house.

Suddenly, a light appeared from nowhere. He wasn't sure where the light was coming from, but it had a soft, welcoming glow and Eugene was drawn to it like a June bug to a lantern. It wasn't an easy walk through bushes and scrub, but when he finally arrived at the light he was welcomed into an old house. There was a table in front of him loaded down with all kinds of food. A woman held out a chair and beckoned him with her hand to sit and eat. Somehow the woman reminded him of his mother, but not entirely—he couldn't quite put his finger on it. As he began to eat, he realized they were not alone. There was also a man at the table sitting in the shadows, so there was no way Eugene could make out his face. But the feeling of joy overtook him as if this was where he belonged. He ate and ate until his belly could hold no more, and when he pushed back from the table, the woman ushered him into another room where she tucked him into the most comfortable feather bed and covered him with a soft quilt. It was heavenly.

When Eugene awoke from his sleep, his back was hurting and his neck was stiff. How could a feather bed give him such a backache he wondered, and it was at that moment terror struck his heart. He had fallen asleep with his back to the tree trunk— the light, the food, the bed . . . it was all a dream and by the looks of the sun, it was now late afternoon.

Eugene jumped to his feet, gathered his pole and buckets, and raced for the house. How could he have allowed himself to fall asleep? With every step, he pleaded with God to spare him from his stepfather's anger. By the time he arrived in the yard, he was out of breath and nearly all the water had been sloshed from the buckets. A sick feeling wrapped itself around his gut as he looked up to the porch and saw Louis standing there, arms folded across his chest and a snarl on his face. *Please God, oh please don't let him kill me.*

"Where the devil have you been all afternoon, boy?" The words just seemed to sizzle out of Louis' mouth.

For a split second, Eugene was tempted to tell his stepfather that *the fish just didn't seem to be bitin' today*, but instead the truth came tumbling out of his mouth along with a very sincere apology. Eugene's politeness must have taken the edge off of Louis' temper. To his surprise, Louis just turned back around and retreated into the house, slamming the door behind him.

Almost feeling guilty for not being chastised further, Eugene quickly made his way to the filet stone with his buckets of fish. He didn't quite know how to respond when Louis chose to leave him alone.

The first bluegill glistened in the sun as Eugene laid it out on the large, flat stone protruding from the ground. Louis had taught him how to filet fish like an expert; for that matter, Louis was the one who had taught him how to fish. But that was back in the day when his mother was alive and Louis didn't drink his nights away. Eugene snuck quietly into the house to get a tin bowl out of the kitchen and tear several pages out of the *Sears* catalog. He pumped some water from the well for his bowl and put the fish that he would fry for supper into the water. The other fish he wrapped in the pages of the catalog and took them into the shed to store in the icebox. A large block of ice was delivered every Monday morning to the house, so tomorrow morning there would be more ice to help keep the fish cold for the rest of the week.

Later that evening, after a tense supper of fish and biscuits, Louis disappeared into the woods behind the house while Eugene was left to clean up the mess in the kitchen. An hour later, Louis emerged from the woods carrying a jug of homemade moonshine. Eugene knew he had to keep busy and stay out of his way for the rest of the evening. But that proved to be a difficult if not impossible task.

Louis sunk down in a hardback chair on the back porch and scrutinized every move Eugene made. He watched him shoo the chickens into the hen house for the night, feed the dog his mush made from supper's leftovers, water the vegetables in the garden, and finally sweep off the back porch steps.

The more Louis drank, the angrier he became. The rage started deep in his gut and began working its way up into his chest. By the time it reached his mouth, vile words began to spew out toward Eugene who stood motionless on the bottom step. Louis had taught the boy not to look a wild animal directly in the eyes if he should ever encounter one. A wild animal would perceive direct eye contact as a challenge, so it was always best to look down.

The boy appeared to be following that principle now, and that small act alone set Louis' blood boiling.

"You slept through your afternoon chores, you lazy, good for nothin' . . ." He noticed with delight, Eugene wince at his choice of words. "Get up here on this porch and take your punishment."

When Eugene didn't move, Louis jumped to his feet and yelled, "NOW!"

Eugene obediently dropped his broom to the ground and climbed the four steps to the top of the porch. Louis ripped off his belt in one motion, grabbed Eugene by the back of the neck, and leaned him over the splintery porch railing. The first blow wasn't as hard as Louis would've liked since he still had a hold on Eugene's neck with his left hand. But then he let go of his grip and reared back to swing with all his might. If Eugene ever pleaded for him to stop, he would take that as a challenge to make it last longer. Louis noticed tears streaming down the boy's face as he silently counted each blow—*seven, eight, nine, ten.* Tonight his rage was the worst he'd ever felt. On the twelfth blow, he let the belt drop with a clank onto the porch and licked his lips to prepare for a long swig from the jug. He was feeling a bit exhausted and definitely thirsty.

He moved over to the bench leaning against the wall of the house and snarled, "Now come 'ere and sit down beside me."

Eugene crept slowly toward him and eased down onto the bench, letting the slightest whimper escape his mouth. Before Louis even gave it a conscious thought, he struck Eugene hard across the face with the back of his hand.

Seeing the defenseless boy lying on the floor of the porch gave Louis an exhilarating feeling. He knew that stopping now was not an option. He'd never struck Eugene in the face before—he didn't want the boy going to school with visible bruises. He'd just as soon keep the sheriff from coming out to his place to question him about it. That would only compromise the whiskey still he had running in the woods behind the house. But this was summer, and there was nobody to see the bruises now.

"Go get that broom and start sweepin' this porch."

Eugene silently rose to his feet and picked up the broom out in the yard. He started sweeping the other end of the porch, too far away for Louis to reach him.

"Boy, come sweep over here where I'm sittin'."

Louis snickered at the kind of control he held over this boy. Just as Eugene got close enough, he kicked the broom out of his hands then whispered in a low voice, "Pick it up."

Lifting the broom, Eugene started to sweep again and had it kicked out of his hands for the second time.

"I said, pick it UP."

With trembling hands, Eugene obediently picked up the broom, but this time Louis snatched it out of his hands and unleashed a beating on him like never before. When it was over, he picked the boy up by the back of his overalls, carried him into the house, carelessly banging his head against the doorframe, and threw him onto his pallet with a heavy thud. Louis stood over him, laughing at the *pile of fodder* crumpled at his feet. "Sleep tight; don't let the bed bugs bite."

For several long minutes, Eugene lay completely still as his stepfather's wicked laughter echoed through his head. When he finally tried to move, every inch of his body screamed in pain. *Lord, I need your help; I think I'm dying.* And with that thought, Eugene mercifully slipped into unconsciousness.

A few hours later, Eugene awoke to Louis' loud snoring in the next room. Only one thought crossed the boy's mind: if he didn't get to the outhouse soon, there was going to be an accident. He knew Louis was sleeping off a long evening of drinking and wouldn't wake up even if he slammed the door. But just to be safe, Eugene crawled quietly across the floor and into the kitchen where he used the table to pull himself to his feet. It was a slow and painful process. Eugene silently unlatched the door and stepped out onto the back porch. His eyes moved to the end of the porch where he'd suffered the worst beating of his life. He suddenly felt nauseated and had to willfully hold back the lurching of his stomach. Just as he turned in the dark to negotiate the steps, Eugene caught a glimpse of it. He blinked hard once, then twice, but it was still there. It was the soft, welcoming glow of a light in the distance. Somehow that light was calling him. He couldn't explain it if he had to, but just staring at it filled him with a sense of hope—the kind of hope he'd given up on long ago.

Eugene glanced over his shoulder at Louis' window in the back of the house. Repulsion cramped his stomach again and made his head hurt even worse, so he quickly turned back to the light. At that moment, he was certain that he would not spend another minute on his stepfather's property. After relieving himself in the outhouse, Eugene started walking away from the house without giving much thought to where the light was leading him. Every step away from Louis gave him the courage to take yet another. There were times he lost sight of the light through the trees, but he always knew he was walking in the right direction. Twice he crossed a narrow stream and finally came out on an old dirt road, which he followed step after painful step. The light was much farther away than he had anticipated, but he was determined to persevere.

Eugene felt he was close now, and he turned off the road onto a path through the woods that led him up a steep hill. Emerging from the trees, he now saw that the light was coming from a house on the other side of an open pasture, and he could just make out its outline in the dark. The grass in the pasture felt cool and soothing to his bare feet, but suddenly his view of the house and the light became obstructed. Cold chills crept up the back of his neck as Eugene realized he was not alone. Something enormous bumped up against him and he was shoved up against another huge object, and before he knew it, he was flying through the air landing with a thud in the grass. This time, Eugene couldn't be quiet. He covered his head and began to scream with fright and cry out in pain. He could hear snorts and whinnies and hooves pawing at the ground, and he knew he was about to be trampled by wild horses. Just as he thought he was surely about to die, Eugene was swooped up into a pair of strong arms and held tightly against a warm body. He sensed swift movement toward the light, and then he was enveloped in total darkness.

Chapter 2

Franklin didn't know what to make of the boy. Surely the horses hadn't done this much damage before he could get to him. Rachel rushed into the room with a basin of water and a washcloth, nudging Franklin out of the way so she could start to work on the boy. As she gently removed his overalls, she let out a muffled cry. He was bruised and bleeding from head to toe. Franklin was certain his thoroughbreds had not inflicted these wounds, but who would have done such a terrible thing?

"Why, he can't be more than ten or twelve years old," she whispered.

Franklin nodded his head in agreement but knew better than to get in Rachel's way. Her gentle hands washed the boy's whole body clean and dressed the open wounds. Finally, Franklin helped her cover him in one of his softest shirts. Lovingly, his wife pulled the light quilt up around the boy's shoulders and told Franklin to get himself to bed.

"I'll stay by his side, in case he wakes up during the night," she said.

Franklin took a long look at the boy, and before he left the room, he put one big strong hand on the boy's forehead, clasping Rachel's hand with the other. "Our Father in heaven, you're the only one to know what's caused this boy's troubles. Would you touch his body and heal his wounds? In Jesus' precious name and Amen."

"Amen," Rachel echoed. "Now get on to bed, Franklin. I'll let you know if he wakes up before morning."

***

As the morning sun began to stream through the windows and the numerous gaps in their house, Franklin lightly touched Rachel on the shoulder. She had been sleeping in a straight back chair with her head down on the boy's bed. Instantly she sat up and noticed Franklin standing over her, dressed and ready for the day.

"How's he doin'?" Franklin asked in a hushed voice.

Rachel began to hastily rearrange the quilt as tears welled up in her eyes. "He hasn't moved all night long. I hope he's going be all right. I just can't stand the thought of someone treating this boy so horribly," she whispered.

"Who do you think he's belongin' to, Rach?" The concern in Franklin's voice matched her own.

"I don't have any idea, but there's no way I'll let this boy go back to someone who beats him like this." Rachel had a burning conviction in her eyes that said you'd have to go through her to ever lay a hand on this boy again.

All during breakfast, Rachel kept leaving her husband at the table to check on the boy. She had no intention of letting him wake up in a strange house all alone. His tanned face looked so sweet and peaceful in contrast to the wounds on his body, which spoke to the horror he must have faced the night before. On her third trip to his room, she couldn't help but smooth her hand across his dark hair. God had never seen fit to give her a child of her own, but even at her advanced age she had a fierce maternal instinct.

Franklin carried his cup and plate to the wash bucket and told Rachel to holler for him as soon as the boy woke up. "I done checked on the horses at first light this mornin'" he said. "They was awful spooked last night so I need to have a long talk with 'em today." Rachel nodded to her husband even as she headed to the back room for the fourth time.

The day crept by slowly for Rachel as she waited for the boy to show some signs of waking up. She soaked a clean cloth and squeezed water into his mouth every couple of hours and changed the dressing on his wounds. When Franklin finally came back to the house just before supper, he found Rachel sitting on the bed with the boy wrapped in her arms, his head against her breast. She was quietly singing hymns as she stroked his hair. She looked up as Franklin entered the room. "He hasn't made so much as a sound all day."

"I 'specs he needs all the rest he can get so he can heal."

Rachel thought for a long moment before asking Franklin the question she'd been pondering. "If he doesn't wake up in the morning, do we dare send for Dr. Randall in Winchester?"

"Rach, you know that ain't safe. We gotta trust that the Almighty will lay His healin' hand on this boy."

This time it was Rachel who broke out in prayer. With tears streaming down her cheeks, she pleaded to the Great Physician to visit Himself on this boy. She knew her emotions were running rampant from her lack of sleep, but from the moment she'd laid eyes on the boy last night she'd felt drawn to him. "I feel like he's my own flesh and blood, Franklin. We have to protect him."

"We're gonna protect him; don't you worry none. God's gonna heal him and we're gonna take care of him." Franklin helped his wife ease out from under the boy and laid him gently back on the feather pillow. "Yes sir, we're gonna protect you, little man. You just sleep now. When God taps you on the shoulder and tells ya it's time, you'll be wakin' up and we'll be here to protect ya."

Turning from the bed Franklin opened his arms wide to Rachel. He just held her close, neither of them speaking a word as she pressed her face into his chest. She had been sixteen when Franklin took her from the plantation as his wife, and he'd practically been the only person in her life for the past thirty-eight years. It had been a lonely existence at times. Franklin was a simple man. He didn't require anything more in life other than his wife and his horses. But Rachel ran deep. She was a passionate woman with a deep love for Franklin and an even deeper love for God. She was a well-educated woman, considering her background, and every night she would read the Bible to Franklin and engage him in deep, spiritual conversations—at least as deep as Franklin could go. She longed for something more, but for the last several years she didn't know what she was longing for. Somehow she felt like the boy in that bed was the key to her longing.

Later that night, Rachel read the Bible to Franklin as they sat beside the boy's bed. She didn't feel much like talking so she just let God's word stand alone.

"O LORD, thou hast brought up my soul from the grave; thou hast kept me alive, that I should not go down to the pit. Sing unto the LORD, O ye saints of his, and give thanks at the remembrance of his holiness. For his anger endureth but a moment; in his favour is life; weeping may endure for a night, but joy cometh in the morning."

Franklin leaned back in his chair. "Uh huh, that's the truth."

A full hour passed in silence before Rachel noticed Franklin's head begin to nod. "I'll be fine right here; you go on to bed."

Franklin rose from his chair, leaned down, and kissed Rachel full on the lips. "Good night, Rach. He's gonna wake up; don't you worry none."

Rachel gently rested her hand on the boy's cheek and smoothed his hair one more time. *Lord, I have no words left; I feel completely empty. Please let your Holy Spirit moan and groan on behalf of my boy.* This night was not like the first one—she could no longer rest beside his bed. Rachel spent long hours walking about the room, lifting her hands to God, not knowing how to ask but leaving her heart open and bare before her Savior. Throughout the long vigil, audible moans escaped her mouth, but nothing seemed to take the weight off of her chest. It felt like she was carrying a heavy boulder as she paced beside his bed. There was no comfort to be found this night.

Franklin woke before sun up to the smell of bacon frying. He quickly dressed and hurried to the kitchen to find one of the finest breakfasts he'd ever seen. Rachel was already putting hot biscuits on the table beside a large slab of butter and his favorite gravy. Eggs and bacon were to follow. His mouth began to water as he eyed the cream and fresh strawberries from the garden.

"We must be feedin' General Grant's army this mornin'."

Rachel ignored his good-natured jab. She would've gone stark raving mad if she hadn't found an outlet for her emotions. Cooking was the only thing that came to mind, and thus far it seemed to be doing the trick. "Set yourself down and eat," she said.

"Not unlessen you eat with me," he replied.

Rachel wiped her hands on her apron and joined him at the table. Taking her hand, Franklin asked a blessing over the food and then over the boy who lay in the next room. At the mention of the boy, Rachel had to quell the urge to go check on him. Instead, she took a biscuit, opened it up, and began to spread a thin layer of butter.

"Is this heaven?"

Rachel couldn't move—she wasn't even sure she was breathing.

"Am I in heaven?" This time, the boy's voice came stronger, not as hesitant as before.

Rachel resisted the urge to run to him and throw her arms around him. After all, they were strangers as far as he was concerned. She slowly stood, held out a chair for him, and beckoned him with her hand to join them at the table.

Eugene couldn't believe his eyes. He was ravenously hungry so there was no need to offer the invitation twice. It dawned on him after his first few steps that this must not be heaven, or he surely wouldn't be in so much pain. But he continued slowly across the floor and sat down gingerly in the chair.

"What's yer name, Son?" Franklin had already fixed up a heaping plate of food and slid it in front of him.

"Eugene."

"Well, that's a fine name. My name is Franklin."

"That's a fine name too," Eugene replied with a slight grin. He downed all of his eggs and one whole biscuit before taking a long swig from his milk glass.

"And my name is Rachel."

Eugene stopped in mid-gulp and just stared at her. Rachel didn't quite know what to make of the look on his face until he spoke his next words.

"That was my mother's name."

Chapter 3

Eugene walked at a snail's pace from the outhouse, with Franklin by his side. He couldn't help but notice all the holes in the house. There were some places you could see from one end of the house to the other. Something Eugene just couldn't quite figure out was how Franklin and Rachel could afford to eat such a feast for breakfast if they were so poor.

A couple of times Franklin tried to help him up the steps of the porch, but Eugene insisted he could walk on his own. By the time he got back into the house, though, Eugene had to admit he was feeling a bit dizzy. Rachel had been anxiously waiting for him to return and ushered him right back into bed. There was no argument from Eugene. He appreciated how she covered him up and told him he was safe now. There was a warm breeze blowing through the house and before he knew it, he began to drift off to sleep.

Rachel withheld no affection from the boy and bent to kiss him on the forehead. "I'll be close by if you need anything."

Eugene greatly appreciated the attention. He hadn't felt this peaceful or content in a very long time. Rachel watched him for just a few moments before she returned to her work. She was already busy cutting down a pair of Franklin's overalls and sewing up the sides so they would fit Eugene.

Eugene. She liked saying his name out loud. When she finished with the overalls, she started working on a shirt. Her heart soared to heights it hadn't been in a very long time. As she worked she thanked God over and over again for His divine intervention. The words she had read from the Great Book last night kept flooding her soul: *joy cometh in the morning.*

***

On his fourth day with Franklin and Rachel, Eugene began to feel more like himself. He hadn't been able to see much of the farm yet, but he had enjoyed sitting on the front porch watching the horses in the pasture. Even though one of them had given him a hard, swift kick, he wasn't afraid of them. He'd always had a love for horses even though he hadn't had much of a chance to be around them. According to his mother he'd come by that love naturally. His father had lived and worked around horses all his life.

It was a hot July day, the noon meal finished, and dishes washed. Franklin and Rachel joined Eugene in the shade of the front porch. There was such an easy relationship between the three of them now. Eugene had no desire to leave this remote farm—as far as he was concerned, it really was heaven. He felt safe as he surveyed the thick woods surrounding the house and pasture. The only way their farm could be reached was by the steep path leading from the road. It was a sanctuary of sorts.

Suddenly, Franklin jumped to his feet and moved swiftly toward Eugene. "Get in the house right now!" Eugene was used to taking orders, but he was startled by Franklin's behavior. "Rachel, you stay with him, you hear me!"

Rachel put her hand on Eugene's back and nearly shoved him through the door. A man was emerging from the trail in the woods and walking across the pasture. Franklin purposely moved away from the house to meet the stranger. Rachel kept Eugene behind her as she watched anxiously from the kitchen window. She could see the two men standing in the pasture and watched as the stranger gestured toward the house. All of a sudden the man brushed past Franklin and began striding toward them.

"You stay behind . . ." her voice trailed off when she turned toward Eugene. There was not an ounce of color left in his face.

"That's Louis." Eugene's voice was a mere whisper, but his words sent Rachel into a whirlwind of motion. While he had never shared the details of Louis' abuse, he had confirmed that the condition he arrived in was a direct result of his stepfather's hand.

Before he knew it, he was being pushed down deep into the feather bed and covered with a layer of quilts.

"Don't you move or make a sound. Franklin will protect you, I promise."

There were so many boards missing on the side of the house Louis could see movement inside. "Who've you got in the house?"

"Jus' my wife. We've lived up here more'n thirty years."

"Lemme talk to her; I wanna know if she's seen my boy."

Franklin stepped between the man and the house. "Sir, we ain't seen yer boy; we don't get much company up here."

"I'll just step inside and have a little chat with your woman." Louis walked around Franklin and headed for the porch steps.

"Sir," Rachel said as she emerged from the house, "we haven't seen your son." She hoped her voice didn't sound as shaky as she felt, and she prayed that God would forgive her of the lie she just told.

The look on Louis' face was one of utter shock. His tone was full of disdain as he asked her, "You mean to say you're married to this colored?"

This time she didn't have to control a shaky voice; it came out clear and strong. "For thirty-eight years to be exact."

"This is downright disgustin'. You're nothin' but a . . ."

Louis didn't have a chance to finish his sentence. Franklin had already snatched him by the arm and flung him on the ground so hard he had the breath knocked out of him.

"You'll not be talkin' that way to my wife." Franklin was a gentle man, but he would die before he let someone disrespect his wife. Louis didn't deserve an ounce of common courtesy, not after what he'd done to Eugene. Franklin looked like he wanted to kick his backside all the way across the pasture, but Louis was already on his feet heading for the trail in the woods. When he got to the far side of the pasture, he turned and yelled some of the most hateful, vile language the two of them had heard in a very long time. As he disappeared down the path, Franklin turned to Rachel with the most apologetic look on his face. "I'm so sorry you had to hear that, Rach." He sat down on the edge of the porch, keeping a watchful eye on the woods just in case Louis decided to return. "Jus' think 'bout what Eugene's life musta been like with that man."

"Oh Franklin, it breaks my heart to even imagine it." Just then, she realized Eugene must be about to suffocate under all those quilts. Sure enough, he was sweating plenty when she finally peeled back all the layers of his hiding place. But as hot as he had been under the covers, he couldn't seem to stop shaking.

"I heard what he said to you and Franklin." Eugene felt like he should apologize for the words his stepfather had used. But all of a sudden he thought he was going to be sick. Without much warning, he started to heave and before Rachel could bring a bowl from the kitchen, he had thrown up all over the floor beside the bed.

"It's all right, darlin'." Rachel rubbed his back soothingly. "There's nothing to be ashamed of; you're just a bundle of nerves and I don't blame you."

Rachel brought a cool, damp cloth to wipe his face and helped him into the other room. There wasn't much furniture in the whole house, but there was a chair and small sofa in the room next to the kitchen along with a table near the fireplace. Eugene noticed the open Bible sitting on the table by a kerosene lamp. Rachel told him to sit down on the sofa and relax while she cleaned up the floor. He must have apologized to her half a dozen times before the task was done. He had to admit he was feeling better, but the sight of Louis had been almost more than he could bear.

That night, Franklin and Eugene sat side by side on the sofa while Rachel sat in the chair by the kerosene lamp and read from the Bible. Eugene was comfortable in his nightshirt. Before long he began to yawn, and soon he was fast asleep on Franklin's shoulder. Franklin didn't quite know what to do. In all his sixty years, he'd never had a son of his own, but it sure felt good having this boy lean up against him.

Franklin sat as still as possible while he and Rachel carried on a quiet conversation. "Do ya think it's right for us to keep him, Rach?"

Rachel looked as if she'd been wrestling with the same question. "I don't think it would be right for us to send him back to that stepfather of his. That awful man might kill him."

"But is it right for *us* to keep him?" Franklin asked once again.

"Oh Franklin, I've spent so much time praying about that very thing, but today the Lord has seen fit to give me peace. I have the distinct feeling that God brought Eugene here for us to take care of him." Rachel leaned forward in her chair as if she would touch the boy, but must have thought better of it. Instead, she briefly rested her hand on Franklin's knee then sat back in the chair as she continued. "He has no real family left and we've been given an opportunity to provide him with a family. So yes, I think it's right, because I know for certain it would be wrong for us to turn him away."

That was just what Franklin needed to hear. Even though he had carried doubts about keeping Eugene, he knew for sure it would be an outright sin to put him back in Louis' hands. Still, he had a gnawing feeling in the pit of his stomach.

Rachel looked at her husband for a few moments before she asked, "What's bothering you?"

Franklin shook his head gently, not wanting to wake Eugene. He needed to say something to his wife, but he knew it was going to upset her. He took a good long look at the boy now drooling on his sleeve, then changed his mind. "It's nothin', Rach."

"I'm sorry, but I know trouble in your eyes when I see it. Tell me what you're thinking."

A deep breath barely escaped through Franklin's closed lips. How could he possibly tell Rachel that he would be hanged if anyone discovered Eugene with them? He'd seen far too many Negro men snatched from their loved ones and dragged to their death or hung from a tree. Most of the time, it was for no good reason at all. He couldn't bear to think about what would become of his precious Rach if that should happen. Looking at her now, he felt certain he should keep such disturbing thoughts to himself. But he determined right then and there, he would do everything in his power to keep Rachel and the boy safe.

With that matter settled in his mind, he had to think of something right quick to say to his wife. "What'r we gonna do with him when school starts? We surely can't send him into town." Franklin was relieved when Rachel picked right up on his question.

"We'll have to school him here, I suppose. When we go to the horse auction in October, I can purchase some books and tablets and have school right here on the farm." Rachel was visibly excited about the prospect of teaching Eugene everything she knew, including the French language.

"And I'll teach him 'bout horses," Franklin said proudly.

"Yes, you'll teach him about horses."

Franklin didn't know how long it had been since he'd seen Rachel this excited about something. She'd always been the most beautiful woman he'd ever laid eyes on. He loved her sparkling brown eyes and dark, wavy hair that reminded him of a waterfall when she let it down. But tonight there was an extra gleam in those eyes that made her even more appealing, if that could be possible.

Rachel went into Eugene's room and turned down the bed while Franklin gathered up the boy in his arms. He laid him gently in the bed, and Rachel pulled the light quilt up to his chest. When she kissed the boy softly on the cheek, she noticed Franklin watching her.

"You got one o' them for me?" he asked, with a twinkle in his eyes.

She was blushing as they walked out of the room hand in hand.

Chapter 4

The next morning Franklin asked Eugene to join him out in the pasture after breakfast. "There's somethin' I wanna show ya." Eugene was excited about getting out of the house and seeing more of the farm. After all, he'd been here for five days and he was curious about where Franklin went every morning.

"Do you think he's ready?" Rachel was showing every bit the concern of a mother.

Franklin and Eugene looked at each other across the table and shared a smile.

"He's a tad bit sore, but thank the Lord t'ain't no broken bones that need healin'." Eugene nodded in agreement, and Franklin added, "We'll be takin' it easy today."

Rachel cleared her throat and looked over at Eugene as he finished his biscuit. "Eugene, Franklin and I have been discussing how you came to be with us here on the farm."

Eugene immediately sat stock-still; he didn't so much as blink. He was suddenly afraid they were going to tell him it was time to go back to his stepfather, Louis.

Rachel looked a bit uneasy as she continued, "If you have somewhere else you'd rather live, we understand. Franklin will be glad to take you wherever you want to go. I just," she corrected herself, "*we* just want you to know how much we care about you."

A giant tear slid down the boy's face, and Rachel prepared herself for his response.

Slowly Eugene said, "Isn't this where I'm supposed to be?" He wiped the tear off of his cheek and added, "Please don't send me away."

Rachel shuddered. "Oh honey, I didn't mean for you to

think we didn't want you to stay. We've been so blessed to have you here. I guess what I'm trying to ask you is, would you like to become a part of our family?"

Eugene's eyes grew wide as he looked between the two and sweetly replied, "If it wouldn't be too much trouble."

Franklin chuckled and said, "No trouble at all. We want ya to stay."

Relief flooded through all three at the very same time. Rachel stood and kissed the top of Eugene's head while keeping her eyes on Franklin. "He's had a hard week; please take care of him." Franklin chuckled again as his chair scraped the floor.

Eugene followed Franklin out the door to the sounds of Rachel cleaning up the kitchen. He walked slowly behind Franklin across the pasture toward a big oak tree in the far corner. Franklin took smaller steps than his six-foot frame was used to, knowing the boy would need to walk at a more gingerly pace.

For the first time, Eugene started thinking about Franklin and Rachel's relationship. In his mind they were perfect for each other. He hadn't even given conscious thought to the fact that Franklin was a black man and Rachel was a white woman, not until his stepfather had yelled those ugly things about them. Rachel was so pretty—tall and slender just like his real mother had been. Still there was something about her he couldn't quite put his finger on. Except for the way she looked and talked, she seemed more like Franklin's kind than his kind. *Maybe it's from living with Franklin all these years.*

"Horses'r natural prey," Franklin broke into Eugene's thoughts. "They gotta stick together so they're safe. You always see 'em in herds 'cause they're social creatures and they watch out for one another." Franklin dropped back to walk beside Eugene. "That's why they kicked you outta the way the other night, so they could protect each other. They didn't know you wasn't there to harm 'em."

Once they reached the oak tree, Franklin sat down in the shade and motioned for Eugene to do the same. He pulled a pocketknife out of his overalls, picked up a good stick off the ground, and started whittling. Eugene leaned back against the tree and listened as Franklin began to whistle. By the time Franklin was finished whistling his lively tune, seven magnificent horses, two mules, and one milk cow were standing in a semi-circle around them. Eugene didn't dare move; it felt like some sort of sacred gathering.

Franklin slowly rose to his feet and began talking in a low, peaceful tone of voice. He took the palms of his hands and started rubbing one of the horse's eyes. "You're in a safe place now; t'ain't no one ever gonna harm ya again." The horse put his head lower and nuzzled up against Franklin's chest, clearly enjoying having his eyes rubbed. He moved slowly from one animal to another, giving each of them equal time. As he rubbed underneath one of the horse's bellies, he continued his soothing talk. "God made every creature special. We're all made different but we all deserve respect. You're respected here." The words just rolled off his tongue, and Eugene didn't know if Franklin was talking to him or the horses. "I'll never let no one harm ya." His strong hand was scratching one of the horses at the base of its mane between the withers. "If'n anyone comes along, they'll have to go through me to get to you—I'll be your protector."

Franklin raised the head of one of the mares, placed his nose right up to her nostril, and blew softly. It was amazing to watch this beautiful animal's response. She lowered her head into Franklin's and they stood forehead to forehead for a good long minute, all the while he spoke his soothing words. For the first time in nearly a year, Eugene started to feel safe.

"The Lord Almighty's watchin' out for us—we're in the palm of His hand." He was scratching behind the mule's ears, and the mule responded by putting his head over Franklin's shoulder.

Eugene was curious to see what Franklin was going to do with the milk cow. She was definitely on the outside of the semi-circle, but she seemed to be accepted by the herd just the same. He reached up under her chin and began to scratch. She rewarded him with a good long lick across his arm. Franklin let out a good-natured chuckle.

"You see how all their heads'r low?" Franklin was speaking directly to Eugene now but still walking slowly among the horses. "That's cuz they're feelin' comfortable and safe. If'n a coyote was to come outta those woods, all their heads'd fly up and their ears'd be pinned back. That's when they'd start talkin' 'mong themselves and close up ranks." He raised up one of the horse's hooves and rubbed the frog with his thumb. Oftentimes the padding in the sole of the hoof would become bruised or swollen, and most of the horses enjoyed the massage. Franklin continued his teaching. "Not all their talkin's out loud, ya know. Sometimes jus' the way they stomp the ground or throw their head is sayin' just as much as their neighs and whinnies."

The morning was already gone when Eugene and Franklin started back for the house. Franklin put his arm around the boy's shoulders and kept him close as they walked. Rachel saw them coming from her position at the kitchen window. She was overwhelmed with emotion at the sight of the two of them. There was no holding back the tears as she prayed out loud to God. "O Lord, you have lifted me from the pit—I am a blessed woman indeed! Help me to be worthy of this special gift."

Rachel kept her back to the pair as they entered the kitchen, hoping they wouldn't notice her tears. She playfully slapped Franklin's big hand away from the ham and was surprised when she had to slap Eugene's hand away too. Just hearing him giggle made her heart skip a beat. It seemed like she'd been waiting all her life to hear that sound.

As the next few days passed, Eugene gradually became a part of the life on the farm. He started milking the cow early in the morning and took care of the chickens just the way he used to when he lived with Louis. But his favorite part of the day was going to the old oak tree with Franklin.

"It's time for you to become part o' the herd." Those were the words Eugene was waiting to hear, even though they caused him a bit of nervousness.

Just like every day, the herd gathered as Franklin whistled.

But this time he asked Eugene to stand up with him. Franklin pulled him close to his side and the two began moving in unison to each of the animals. "Put your hand on top o' mine," Franklin whispered. Together they began to rub the horse's eye. As soon as the animal's head dipped low, Franklin's hand gently slipped out from under Eugene's and the boy continued rubbing just the way Franklin had.

"Now speak softly to him." At first, Eugene didn't know what to say, but the words began to flow as he moved slowly with Franklin from one horse to the next. Before he knew it, details of what his life had been like with Louis came tumbling from his mouth. His connection with these majestic animals grew stronger and stronger as he shared the horrible details of his mistreatment. Eugene couldn't have stopped his words if he'd tried, but his voice remained calm as he held nothing back. He had felt so guilty after his mother's death. Louis had reminded him day after day why it would've been better for Eugene to be dead instead of his mother. How many times had he wished it to be so? Somehow her death weighed heavily on his conscience.

Hours passed without boy or horse being aware, and Franklin left the herd without notice as well. Eugene remembered how Franklin told him each horse has a personality of its own, just like humans. *They've all got places they like rubbed or scratched that brings 'em pleasure* and Eugene knew by now what each animal loved. He finally looked back to notice Franklin standing next to the oak with a furrowed brow. Slowly Eugene walked away from the herd and toward Franklin. For a long moment they just stared at each other, neither one breaking eye contact.

"Son, I'm so sorry I couldn't protect ya. If'n I only knew . . ."

Eugene was in Franklin's arms as fast as he could get to him—both man and boy sobbing and clinging to each other.

When Franklin felt the boy's breathing begin to calm, he released him without any signs of embarrassment. Eugene wiped his eyes as they turned to make their way back to the house. Not another word was spoken between them, but Eugene had a feeling he had just been utterly cleansed of the past. He no longer carried his heavy burden of guilt—the herd was carrying it now.

The afternoon meal was a bit quiet, not as lively as the days before. Franklin was the first to break the silence. "Eugene's a part of the herd now, *Mama*."

Rachel just stared at Franklin who continued eating his fried chicken as if he'd been calling her *Mama* all his life. She rarely laughed out loud but she couldn't help it now. Joy just bubbled up inside of her, and laughter was the only way she could release it.

"What's so funny, Mama?" She now stared at Eugene who was wearing the biggest grin on his face she'd ever seen. She couldn't help but touch his arm as she rose to bring him the pitcher of milk. As Rachel passed the kitchen window, she noticed a small movement out of the corner of her eye. With a closer look she could just make out the shape of a man on horseback coming up the trail in the woods.

She turned from the window flushed with fear. "Franklin, we've got company!"

Franklin's chair overturned as he jumped to his feet and ran out on the porch. Seconds later he returned with hurried instructions. "You gotta hide him right, Rach. It's the sheriff."

Rachel ran into the other room telling Eugene to follow. She threw back the rug on the floor in front of the fireplace, put her finger in a small knothole in the wooden floor and lifted a trapdoor. There was no time to light the lantern but Eugene could just make out the first few steps from the light in the room. Rachel took Eugene by the hand and fairly pulled him down the first three steps. "Sit on that step and take hold of this one." The steps were open slats so he sat down and wrapped his arm around the one above it. "It's going to be dark—very dark—but you'll be fine. Just don't move or make a sound. I'll come back for you just like before. I promise."

Rachel knew she had a lot of work to do in a matter of seconds. She ran to the table, righted Franklin's chair and grabbed Eugene's plate and glass off the table. She nearly threw them in the wash bucket after clearing the food off in the scrap pile on the counter with one sweep of her hand. Without using soap, she pulled them from the water, hastily dried them with a cloth, and put them back in the cupboard. Before joining her husband on the porch, she ran back to Eugene's room to make sure there were no visible signs of anyone living there.

"What's your name, boy?" The sheriff had already dismounted and was walking up the steps of the porch toward Franklin.

"Franklin, sir, and this is my wife, Rachel." Rachel nodded to the sheriff who stared at her for a moment through narrowed eyes but didn't acknowledge her presence.

"You gotta last name?"

"Hawkins, sir."

"Well, I'm searchin' the county for a boy that's been kidnapped. You mind if I go inside and have a look around?"

They were given no choice in the matter. The sheriff was already opening the screen door into the kitchen, so they followed him in silence. Rachel noticed he didn't bother to remove his hat. "You must be awful cold up here in the winter with so many boards missin' on the side of your house." He had a gleam in his eye as he turned toward Franklin.

"Yessir, that's the truth."

Rachel's eyes immediately swept the table to make sure she hadn't forgotten anything. Suddenly, her eyes focused on a lone fork sitting on the table right where Eugene had been eating. Her breathing began to speed up along with the pace of her heart.

"Looks like I interrupted dinner. Well, I haven't eaten yet; I may have to have me a bite."

Rachel immediately moved to the stove to take his focus away from the table. "I'll be glad to fix up a lunch you can take with you." She hoped her voice sounded natural to the sheriff even though it didn't sound natural to her.

"Do that."

Franklin followed the sheriff as he made his way through

41

the other three rooms of the house. Seeing nothing of interest he turned and moved back into the kitchen. Rachel held out a clean kitchen cloth tied up with a couple of pieces of fried chicken along with a biscuit. He took it from her without a word of thanks and moved out onto the porch.

"I noticed you had a few horses in the pasture. They don't look so good."

"No sir, they're not the best horses 'round here," Franklin replied.

The sheriff stared back at the house. "I expect you're not too welcome in town, are you?"

"No sir, we just stays to ourself."

The sheriff swung his leg up in the saddle and turned his horse toward the trail in the woods. "Keep it that way." He didn't so much as look back over his shoulder as he opened the cloth and started eating his biscuit.

This time, Rachel thought *she* was going to be sick. When Franklin returned to the kitchen, she was bent at the waist, her hands on her knees.

"Rach, you all right? You look like yer gonna pass out."

She raised up and took one long, deep breath. "I'll be fine."

"You did real good hidin' Eugene. I'm gonna go outside and keep watch. You can get him out now."

Eugene had heard the muffled voices above and the footsteps on the floor as he sat perched on the steps in total darkness. As he waited patiently an overwhelming sense of peace had taken over. He now believed God was watching over the three of them, and Franklin would protect him from harm. Even in the intense darkness he began to trust again. He thought it odd that there wasn't one smidgen of light sneaking through the floorboards above. *How could the house be in such bad shape but have such a solid floor?*

Rachel threw back the rug and lifted the trapdoor. "It's all right now; he's gone."

Eugene's hands instantly flew up to cover his eyes, the light was so intense. He felt Rachel's hand come up underneath his arm to lead him gently back up the steps. He still couldn't open his eyes fully but could hear the trapdoor closing and the rug being swept back into place.

"Is that your cellar?"

"You might call it that. I'm sorry you had to sit down there for so long."

"It was better than bein' pushed under those quilts."

There was that giggle again. As long as she lived, Rachel would never tire of hearing it.

That evening after the Bible reading, Franklin told Rachel and Eugene what the sheriff had said about the horses *not lookin' so good*. Eugene's mouth dropped wide open and Rachel declared with a passion that Franklin had some of the finest thoroughbreds in Kentucky grazing right out there in that pasture.

"Some people only believe what they see on the outside." Franklin spoke to them in a low voice as if he were whispering to his horses. "The sheriff seen the holes in our house, and the mules 'mong the horses . . ." He paused for a second, and looked tenderly toward his wife. "Then he seen the woman I live with and he be thinkin' the worst. That's how some people is—they got blinders on. They only see what's in front of 'em with their eyes and don't bother none to look what's inside a person's heart."

Franklin sat back and contemplated the close call they'd had this afternoon. He knew it was purely by the providence of God that the three of them were together, safe and sound tonight. *Lord, please keep Eugene hid with us as long as you see fit.*

Even after putting it in the Lord's hands, he still worried about how long they could keep him safe.

Chapter 5

It was the last day of August, and Eugene had now spent two full months on the farm. As soon as the sun started leaking through the slats in his room, he was dressed and ready to plunge into a new day.

"Good morning, Eugene." Rachel was at the stove cooking breakfast as he walked through the kitchen. "As soon as you're done with the milking, we've got something special to do today."

Eugene's eyes lit up. "What is it?"

"You'll see soon enough. Now get going."

Eugene ran outside, grabbed the bucket, and started whistling for the milk cow. When she appeared, he tied her to the corral post and situated his milking stump. He worked quickly today, and had the bucket full in record time. Eugene still took a second to scratch under her soft chin and tell her what a good girl she was before he released her. Then he grabbed the bucket and sprinted the short distance back to the house. Franklin emerged from the shed at the same time, and followed the trail of milk all the way into the kitchen.

Eugene was surprised that breakfast wasn't on the table when he returned. Instead, Rachel had packed it away in a basket. Before he could ask what was going on, Franklin arrived holding a thin, leather strap. "I found just what we need, Rach." Franklin held the strap up high for her to see. Then he added, "Are you'ns ready to go?"

Eugene felt like there was some kind of conspiracy going on here. His brow was furrowed when he asked, "Where are we goin'?"

Franklin ruffed up his hair. "We're headin' down to the stream this mornin'. We got somethin' important we gotta take care of."

Eugene asked a wagonload of questions as they walked through the woods, but after each one he was told to *wait* or *be patient*. Finally, the stream came into view and Eugene wondered why he hadn't been down here before.

"How come I didn't know about this stream?"

Franklin gave him a serious look. "We don't want you comin' down here alone, Eugene. You understand what I'm sayin'?"

When Eugene didn't answer right away, Rachel said, "Eugene, it's not safe for you to be away from the house and pasture." She saw the disappointed look on his face. "It won't always be like that, but for now, you need to do what we ask. Do you understand?"

Eugene let out a disappointed, "Yes."

Rachel tilted her head and raised her brow. "Yes, what?"

"Yes ma'am," he said obediently.

Eugene watched Franklin take the leather strap and bend down to soak it in the stream. When he rose up he said, "Gimme yer hands."

Rachel stretched out her hand, palm down, toward Franklin and motioned for Eugene to do the same. Slowly he raised his hand, until it was level with hers. She gently turned her hand up and intertwined her fingers with his. When Franklin started tying the strap around their wrists, Eugene looked curiously at Rachel. Her eyes were focused on his, and they were brimming with tears. Neither of them spoke as they gradually turned their attention back to Franklin who had finished tying the knot, and was now covering both of their wrists with his strong hands.

"I be a witness, 'long with the Lord, that the two of you be bound. T'ain't nothin' on earth can break this bond 'tween mother and son. You'ns are bound by God and by water."

Only the rippling murmur of the stream could be heard as Franklin unbound their wrists. Rachel took the strap and dipped it into the cool water while Franklin moved to Eugene's side. Tears streamed down her cheeks as she tied the strap firmly around her son and husband's wrist.

"As God is my witness, this cord will never be broken. It binds Franklin and Eugene together for life, as father and son." She looked at them both with deep emotion. "You are bound by God and by water."

As soon as Rachel removed the strap, Eugene threw himself into her open arms. He thought for a second he might not be able to breathe, she held him so tight. But he didn't care, he belonged to her, and that's all that mattered. When she released him she turned him toward Franklin, who stretched out his strong arms and picked Eugene clear up off the ground.

"Son," was all Franklin said.

"Papa," was Eugene's response.

Later, as the three ate their breakfast by the stream, Eugene asked, "Where'd you learn to do that?"

Franklin answered first. "That tradition goes way on back. I seen my people do that many a time to make their family bonds. And that's what we be now, a family."

Rachel spoke then. "Eugene, I know how much you loved your real mother—I don't ever want to take her place. But since she's gone, I'm proud to help her raise you to be a man."

Eugene smiled as he nodded his head. "I think she'd like that."

When breakfast was over Eugene and his folks made their way back through the woods. Before the house ever came into view, he'd asked nearly a dozen times when he could go back down to the stream on his own.

Two days later, Franklin took Eugene out into the pasture to separate two of the horses from the herd. These were the two youngest thoroughbreds that would be taken to auction in Lexington in October. Eugene climbed up on top of the corral and noticed the sturdy wooden rails. *How could Papa have such a fine corral and a house that seemed to be falling apart?* He was beginning to

47

wonder what winter really would be like.

"There's lots of folks who break their horses, but if'n you break a horse, you break his spirit." Franklin was walking around in the corral as if he was one of the horses. It almost seemed like he was leading them on a halter, but Franklin didn't even have a rope in his hands.

"T'ain't natural to have a body ridin' ya. We gotta help 'em be comfortable with somethin' on their back, but t'ain't natural, no sirree." Soon Franklin reached for a rope hanging on the fence and continued walking around with it in his hand. "You gotta keep 'em calm and feelin' safe, but you gotta let 'em know who's boss."

Franklin slowly put the rope around one of the horse's necks and his head instantly shot up in the air. Leaning into him with a little pressure, Franklin told the animal who was in control, and his head slowly came back down. Eugene could hear Papa talking to the horse all the while.

"You're in my hands now and you trust me. I been listenin' to you for a long time and you been listenin' to me. I'm never gonna harm ya."

All morning long Franklin transferred the rope from one animal to the other, and before the morning was over, Eugene was leading one horse while Franklin led the other.

Most mornings now were split between training the horses in the corral and being with the herd in the pasture. Occasionally, Eugene would spend his time in the herd by himself while Franklin worked with the horses in the corral. This particular morning the skies had started out clear but by late morning a terrible cloud had blown up and the sky grew frighteningly dark.

Franklin sent Eugene running to the house to tell Mama to take cover and before she could stop him, Eugene was already running back out to the pasture to help Franklin with the horses. He didn't have a clue where Franklin was going, but the animals fell in obediently behind them. The wind was howling now and rain was coming down in sheets as they entered the woods and followed a trail down a short embankment. Eugene could just make out an opening in the side of a low bluff. The horses nearly ran them over as they hurried inside for shelter. Eugene watched in amazement as Franklin took down a lantern hanging on the side of the wall and reached up on a ledge for a box of matches. With the lantern's light they moved farther down the passageway, and the animals were all waiting patiently again for Franklin to take the lead.

Further inside, with the entrance out of sight, they came into a room with hay scattered across the floor and bales stacked up against one wall. Another lantern was sitting on the ledge with matches, and Franklin told Eugene to light it. A post had been driven into the ground that had a wooden peg higher than Eugene could reach. Franklin took the lantern and hung it on the peg so the animals would have light as they waited out the storm. Clearly they had done this many times before.

Eugene suddenly began to worry. "What about Mama?"

"Don't you worry none 'bout Mama. We're 'bout to join her." Franklin motioned to a passage off to their left. "She's probly worryin' 'bout the two of us more. We need to get movin' 'fore she comes lookin' for us."

Franklin held the lantern up high as they wound their way through the cave. When the passage narrowed and the ceiling dropped lower, Franklin had to duck down a bit to keep from hitting his head. When they came out of the narrow passage, they were standing in a well-lit room, and Rachel was waiting for them with hands on her hips.

"I thought I told you to stay with me, young man."

Eugene didn't quite know what to say—he'd never been scolded by Rachel before. But he could see by the look on her face that she was not happy with him.

Franklin said, "I need all the help I can get with the animals, Mama."

"Those horses would've made their way to shelter without either one of you, and you know it."

Eugene now looked at his papa for advice. Franklin motioned ever so slightly with his head toward Rachel. Humbly and apologetically, Eugene reached out and put his arms around his mama. Franklin just chuckled when he saw Rachel's anger melt away. He suspected it had been more about fear than anger that had her all riled up in the first place.

When Eugene pulled away from Rachel, he'd given her a fairly good soaking. She didn't seem to mind. She was enjoying the look of utter amazement on his face.

Eugene couldn't believe what he was seeing. There were lanterns hanging everywhere lighting the room—and the room was huge. He couldn't seem to take it all in at once. There was a bed, a table and chairs, a cabinet full of dishes, a cooking stove, a cedar chest, a bookshelf with books and two rocking chairs. There were even rugs covering the floor.

"Is that . . .?"

Rachel followed his gaze and said, "Yes, those are the stairs leading to the trapdoor in the house."

"Where did all this come from? How come I didn't know about this place? Does anyone else know it's here? Who lives down here? How big is this cave?" The questions just kept coming one right after the other.

Franklin finally broke in when Eugene had to take a breath. "My pappy and me built our house right on top o' this cave more'n forty-five years ago. I lived here ever since I's thirteen." Franklin moved to one rocking chair while Rachel took the other. Eugene continued walking about the room mesmerized by his surroundings while listening to Franklin's story.

Franklin's father, Isaiah, had been a slave on the Hawkins plantation near Lexington all his life. From an early age his master had recognized Isaiah's ability to work with horses and he started out in the stables at age six. By the age of seventeen, he was in charge of his master's stables. By that time the plantation had been passed on to Master Hawkins' son, Samuel. Samuel Hawkins was a kind master and wasn't afraid to roll up his sleeves and work side by side with his slaves.

The mule trade was huge back in those days. Every cotton plantation needed Negro slaves and mules to be successful, and Samuel Hawkins had one of the most successful cotton plantations in Kentucky. So Franklin's father, Isaiah, not only bred and trained horses, but he bred mules.

"My pappy always said the bluegrass in Kentucky made for the best mules. They got the biggest, strongest frames of any mules in the country. Yessir, he made his massa a heap o' money off the mule trade. He could get $100 a mule for an unbroke one and $120 for a broke one."

Eugene became so engrossed in the story that he took a seat on the small footstool at Franklin's feet.

"My pappy fell in love with a slave woman name o' Ruth and they was married on the plantation. I's what they produced 'long with 'bout six others. 'Cept only two of us lived, me and a sister named Sarah. She been gone since I's a young'n, 'long with my mammy."

Eugene wanted to know what happened to his sister and mammy, but didn't dare interrupt. So he moved a little closer, making sure he didn't miss a word.

Franklin went on to talk about what his life had been like on the plantation. His pappy had taken him into the stables from the moment he could walk. Isaiah had recognized his son's God-given ability to tame horses with a gentle hand and voice. Most people simply didn't have the patience that Isaiah and Franklin possessed to train a horse in such a manner. So by the time Franklin turned six, the master of the plantation had put him to work full time in the stables.

Master Hawkins was proud of his horses and mules and knew he owed it all to Isaiah. So when the War between the States ended in '65, Isaiah and Franklin were set free, but Samuel Hawkins wanted to show his appreciation for what they'd done for him. He gave Isaiah a fine stallion and mare from his stables and a piece of land about twenty miles southeast of Lexington.

"The only thing my pappy had to do for Massa Hawkins was sell the first foal back to *him*. Pappy gladly shook hands on that deal."

Eugene caught a look between Rachel and Franklin he couldn't quite figure out. When Franklin winked at her, Rachel began to blush. She quickly rose to her feet and declared it time to go check on the house and the chickens. "Surely the storm's moved on by now," she said.

Eugene hadn't even begun to get all his questions answered. When Franklin headed for the passageway to check on the horses, Eugene decided his best bet was to follow Rachel up the stairs.

"So where'd all this stuff come from down here? There's more in the cave than there is in the house."

Rachel stepped aside and gave him a little nudge up the stairs ahead of her. They lifted the trapdoor together and he held it open as she finished the climb. "Just leave it open; I'll have to go back down and put out the lamps."

"What about *your* family, Mama?" Eugene was having to work awfully hard to get answers to his questions.

"Eugene, someday when you're older I'll tell you all about my life on the Hawkins' plantation and since, but now is not the time." She saw the look on his face and went on. "There are a lot of things you don't understand yet, but someday you will and I promise I'll tell you everything."

"When?"

"Soon enough, Eugene. Soon enough."

Chapter 6

Fall 1912

October brought a fair amount of excitement around the farm. Eugene helped his papa get the big wagon ready for travel and check all the tack and harnesses for the mules. Franklin told him as they worked that the condition of the house kept outsiders thinking they were nothing but poor folks. But the truth was they could buy anything they wanted or needed for an entire year with the sale of just one horse at auction. This year they had two horses for auction, and so far one of the other mares would be producing a foal come March of next year.

Rachel and Franklin sat around the table in the evenings preparing a list of supplies they needed in Lexington. This year she was like a little girl at Christmastime thinking of all the school supplies and clothes she needed to buy for Eugene. She explained to him that the wagon would be light on the trip to Lexington, but it would be loaded down on the way home.

The night before they were to leave, Eugene didn't sleep a wink. He'd been chopping firewood all afternoon and thought sure he'd sleep well that night. But he was too excited to do anything except think about the trip. And when Rachel and Franklin got up in the morning while it was still dark, they found Eugene already dressed and sitting on the floor in front of their bedroom door.

"We're gonna get the wagon ready while Mama fixes breakfast." Franklin took Eugene by the hand and pulled him to his feet, giving him a friendly pat on the behind to show his love. "Your mama's scurryin' and we gotta get outta her way."

Rachel gave her husband a pat on the behind and Franklin yelped as if she'd put a whoopin' on him. She could hear their laughter as they went to work outside.

The sun had barely made its appearance when Franklin pulled the wagon away from the house. "We're gonna stay as far away from Winchester as we can." Eugene turned around from his seat between Franklin and Rachel to make sure the horses' tether was holding at the end of the wagon. "We've got twenty-one miles 'tween here and Lexington, and it'll take all mornin' to get where we're goin'."

Rachel told Eugene he could ride in the back of the wagon anytime he pleased. "But if we meet anyone on the road before we get to the city, you'll need to get under the tarp and stay put until they pass." Rachel and Franklin had already decided they were going to take every precaution to keep Eugene safe on this trip. They had no idea if Louis and the county sheriff were still looking for him, but they didn't want to take any chances around Winchester.

By the time they got to Lexington, Eugene had been underneath the tarp nine times. If Rachel so much as thought she saw another person on the road, she made sure he was nowhere to be seen. Eugene didn't seem to mind and pretended it was a game of hide-and-seek.

Franklin explained that they would have to travel through the heart of the city to get to their campsite. Eugene had never been in a big city before, and he was fascinated by all the activity in Lexington. There was a mix of automobiles and buggies on the streets and people walked hurriedly along the sidewalks. It was much different than the small-town pace Eugene had grown up with.

Rachel purposely moved as far apart from Franklin on the wagon seat as possible. She was looking everywhere except at her husband. Eugene didn't seem to notice; he was far too busy taking in all the sights and smells of the city.

Soon Franklin pointed out the massive auction barn in the distance. "We're goin' straight there in the mornin' for the sale. You won't be able to come with me, but you and Mama can watch from the stands."

Franklin continued driving the mules out of the city and toward the river. "We got us the best campin' spot in the area. There's even a little time for fishin' this afternoon if you like." Eugene had been pretty excited when he saw the fishing pole come out of the shed as they were loading the wagon this morning. The last time he'd been fishing was the day he ran away from Louis. He was looking forward to putting a worm on the end of a hook again.

The campsite was on level ground with shade trees all around and the river just a few yards away. It was too cool to wade into the water, but Eugene slipped off his boot and dipped his foot just to check the temperature. Rachel kept an eye on him as she began to unpack some of their provisions.

"Eugene, you can help me set up the tarp on the wagon." Franklin fitted four long hickory sticks inside slots at the corners of the wagon bed. Each stick had a forked end, and a long pole the length of the wagon was laid across each stick. Eugene worked hard to unfold the heavy tarp and then he and Franklin pulled it up over the sturdy hickory frame. It was long enough to cover the top and the sides of the wagon. Franklin clipped a quilt to the tarp on the open end of the wagon, then flipped it up on top. Rachel could pull it down when she needed privacy to dress. All three of them would be sleeping in the wagon that night on their bedrolls.

After dark around the fire, Rachel explained to Eugene that he wouldn't be able to call Franklin *Papa* while they were in Lexington. Eugene thought it must have something to do with his so-called kidnapping in Winchester, but he couldn't have been further from the truth.

Rachel said, "There are a lot of people who don't look too kindly on our kind of marriage. We've found it a lot easier just to pretend that your papa works for me. He'll be selling *my* horses and helping me with *my* purchases when we go shopping tomorrow."

Eugene noticed it didn't seem to bother Franklin any, but it was obvious Rachel was struggling with it. The whole thing just didn't seem right to him either.

Before bed, Rachel chose to read the story of Abram and Sarai in the book of Genesis. The irony wasn't lost on either husband or son when she read the part where Abram lied to the Egyptians and told them his wife Sarai was really his sister.

The next morning, Franklin hitched the mules to the wagon while Eugene brushed the horses down until their coats were shining brightly in the autumn sun. He talked to them soothingly and told them how much he loved them. It hadn't really occurred to Eugene until now that these two horses would never again be a part of the herd. Just the thought of it put him in a melancholy mood. It was even harder when he stood by Rachel in the stands and watched Franklin lead his first horse into the arena. He was magnificent looking, and Franklin knew just how to show him off.

"The Hawkins name means a lot here at the auction." Rachel put her arm around Eugene's shoulder to comfort him at the loss of one of his horses. "Whenever a thoroughbred from the Hawkins' bloodline is sold, the bidding goes high. Just watch the cards go up."

Sure enough, Eugene watched the bidding for this fine animal go on for several minutes. It was finally sold to a gentleman who looked quite pleased with his purchase. A dozen other horses were auctioned before Franklin returned again with the filly. She was tall and sleek and the bidding once again was brisk. After she was led away, Rachel noticed Eugene wiping tears from his eyes so she suggested they wait outside the barn for Franklin to finish his transactions. She had taught her husband years ago how to sign the Hawkins name so he could complete the paperwork and receive payment. He was paid in cash, and before leaving the barn, he put the money inside each of his boots and covered them up with his pants legs.

Franklin waved to his family when he saw them standing

on the other side of the paddock. Once again, Rachel barely acknowledged his presence and left ample room between them on the wagon seat. Eugene climbed into the back of the wagon looking like he'd just lost his best friend.

As soon as they pulled away from the auction barn, Franklin looked back at him. "I know your first sale is hard, Son; they've been your friends. But they're gonna be fine in their new life; don't you worry none."

That afternoon they shopped in the city for the household items on Rachel's list. Clothing, books, and school supplies were all purchased during that afternoon as well. Eugene was getting about as worn out as an old pair of overalls. He finally left the mercantile and went outside to lie down in the back of the wagon. Franklin just stayed by the wagon and waited for Rachel to motion for him to carry out her purchases. He would've liked to have joined Eugene in the back of that wagon.

That evening was a special treat. There was a tent revival on the other side of the river. After a modest supper by the campfire, they drove the wagon across the wooden bridge and down a dirt road into the countryside. Rapturous harmony drifted through the night air, and they followed the sound until the tent came into view. When they entered underneath, Eugene realized he and Rachel were the only white people inside. He wasn't bothered by that fact and neither was anyone else for that matter. They were all too preoccupied with praising the Lord.

Eugene watched Rachel worship without any inhibition and thought how beautiful her worship must be to God. He had a hard time not watching her, and he noticed his papa having a hard time too. They heard a fiery message that night with plenty of *amen's* to go around. When the preacher offered the invitation for salvation, Eugene knew in his heart that he needed to join the crowd moving forward. Before the night was over, he was baptized in the river with nearly a dozen others seeking a cleansing for their souls. Eugene's burden of guilt no longer lay with the herd—he had given it to Jesus who would carry it from now on.

***

That night, unable to sleep in the wagon because of the day's purchases, Franklin offered to set up a shelter for Rachel. She took one look into the heavens and decided she'd much rather sleep with her men under the stars. All three lay on their bedrolls covered by blankets marveling at God's handiwork. Finally, Eugene asked a question that had been on his mind for a long time. "Mama, I was just wonderin' somethin'."

Rachel turned to see Eugene lying on his side looking at her.

"Who are your people?" he asked.

She understood what he was asking. He was wondering which world she fit in. She gave him the only real answer she had.

"My people are Franklin and Eugene. That's who my people are."

Rachel turned away from Eugene's gaze and pretended to go to sleep. The truth was, she was fully awake and wrestling with the past. She realized Eugene was quite intuitive and his curiosity never ceased to amaze her. How long would it take for him to figure out that there was more to her life than she was telling?

Chapter 7

B ack on the farm Rachel could finally let her guard down, knowing they had kept Eugene safe. She sensed that Eugene hadn't felt all that comfortable in the big city anyway. They had gotten up early this morning and made their last purchases in Lexington before heading home. All of the food items had to be bought last. The butcher had packed up large slabs of beef and pork that Eugene was now helping to hang in the smoke house. All sorts of other food items along with flour, sugar, and salt were packed in the wagon on top of the lumber.

Franklin declared how proud he was of his mules for pulling their heaviest load ever.

They worked long into the evening emptying the contents of the wagon. Eugene helped Rachel carry everything inside while Franklin took care of the wagon and the mules. He then checked on the other five horses before joining his family in the house.

Franklin declared, "I'm so tired I don't even know my name." He ruffed up Eugene's hair as he wound through the maze of crates and boxes. "Let's go to bed, Mama."

Rachel was feeling a little overwhelmed by the task at hand, but wasn't the kind to leave anything undone. However, even she had to admit they all just needed to go to bed. Eugene looked so cute just standing there with his hair all messed up. She opened her arms to him, and he stepped over a crate and allowed himself to be enfolded there. When she finally let go, she took his face in her hands and kissed him on the cheek.

Before he made it to the door of his room, he turned around with a sleepy grin on his face. "I love you, Mama." Rachel never dreamed of such happiness. She knew something inside of her was being fulfilled by this sweet, dark-headed boy. "I love you more," she replied softly.

The next several days were busy with preparations for winter. Eugene and Franklin spent their mornings with the horses and their afternoons working on the room below. The new bed purchased in Lexington was set up for Eugene and a partition was being built to give Rachel a little more privacy. Eugene was very curious about how everything worked below the house.

"Where does the smoke go from the stove?"

"We've got an extra long pipe runnin' right up the wall outside the house so it looks like the smoke's comin' from the stove upstairs. We spend the cold months down here but keep a light glowin' in the house till bedtime every night," Franklin explained.

"Why?"

"'Cause we want people to leave us be. They all just think we're poor folks and don't bother with us none."

"Have you always been like that, I mean, since you lived here?" Eugene still had too many unanswered questions.

"No, t'ain't always been that way. But some things has happened in the past that can't be fixed, so we just keep to ourselves and don't cause no trouble."

Eugene helped Franklin hold up a board for him to nail and asked, "Like what?"

"I'm thinkin' there's some things you need to know now that you're part of this family, but I gotta talk to Mama 'bout it first." Franklin saw the look on Eugene's face. "We're not tryin' to keep secrets from ya, it's just you might need to be a little older, that's all."

That evening there was a definite chill in the air and all three were wearing a jacket when they came to the supper table.

Rachel said, "I think it's time to move downstairs tonight." She had stayed so busy all day that she hadn't been cold until she sat down at the table.

Franklin pulled his jacket a little closer. "I agree with ya, Mama. Eugene 'n' me'll take down whatever you need."

Rachel thanked them and said, "We'll do your lessons downstairs then."

Rachel and Eugene had agreed that the best time for his studies was after the evening meal. There were just too many things that needed to be done on the farm during the day to take time out for lessons. But at night, especially during the winter, it was the perfect time for learning. Franklin always sat nearby listening to each lesson and watching Eugene soak up the knowledge. He was especially fascinated to hear them speaking those fancy French words.

Tonight, as they sat at the table below in comfort, Eugene seemed a bit distracted. Rachel finally put down the book in her hand. "Where are you tonight, Eugene?"

"I'm right here with you."

Rachel laughed. "No, I mean where is your mind? You don't seem to be able to concentrate on the lesson."

Eugene thought for a long moment and finally said, "Well, now that I'm a part of the family, me and Papa think there's some things I need to know."

Rachel shot a look at Franklin that said *what have you been telling him?*

"Now hold on, Mama. I ain't told Eugene nothin'. All's I said is that I'd be talkin' to you 'bout sharin' a few things with him, that's all."

Rachel's voice was low and quiet as she looked Franklin in the eyes. "He's too young to know."

"Mama, he's been through a lot hisself. He doesn't have to know everything right now, but he can know a little bit. 'Sides, he's nearly twelve."

"Yep, I'll be twelve next month!"

Rachel smiled at him then. "I know it; you'll soon be a man." She moved her chair back from the table and acknowledged the nervousness within. "What do you want to know?"

"I want to know why you don't ever go to Winchester, and why don't you and Papa want anyone coming up here from town?"

She didn't know where to start or even if she could. She realized she was about to talk of things that hadn't been spoken of in over twenty years. Franklin had always been there to protect her, but she knew he wasn't able to protect her from the vulnerability she was feeling now.

"Eugene," she took a long deep breath, "something bad happened to me and your papa a long time ago." Eugene's brow became furrowed, and once again, Rachel wasn't sure if she was doing the right thing, but she continued anyway.

"We used to go into Winchester almost once a week to buy what we needed and do business in town. But most folks didn't understand our marriage; you see, most people think I'm white just like you. But my mother was a Negro woman and I was raised among the Negroes on the Hawkins plantation. The other night when you asked who my people are, my people have always been Franklin's people. But folks just don't seem to have an understanding of that, and you can't go around explaining that everywhere you go." Rachel slowly and painfully continued.

"We knew people in town didn't accept us, and sometimes nasty things were said to us right out in public on the street where everyone could hear it. We decided from the very beginning that we would never respond to such filth. But we could only take so much of it. After a while we thought it was best not to go into town very often, at least not together." Her voice shook a little and she looked down at her hands in her lap.

"Our people have always accepted the two of us, so we continued to worship every Sunday at a little church on the outskirts of Winchester. Papa and I had a lot of good friends at that church." Rachel glanced at Franklin, giving him the faintest of smiles before she continued.

"One Sunday after the worship service we were all standing around outside enjoying the fellowship. All of a sudden we heard a noise on the road and about twenty or more white men on horseback came storming up to the church. They were angry about me and your papa coming into *their* town. A lot of horrible things were said by those men, and it wasn't long before violence broke out. Two men from our congregation were killed that day, all because of us."

Eugene suddenly jumped to his feet. "That wasn't your fault, Mama!"

Rachel shook her head. "In some ways it was. We've always felt sad about what happened. Two families lost their husbands and fathers because of us. We made a decision after that to protect our people and never go back."

No one spoke for a very long time. Rachel was re-living the scene again in her mind. She'd been thirty-three years old and Franklin thirty-nine when all of this had taken place. She hadn't shared the whole story of that horrible afternoon with Eugene. She could still feel the hands of those men on her. They had yanked her out of the crowd, called her disgusting names, and said no white woman was permitted to be a part of that church. Rachel had been completely humiliated as they put their hands on her in ways reserved for her husband alone. Franklin had gone wild when he saw the way his wife was being handled. It was a wonder he hadn't been killed that day as well.

Franklin stood up and took Rachel by the hand, pulling her into his arms. "You did fine, Mama." He spoke so softly into her ear Eugene couldn't even hear him. "I love ya, Rach." Another arm came around her waist as Eugene joined in the hug. She was surprised that she'd been able to tell the story without crying, but there was no holding back now. Her men just held her as she wept in their arms.

Chapter 8

Christmas 1912

Rachel and Franklin hadn't had a Christmas tree since the first year of their marriage. Franklin's pappy had always dragged a fairly large fir tree into the cave every December. But for some reason after he passed away, neither he nor Rachel had seen fit to cut down another tree. They hadn't seen much reason for gift giving either—but Eugene changed everything.

"How do you like this one, Mama?" Eugene was excited about finding a good-sized fir tree near the pond on the other side of the pasture. All three of them had been walking through the woods for a good bit of the afternoon trying to find just the right tree.

Rachel took her time walking around the tree, making sure it looked pretty on all sides. Franklin just leaned on his axe handle, as if he expected this tree to be rejected too. So far she had found something wrong with a half dozen or more trees.

"Rach, I was hopin' we could pick us out a tree today."

She ignored her husband's teasing remark and declared, "It's important we find just the right one."

Eugene said, "Mama, no one's going to see it but us." He thought this one looked perfect, but then, he thought the other ones were perfect too.

Rachel finally decided this one would be fine despite its imperfections. Besides, she could see how anxious Eugene was to cut down his first tree.

Franklin took the axe and notched the trunk on one side and then handed it to Eugene. It took him a lot longer than it would've taken Franklin, but when the tree finally fell to the ground, Eugene let out a loud whoop while Rachel clapped and cheered.

Franklin said, "We're gonna carry it all the way back so's not to mess it up before we get it in place. We don't want Mama sendin' us out to chop down another one."

Rachel giggled and pinched him on the side as she picked up the axe off the ground.

On the way back to the cave, Eugene couldn't help but remember last year's Christmas with his stepfather. Louis had actually given him a gift. It was a carved wooden horse that he had played with all day long. That night, Eugene watched in horror as Louis threw it into the fire during a fit of rage, and then made fun of him while he cried.

Eugene shook his head trying to rid himself of that awful memory—it was starting to give him a stomachache. The best thing to do would be to concentrate on this Christmas and not the last one. He wasn't expecting any gifts; he was just thankful to be living on the farm with his new family. That was gift enough.

A few days later when he awoke on Christmas morning, Eugene was surprised to discover a present waiting for him beneath the tree. He excitedly opened the box to find a copy of *The Count of Monte Cristo* by Alexandre Dumas. Throughout the day he and Rachel took turns reading the book out loud. Franklin was just as engrossed in the story as Eugene.

Rachel prepared a fine Christmas dinner, and as usual, there was no lack of conversation around the table.

Eugene asked, "Why don't you ever name the horses, Papa?"

"I'm afraid if I name 'em I'll be too sad to sell 'em." Franklin was reaching for another helping of sweet potatoes.

"How 'bout we name the milk cow then? We won't be selling her."

"Now I think that'd be a fine idea. Whatcha got in mind?"

For the next several minutes, all three of them bantered at least a dozen different names around the table. Finally Rachel said,

"How about Contessa to remind us of the *Count of Monte Cristo?*"

"I think that'd be a good name. What do you think, Papa?" Eugene didn't want to give her a name that Papa didn't agree on.

"Well, that's a mighty fancy name for a cow, but I specs she's deservin' of it after all the milk she's given us over the years."

Eugene couldn't wait to tell Contessa about her new name. "Mama, can I be excused? I want to see how she likes it!"

"I suppose you can have your Christmas pudding when you get back."

Eugene jumped up from the table, grabbed a lantern, and took off down the long passageway. He found Contessa contentedly chomping on hay at the other end of the cave. He wasn't sure if she liked her new name or not, but she certainly did enjoy having her ears scratched. The horses were also in that end of the cave. Franklin kept a lantern burning in their shelter throughout the winter days in case they wanted to come in out of the weather.

Eugene hadn't been with the horses all day, so he stayed with the herd a while and worked his way around to each animal. When he came to the pregnant mare, he began to rub under her belly and couldn't help but notice how much more rounded it was. Suddenly without warning, her tail swished violently into his face and he felt an intense burning pain in the back of his left shoulder. He jumped away from her as fast as he could. Her teeth were bared at him and he could see the blood in her mouth. *What on earth is going on?* Eugene had never been frightened of the horses before, but she was definitely putting a scare into him now. He tried to look over his shoulder to see what she had done, but he couldn't see the wound. He knew he was hurt pretty bad though, so he grabbed the lantern and made his way back down the passageway.

Franklin and Rachel were still sitting at the table talking when they saw Eugene come through the opening at the other end of the room. Instantly Rachel's eyes were drawn to the torn shirt and she noticed the look of confusion on his face.

"The pregnant mare . . ." Eugene's voice was higher pitched than normal. "She attacked me." Both Rachel and Franklin reached him at the same time.

"What happened?" Rachel was gently pulling back the torn portion of his shirt to try to get a look at the wound—it didn't look good.

"Franklin, please hold the light up for me." She sat Eugene down on the end of his bed and helped him remove his shirt. No doubt about it, the mare had ripped into the back of his shoulder and left a gaping wound.

Rachel said, "Stay with him, Papa."

There was hot water in the kettle on the stove, and Rachel hurriedly poured some into a bowl and mixed it with cool water from the pitcher. As she was gathering up her supplies, Eugene asked Papa, "Why would the mare do that to me? She knows how much I love her."

Franklin held the light a little higher as Rachel began to clean the wound. Eugene flinched at the pain, and Rachel apologized for causing him further discomfort.

Franklin explained, "Son, she's got a foal in her belly, and sometimes a gentle mare can get upset and bite or kick when she's never done such a thing before. I've even seen the orneriest mares come to be gentle when they're with foal. T'ain't no explainin' it; just the way o' nature. But she's got to be respectful. I'll have me a talk with her tonight."

Rachel had a grave look on her face when she turned to Franklin. "That talk will have to wait. I'll need your help to sew him up."

Eugene's breathing suddenly increased dramatically. Rachel sat down in front of him on the bed and rested her hand on the side of his face. "Eugene, that wound won't heal without being sewn up. I'm so sorry, darlin'." He nodded slightly, doing his best to look brave, but he was scared to death inside. As she rose to her feet, she kissed his forehead and told him to lie down on his stomach.

Franklin put a lamp on the small, bedside table and

brought another one to hang up high. He moved to the other side of the bed and sat down to hold Eugene steady.

Rachel sterilized the needle in the alcohol they kept for medicinal purposes. When Eugene saw her threading the needle, he scrunched his eyes tighter than a screw sunk deep into a piece of wood. He was so tense.

"Darlin' I need that shoulder to be relaxed so I can stitch it up smoothly." Eugene watched her put down the needle and felt her rubbing his arms and back as she began to hum softly. Her warm hands were soothing, and he sensed his muscles beginning to relax. Soon Rachel fell silent as she picked up the needle again and started her first stitch. It was a stinging pain, and he couldn't stop himself from crying out once or twice. But he used every smidgen of willpower not to move or tense up his shoulder again.

Franklin laid a gentle hand on Eugene's right arm and said, "You're a strong boy, Eugene. You keep bein' brave. If'n I could take these stitches for ya, I would."

It took several long minutes before Rachel finally tied off the last stitch and cut the thread. But that wasn't the worst of it. She still had to put alcohol on the wound to keep it from getting infected. "Eugene, you need to hold on to your papa's hand."

She soaked a cloth with alcohol and gently dabbed it on the wound. The pain was almost more than Eugene could bear. He pressed his face into the pillow then and let out a deep, guttural sound.

Rachel continued to apologize. "I'm sorry, Eugene, I'm so, so sorry."

After she finished, Rachel covered the wound the best she could, then continued to sit with him, rubbing her hand on his lower back. "It's over now, Son; I'm so proud of you."

Eugene slowly moved into a sitting position. His eyes were moist but he managed a grin when he looked at Rachel. "You did save me some pudding, didn't you?"

Rachel laughed and smoothed her hand across his hair. "The rest of the pudding belongs to you."

***

When Franklin returned from the other end of the cave an hour later, Eugene was in his nightshirt while Rachel sat by his bed reading to him. They stopped reading to find out how the mare was doing. Franklin explained that it would be best for Eugene to stay away from her until she gave birth.

"I don't reckon she'll attack you again in the herd, but for some reason she just don't wanna be touched." Franklin had been firm with her when she swished her tail at him and stomped her front hoof. But he refused to give her the upper hand. He leaned steadily into her neck and held her head low with his hand on her muzzle while telling her gently what he expected of her. Finally, the mare gave in to his discipline and allowed him to rub her belly.

"Have I missed much o' the story?" Franklin asked as he took a seat on the end of the bed.

Excitedly Eugene caught him up on what he'd missed. "Edmund was falsely accused of plotting with Napoleon Bonaparte and he's been thrown into the prison at Chateau D'If."

At the end of the next chapter, Rachel closed the book and declared it time for bed. She reminded Eugene that he would need to sleep on his right side and try not to lie on the stitches. He didn't think he'd need to be reminded of that. It was fairly painful even with the bandage wrapped around his shoulder.

Franklin took both of their hands in his and led them in prayer before bed. He expressed his thanks to God for sending His son as a little baby all those years ago. Then he asked the Almighty to touch Eugene and heal him once again. This time, Eugene was able to voice his own *amen*.

The next few days couldn't go by fast enough for Eugene. His twelfth birthday was coming up on Wednesday and his papa had already told him there'd be a surprise for him on that day.

Rachel was taking advantage of the sunny days God had given them the week after Christmas. Thus far they were having a mild winter. She always made it a point to spend as much time in the sunshine as possible during these months. It just wasn't good to be deep under the earth for very long. Franklin always made sure he laid a fire for her in the upstairs fireplace so the house would have a little warmth.

Wednesday morning after the men went out to do their chores, Rachel started to work on a chocolate cake for Eugene in the upper kitchen. She had made sure to buy all the right ingredients during their visit to Lexington earlier in the fall. At the noon meal, Eugene could see the cake sitting on the counter.

"Eugene, slow down before you get a stomachache." Rachel couldn't believe the speed with which he was putting the food away.

"I ain't seen a chocolate cake in years," he said excitedly.

"I *haven't* seen a chocolate cake," Rachel corrected.

Franklin's eyebrows were raised when Eugene looked over at him. He returned his attention back to Rachel.

"How come you correct me and not Papa?"

"Because I got your papa when it was too late, but it's not too late for you, young man. Besides, I'm hoping someday you'll attend the university in Lexington."

"Not if it means I have to leave here." Eugene couldn't imagine the thought of leaving Franklin and Rachel and the horses.

"You've got a few more birthdays before we have to worry about that," Rachel replied. "We'll just count our blessings for every day we have together."

Franklin chimed in, "Are we gonna cut the cake or what? I'm thinkin' I can't wait another minute." His wink to Eugene didn't escape Rachel. She wasn't quite done eating, but she brought the cake to the table anyway and cut two slices for the men. Eugene thought it was the most heavenly thing he'd ever put in his mouth.

Franklin finished his cake and pushed back from the table. Moments later he returned from the bedroom carrying a long box.

"This is for you, Son. Happy birthday!" Franklin put the

box in Eugene's lap and lifted the lid.

Eugene didn't know what to say. He took a deep breath, and with wide eyes, he asked, "Is this for me?"

"Uh huh, that's yours to keep. It's a Winchester rifle, lever-action 1894. I've got a model 1866."

Eugene took it out of the box and held it lovingly. "Wow, I can't believe it! Where'd you get it?"

"You was sleepin' in the wagon in Lexington when I hid it under the tarp."

Franklin put a box of .30–30 cartridges on the table. "You need to do some target practice 'fore we go huntin'. What do ya say we get to it?"

Eugene was on his feet in a flash.

Rachel put her hand in the air and said, "Hold on just a minute you two. I need to check Eugene's stitches."

Eugene knew better than to argue with his mama, so he put down the rifle and unbuttoned his flannel shirt. The wound seemed to be healing nicely and looked like it wouldn't leave too bad of a scar. The entire time Rachel was examining her handiwork, she was spouting a lecture on gun safety. Both men said, "Yes, ma'am," in all the proper places.

She lifted his shirt back up on his shoulder and said, "Less than a week and I'll be able to take the stitches out."

"Thanks, Mama." Eugene turned and gave her a quick embrace. "And thanks for the rifle!" He was out the door so fast, with only one arm in his coat; he didn't even hear Rachel wish him a happy birthday.

When the men returned to the house in the late afternoon, Rachel was checking the laundry lying over a rack near the fire. She'd been scrubbing clothes for the better part of the day. Franklin immediately went downstairs, but Eugene sat down on the couch admiring his rifle.

"That's not loaded is it?" Rachel asked. Having an unloaded rifle in the house was one of the stipulations in her previous lecture.

"No, ma'am."

Franklin came up the stairs with his coat still on and a bag over his shoulder. He kissed Rachel on the cheek and told her not to wait up. "You'ns go on to bed without me. I'll be home late tonight," he said.

Rachel followed her husband to the door. They stood in the kitchen for a very long time speaking in hushed tones. Eugene stayed on the couch taking aim at the clothes on the rack. He hurriedly lowered the rifle to his lap at the sound of his mama's footsteps.

When Rachel returned to the room she'd been crying.

"Mama?" Eugene asked softly.

"Not now, Eugene." She felt bad to put the boy off, but she knew she was too emotional to talk to him at the moment. Surprisingly, Eugene quietly walked out onto the porch and sat down on the steps with his rifle across his lap.

Rachel took a seat by the fire to warm her body. She was suddenly feeling chilled and worried about Franklin. Every New Year's Day Rachel did the same thing. She sat alone by the fire and prayed fervently for the safety of her husband.

Chapter 9

Rachel lay awake in the dim light of the cave below. She always kept a lantern burning at its lowest setting to give just enough light if anyone should need to get up during the night. She could hear Eugene squirming in his bed and knew he must be as anxious for Franklin's return as she was. *O God, please send an angel to watch over your servant tonight.*

At that moment, a jittery voice drifted across the room. "Mama? Is Papa coming home?"

She couldn't explain her silence; there just seemed no way to answer his question.

"Mama?"

Rachel knew Eugene was worried, so she moved over and held the covers open for him. "Come here."

He didn't hesitate a second to run across the room barefoot and climb in beside her. "Where'd he go, Mama?"

Rachel still remained silent. The truth was she was just trying to keep her voice from shaking. She'd always been worried in the past, but this year was harder than ever before. Eugene had changed everything.

Finally, Rachel felt an inkling of composure return. "You remember I told you about what happened in town at church?"

"Uh huh."

"Well, every year on January first, Papa goes to the two families who lost their man and leaves something for them."

Eugene propped himself up on his elbows. "You mean he's in town?"

"Yes."

"What if someone sees him?"

"That's why he waits till dark. He makes sure no one will see him."

"What does he leave 'em?"

"Mostly enough money to help them get by for the year. This time he took a slab of meat for both of the families too. Sometimes I'll make them a quilt or blanket, but I've been a little distracted these past few months." For the first time, Rachel allowed herself to give Eugene the hint of a smile.

He dropped back on the pillow, looking up in the dim light. "Does he talk to 'em?"

Franklin's strong voice suddenly bellowed out from the other side of the room. "I talked to 'em this time."

Franklin was nearly knocked to the ground by wife and son as he emerged from the passage in the far wall. He put down the lantern and engulfed them in his arms.

Rachel put on her robe and threw a quilt around Eugene's shoulders as they all sat down on the bed to hear Franklin's account of the night.

He explained to Eugene that both families live on the far side of Winchester, so he had to skirt around the whole town to get to their houses. This time he knew he couldn't just leave the meat out on the porch at night. Critters would come along and drag it off.

"Lights were still burnin' in the Reed household. I was gonna leave everything on the porch and knock then go away. But for some strange reason I was still standin' there when Sam's widow woman come to the door. We was just starin' at each other for the longest time."

Franklin said when Anna finally recognized him she took hold of his arm and told him to come in.

"You know all their chillens are grown and gone 'cept little Emma? She's still livin' with her mama and helpin' take care of her." Little Emma had been a babe in her mother's arms when the incident had taken place.

Rachel could see that Eugene was fascinated with everything Franklin was saying. "Did she know you'd been giving her the money all these years?" he asked.

"No sir, she was thinkin' some white person in town was feelin' bad 'bout what happened and tryin' to make their conscience feel better." He slipped his hand underneath Rachel's and held it gently. "She never dreamt it be you and me, Mama."

Rachel would dearly love to see her old friend again. While Eugene fulfilled her longing for a child, there was still a void in her life that only a woman friend could fill. It had been a long time since she'd been able to share the joys and sorrows of life with another woman.

Franklin suddenly gathered Rachel in his arms and gave her a tight hug. When he released her, he noticed the questioning look on her face.

"That hug comes from Anna. I gave her one from you too."

Franklin went on to explain that by the time he made it over to Clara Eton's place, all the lights were out and he didn't want to disturb her. He left the money in the bucket on the back porch like always but dropped the meat back at the Reed place.

"Anna said she'd be happy to take it over to Clara's in the mornin'."

Rachel didn't seem to want to let go of Franklin's hand, but she knew it was time for all of them to get some sleep. She rose to take Eugene back to bed but Franklin put his hand on her shoulder and said, "I got him, Rach." As she took her robe off and slipped back into bed, she could hear the conversation across the room. "I'm sorry you was worried 'bout me tonight." Franklin pulled the quilt up around his son's shoulders.

Eugene covered a sizeable yawn, then said, "I was prayin', but I didn't know what to pray for. Now I know. Thanks for telling me."

"Now that you're a man there's lots more I need to tell ya, but we got plenty o' time for that. You sleep now and I'll see you in the mornin'." Eugene sat up in the bed and put his arms around his papa's neck. Franklin gave him as strong a hug as he dared without messing up Rachel's stitches.

***

January brought a light snow that disappeared as quickly as it fell. Eugene was disappointed because he had always loved a good snow when he had lived in town. It never seemed to matter how cold the temperature was though; he was outside every day all day. That's the way he liked it. Rachel had a hard time just pinning him down long enough to take out his stitches. They came out nicely, but she apologized for the curved scar on the back of his shoulder. He didn't care; who was going to see the back of his shoulder anyway? Rachel agreed and told him she was just thankful to have kept it from getting infected.

Just a week after his birthday, Eugene finally got to go hunting for the first time. Franklin hadn't been hunting in years. When he and his pappy had moved up here in '65, that's the only way they had survived. But by the time he brought Rachel to the farm in the fall of '74, he had already sold three horses to Master Hawkins and four more at auction. There was really no need for hunting anymore. They could afford to buy everything they needed in Winchester and Lexington.

"Now if'n we shoot somethin' we're gonna eat it. We're not gonna kill one o' God's creatures for nothin'." Franklin didn't even have his rifle with him. He hadn't bought cartridges for it in years, but he sure was curious to see Eugene try his hand at hunting. They spotted two squirrels, one deer, and spooked three rabbits before Eugene finally got his first kill. He'd missed both squirrels and didn't have the heart to shoot the deer, but he dropped the third rabbit before it hit its stride.

When they got home later that morning, Eugene burst into the house holding up his prize rabbit by the hind legs. Franklin leaned on the water pump outside just laughing. He knew exactly what was coming.

"Get that rabbit out of this house, young man! I'll be glad to cook anything you bring home, but I don't want to see it until it's ready for the cooking pot."

"Yes, ma'am, sorry, Mama. But ain't he a beauty!"

"ISN'T, Eugene, isn't he a beauty and yes, he is." Rachel had her hand on his back pushing him toward the door. "Take that poor creature outside and tell your papa he can stop laughing now."

It wasn't long before Eugene could hit just about anything he spotted. But the prize kill for his first hunting season came in February when he dropped his first elk. Even Rachel agreed that the antlers needed to be mounted over the fireplace. The elk steaks were a little on the tough side, but the animal provided meat for their family all the way through the first three months of 1913.

At the end of March, Franklin began to ready the family for a new birth. Eugene had been riding around the property all afternoon on his favorite horse, while Franklin had spent the day with his mare in the pasture. Papa met Eugene in the shed as he was putting away the horse tack. "It's gettin' close to the mare's time. We're gonna separate her from the herd so she can have a place all her own to foal."

Eugene walked a fair distance behind his papa as he led the mare to the cave, and a wooden gate was pulled up in front of the entrance to keep the other animals away. Together they prepared a comfortable space for the mare in the shelter. Franklin explained that they needed to keep fresh hay on the floor and the shelter well lit.

"Most mares like to foal late at night or early mornin'. Those'r peaceful times and they want to be alone," Franklin explained.

"What about us? Can we watch?" Eugene asked. He didn't want to miss a thing.

"We need to watch in case there's any trouble." Franklin had been through more than a few difficult births over the years, but he had never lost a foal.

"How do we know when it's time for her to foal?"

"When she starts havin' contractions, she'll be restless and pace 'round the room. She might even bite or nudge her own side. When that starts happenin' you know it won't be long."

Just then, Rachel appeared in the shelter from the passageway. "How's our girl doing?"

"Nothin's happenin' yet, Mama. But Papa thinks it's gonna be tonight."

Rachel moved to Franklin and put her hand through the crook of his arm drawing him close to her. She looked at Eugene and said, "I don't think I'll ever grow tired of watching a mare foal. It's a miracle from God."

Franklin leaned into his wife grinning and said, "We've stayed up many a night together waitin' for that miracle to happen. Last spring we had two mares foal in three days' time. Not much sleep to be had then."

Rachel smiled and said, "If nothing is happening yet, how about a little supper of cornbread and beans before the vigil begins?"

Eugene didn't appear to want to leave the mare but Franklin put him at ease by saying, "That sounds good, Mama. We gotta keep up our energy if'n we're gonna be able to help the mare tonight."

When they sat down at the table in the lower house, Eugene blessed the meal and made sure he included the mare and her foal. Sure enough, by the time Rachel cleaned up the dishes and joined the men in the shelter, the mare was already having contractions. She was pacing and pawing the ground and showing all the signs of discomfort. Within an hour, her water broke and she moved to fresh hay and lay down on the floor. It was then that she started to nicker and whinny.

"Is she all right?" Eugene kept his voice low.

Franklin put his hand on Eugene's back and rubbed up and down. "She's fine. It won't be long now."

The mare couldn't seem to decide if she was in the right spot or not. She got up twice and repositioned herself on the floor. Finally, the foal's head presented itself and its whole body just seemed to come sliding right out onto the hay. He lifted his head and neck and instantly rolled onto his chest.

Franklin was watching closely to make sure the foal had broken through the sac that was surrounding him. If not, he would have to tear it open himself and clear the foal's nasal passages.

"He's breathing!" Rachel cried.

Eugene could see the rhythmic movement of his little chest and felt a wave of relief wash over him. He realized he hadn't taken a breath himself since the foal had been born.

The mare was resting quietly now, but her foal was on the move. Eugene laughed when the little guy started creeping forward and his ears flopped to the side. His head seemed a little wobbly at first while he figured out his next move. Several minutes passed before his skinny little forelegs lifted his chest off the ground. He held that position for only a few seconds before he landed back on the floor spread eagle. His hind legs weren't strong enough to fully support him yet, but the next attempt sent him staggering a few steps before he crumpled to the ground. After a few more attempts, he decided it was time to rest. It was at that moment that Franklin introduced himself to the foal. He squatted down next to him and began rubbing his neck and chest. The mare moved close to Franklin so he put his palm up to her muzzle and talked soothingly to her, even though his words were meant for Eugene.

"I don't wanna interfere none with the bondin' 'tween mother and foal, but right now, this little fella's fearless. It's the perfect time to introduce myself to him."

Finally he said, "Come 'ere, Son." Franklin put his palm back up to the mare's muzzle as Eugene presented himself to the foal. Eugene was so full of love for the colt he wanted to throw his arms around his neck and squeeze him tight. But he wisely kept his emotions in check and imitated Franklin's every move, talking to him all the while.

Before an hour had passed, the foal was standing on his own again and this time taking a few shaky steps. Once again, Eugene's laughter echoed throughout the cave.

Rachel said, "Believe it or not, Eugene, you'll see this little guy galloping in the pasture tomorrow morning."

Franklin confirmed Rachel's declaration. "Uh huh, but right now he's probly thinkin' how hungry he is."

As if he'd understood what Franklin was saying, the little foal moved over to his mama's side. It didn't take him long to find what he was looking for and he began to nurse loudly. He only nursed for a short time before he decided a nap was in order. Still without much coordination, he collapsed on the hay and the mare moved close by to watch over her foal.

Franklin busied himself cleaning up the shelter while Eugene spread fresh hay where the birth had taken place. When that chore was done, Franklin declared it was time to leave mother and son alone so they could get to know each other better.

"Eugene, let's you and me go up on the porch and have us a little talk." The two men put on their jackets and went outside in the cool night air. They sat down on the top step and looked up at the stars for a long time. Eugene just waited patiently for his papa to tell him what was on his mind.

After a while, Franklin took in a deep breath and let it out slowly. "Son, I think it's time for you to know how things is 'tween a man and a woman."

Rachel was sitting by the lantern reading the Bible when her men came into the house. Eugene seemed to be a little embarrassed when she looked up, so she asked them to have a seat on the sofa while she finished reading the passage out loud. She'd been reading the story of Ruth and Boaz, and once again the irony wasn't lost on either husband or son.

After Eugene went to bed, his folks stayed up and conversed in hushed voices. "How did your little talk go?"

Franklin grinned. "It went fine, just fine. After watchin' the mare foal tonight, it was a lot easier to explain how things is, if ya know what I mean."

Rachel smiled and could only imagine the questions Eugene might have asked.

Franklin said quietly, "He asked me 'bout you. He's got some things he's tryin' to put together in his mind." He took

Rachel's hand and pulled her onto the sofa beside him. She nestled up close to his side thinking about the new little foal in the shelter and wondering how long she had before Eugene asked the right question.

Chapter 10

After breakfast the next morning, Rachel joined Franklin and Eugene in the pasture to watch the little colt kick up his heels. All three of them were laughing as they watched his escapades. Not having another young playmate, he was doing his best to get his mama to play with him. He ran circles around her while kicking out his feet and jumping straight up in the air. The little fella just seemed to bring a joy to the farm that said winter was over and spring was here.

Rachel took in the scent of the fresh morning air and with it came an overwhelming contentment. "We are so blessed."

"Yes'm, we're blessed indeed," Franklin replied.

Rachel couldn't remember the last time she'd joined Franklin at the oak tree, but this morning she found a spot and sat down with her back to the tree.

As the animals gathered around, she couldn't help but feel the presence of God in their midst. This morning Franklin held back so Rachel could see Eugene's gift. Not everyone had the patience to train a horse in such a way. It took a very special person to listen to what each animal had to say and become one of them. Franklin may have taught Eugene the technique, but *the gift* had come directly from God. There was no doubt about it.

The mare and her foal were the last to join the herd this morning. As they approached, the foal collapsed on the ground in the shade to take a nap. Eugene carefully reintroduced himself to the mare. She appeared to harbor no animosity toward him as he approached. All of his words were tender and soothing, but he patiently took the time to listen to her. Her demeanor told him that everything was fine between them. Scratching her head between her ears brought just the response he'd been waiting for. Her head dropped down over his shoulder while Eugene showed his affection for her.

Rachel was tense as she watched the mare's head drop down over Eugene's left shoulder. Franklin turned to her and said, "Relax Rach, she's herself again."

As Franklin began to walk among the herd, Eugene eased gently away and sat down beside Rachel. "How come you never had children, Mama?"

Eugene never ceased to amaze her with all of his questions. She didn't blame him though—they'd been together for nine months and there were still so many things he didn't know.

"Eugene," she let out a faint sigh, "for some reason, which only the Lord knows, your papa and I weren't able to have children." She glanced over at him sitting beside her. "That is, until you came along." Both of them shared a soft laugh.

Down deep Rachel knew more questions were coming. She decided to sit quietly and wait for the next one and the next one and the next one . . .

Eugene didn't miss a beat. "If your mama was a Negro woman, was your papa a white man?"

There it was. She wondered how long it would take for him to ask that question. But for some reason, today she found herself ready and almost eager to talk about the past.

"Yes, Eugene, my father was Samuel Hawkins, owner of the plantation where your papa and I were born." Rachel decided to start at the beginning, so Eugene would understand how things were back then.

"My mother's name was Naomi, and she was born into slavery on the Hawkins plantation. When she was old enough, she became what was known as a domestic slave. She worked in the big house cleaning and washing and taking care of all the family's nice things."

"Did she live in the big house?"

"No, every night she returned to the slave quarters on the other side of the plantation. The Hawkinses owned hundreds of slaves, so the slave quarters were almost like a little town all to itself. But every morning she'd walk over to the main house." Rachel wanted Eugene to know how cruel slavery really was, but now was not the time. That conversation would be reckoned with in the future, so she continued by simply saying, "It was hard being a domestic slave, but the field slaves had it much worse. Working in the cotton fields was backbreaking work out in the hot sun all day long."

Franklin moved away from the herd and sat down on an old log nearby. Rachel felt certain he hadn't thought about his mother and sister in a very long time. She was going to have to tell their story before she could finish the one about her own mother. She looked at her husband tenderly then turned her attention back to Eugene. "Your papa's mother was named Ruth and his sister was named Sarah. Both of them were personal slaves to Master Hawkins' wife, Elizabeth, and oldest daughter, Isabella. Samuel and Elizabeth Hawkins had three other children: two sons, and another daughter that was just a babe. One morning, I believe it was early June . . ."

"In '56 . . ." Franklin's voice broke in.

"Yes, in June of 1856, Elizabeth and Isabella Hawkins went into Lexington for a day of shopping. They were driven to town in a fancy carriage with fine horses and the best driver on the plantation. Papa, do you remember his name?"

"Ezekiel. His name was Ezekiel."

Rachel watched their horses slowly move away from the oak and start grazing in the warm sunshine. The newest member of the herd woke up suddenly and moved out in search of his mother. Only Contessa remained in the shade chewing her cud and listening to Rachel's story.

"Whenever Elizabeth and Isabella went into Lexington, they always took their personal slaves, so your papa's mother and sister were in the carriage too. That afternoon while they were on the road back to the plantation, a terrible storm came up. The river rose very suddenly over a low section of the road. Ezekiel must have thought they could make it across the water in the road, but the carriage was swept into the river and they all drowned."

"All of 'em?" Eugene sat straight up, and appeared to be distressed.

Rachel looked at him with compassion in her eyes. "Yes, all of them."

Franklin spoke up then. "Most o' the slaves went out with torches all night searchin' the woods 'n' river. My pappy was one of 'em and Massa Hawkins too. I's only four years old, so I ain't got much recollection of that night. But I do recall the loud wailin' in the slave quarters all the next day."

Rachel said, "Their bodies were found in the morning washed down river. Sarah's body was the only one they never found."

Franklin slowly rose to his feet and started walking toward the house. Rachel and Eugene followed silently until they all sat down on the top step of the front porch. For some reason, that top step seemed to be the place where important family matters were discussed.

Franklin picked up again, where Rachel had left off. "My pappy never stopped lookin' for Sarah as long as we lived on that plantation. Sometimes he'd be up way before dawn, walkin' 'long the river. He told me her soul would never find rest unlessen we could give her a proper burial."

Eugene asked with all sincerity, "Do you think that's true?"

Franklin shook his head. "I'm thinkin' the good Lord takes care of those that can't be found."

Rachel was now contemplating how she would tell Eugene about her mother and Samuel Hawkins when he asked his next question.

"Did Mr. Samuel marry your mother?"

So much for working her way around to it *slowly*! Eugene had a way of getting right to the heart of the matter. He was sitting on the other side of Franklin, so she leaned forward, resting her elbows on the top of her legs. "Mr. Samuel was a sad and lonely man after he lost his wife, Elizabeth. It wasn't long before he fell in love with one of his house slaves. It was said that she was a very beautiful woman."

"Your mama?"

"Yes, my mother, Naomi. Eugene," Rachel took a deep breath, "he didn't marry her, but he did things with her that are reserved for the marriage bed alone."

Eugene interrupted. "Me and Papa talked about that very thing last night, didn't we, Papa?" Eugene didn't seem to be embarrassed now. As a matter of fact, he winked at Franklin as if they shared a secret Rachel didn't know about.

Franklin just chuckled and nodded for Rachel to continue.

"After a while, Naomi discovered she was with child and there were some on the plantation who suspected that Mr. Samuel was the father. But when it came time for her delivery, it was a very difficult one. She spent an entire day and night in horrible pain but couldn't seem to deliver the baby. By morning she knew she was dying, and she asked for Mr. Samuel to come to her. That's how they all knew for sure that the baby was his. He refused to leave Naomi's side even as her labor continued until late that night. Finally, I was born and laid in my mother's arms while she was dying. She told Mr. Samuel that her baby's name was to be Rachel, and she made him promise to take care of me. They say we were both in his arms when she died."

Eugene was shaking his head but seemed to be out of questions for the moment.

"I needed my mother's milk if I was going to survive, so they gave me to someone who was already nursing her own baby, and she nursed me along with her own. But when I was old enough, Mr. Samuel came for me and had me educated by a tutor alongside his youngest daughter, Catherine."

"Did you live in the big house?"

"No, someone always came and got me after my lessons, and I was raised in the slave quarters by the same woman who had been my nurse. Her name was Jessie. I think Master Hawkins took care of her because she never had to work on the plantation. She just took care of me along with her other children. But when

I turned seven, the war ended and Master Hawkins let all of his slaves go free. A lot of us had nowhere to go, so we just stayed on the plantation and worked for him of our own free will. But from that time on, I worked in the house for pay. He still provided a tutor for me until I was sixteen, and after my lessons every day, I was one of his household servants."

"Did you live in the big house then?"

"No, I always went back to Jessie every night. As far as I was concerned, she was my mother."

"How'd you meet Papa?"

"Well, one day when I was fifteen, I was working in the front parlor when someone came to the door. It was a nice-looking young man with his hat in his hand saying he had a fine horse to sell to Mr. Hawkins. I let him in and he introduced himself to me as Franklin." Rachel noticed Franklin was grinning from ear to ear. "He said he already knew who *I* was. I took him back to Mr. Samuel's study . . ."

"And I was watchin' her instead of where I was goin'," Franklin interrupted. "I run smack into a table in the hallway, and she was laughin' the whole time I was talkin' to Mr. Hawkins."

Rachel said, "It seems to me you were in a bit of trouble, too, when you got back home to your pappy."

Eugene's laughter told Rachel he was enjoying this part of the story as he listened to them banter back and forth.

"I was in trouble for sure, when I got back here. I stayed a whole extra day at the plantation just so I could see the beautiful Miss Rachel one more time 'fore I went home. Yessa, Pappy let me have it good."

"What did you tell him?" Eugene asked.

"Well Son, I told him I was goin' back to that plantation and get me a wife same time next year. Pappy just laughed, but he wasn't laughin' no more when I brought your mama home. We got married right there on the plantation and came home husband and wife." Franklin stuck his chest out looking every bit as proud as he had been thirty-eight years ago.

For several minutes they sat on the porch laughing and

reminiscing about their younger days until Eugene had one more question for Franklin.

"What happened to your pappy?"

"The Lord called him home a year an' a half after I brought your mama here. Some kind o' sickness like pneumonia or somethin'." There was a long pause while everyone contemplated his passing. "We been up here all by ourself ever since."

After that day, Eugene had a better understanding of his folks, and felt a keen sense of loyalty and love for them both. It wasn't long before they gave him a free reign of the farm—even the stream wasn't off limits anymore. But he was always mindful to be on the lookout for anyone who might wander onto their land. He knew his mama worried about him when he was hunting or riding, but as the years went by, few people ever bothered to make their way up the steep path in the woods.

Eugene loved his peculiar, carefree days. His life had been so hard until the Lord led him to Franklin and Rachel. Even though he savored every day on the farm, he had no way of knowing how short those untroubled days would turn out to be.

Chapter 11

1917

October of 1917 brought one of the most beautiful autumns Rachel had ever seen. They'd had a very dry summer, and as a result, the leaves were showing off in bright and brilliant colors. It made for a most pleasant trip to Lexington this year.

At age sixteen, Eugene was growing into a tall, handsome young man, and she watched him as he drove the wagon. It was uncanny how much he looked like her with his dark hair and deep brown eyes. Rachel marveled over the fact that Eugene had lived with them for over five years. He was no longer a young boy; she had to remind herself there were *two* men living with her now.

Rachel turned to check on Franklin who was sitting in the back of the wagon keeping a watchful eye on his prize thoroughbred. This horse was one of the finest he'd ever bred, but she had never known her husband to take the credit for his magnificent animals. Franklin was a humble man and always gave credit to the Lord for everything.

"How's he doin' back there, Papa," Eugene called over his shoulder. He seemed to be just as concerned about the horse as Franklin was. It was obvious this one was special.

"Doin' fine, just fine."

That hadn't been the case at this one's birth. In fact, this particular horse owed his life to Eugene.

Franklin had taken sick a couple of springs back when one of the mares was about to foal. Rachel and Eugene had forced Papa to stay in bed while they kept watch through the night. As much as Franklin wanted to be with his mare, he knew she'd be in good hands. But just before dawn when the foal was born, he wasn't able to break through the protective sac to take his first breath. Eugene and Rachel gave him a minute to see if he could struggle through. When it was obvious he wasn't able, Eugene tore the sac and cleaned out his nasal passages. When he still didn't take a breath, Eugene closed up one of the foal's nostrils with his palm and blew air into the other nostril. Rachel had cried when the precious foal finally gasped for air. Eugene was close to tears himself before it was all over. That morning Rachel and Eugene decided to name the foal. As they sat exhausted side-by-side watching him take his first awkward steps, they named him *Morceau de ciel,* French for *piece of heaven.* Before long they were just calling him Morceau.

The horse drew a lot of looks as they passed through Lexington. He was jet black with four perfect white socks, highly unusual coloring. He stood seventeen hands high with powerful chest muscles and a long, sleek body.

Two foals had been born on the farm last spring, and Franklin and Eugene had discussed taking one of them to auction this year while keeping Morceau on the farm as a stud. But he possessed a wild spirit, and the herd was kept in a constant state of turmoil because of him. Even now he was wearing blinders just so they could make it through the city safely.

The road along the river to their campsite had changed from the previous year. It was wider than before, and Rachel noticed it seemed to be well traveled. Before they made it to their usual site, it became obvious why. A National Guard unit was camping all along the river, and Eugene had driven right into their camp. He pulled the wagon to a halt as the three of them sat and stared at the scene.

Rachel jumped when a man on her side of the wagon asked, "Can I help you folks?" He was addressing Rachel and Eugene while clearly keeping his eye on Franklin, who was still sitting in the back of the wagon.

Eugene responded to the guardsman. "Sir, we're in town for the horse auction tomorrow and used to have a camping spot down here by the river. I see it's not available so we'll just be heading back into town now."

The guardsman leaned in a little too close for Rachel's comfort. "You better keep an eye on your colored back there. We just had us a race riot last month in the city."

Neither Rachel nor Eugene knew how to respond; both just sat there at a loss for words.

"Tension's runnin' a bit high these days with the war and all."

Eugene started to say something, but Rachel already had her hand on his arm to stop him.

"We'll just be moving along now, Son. Please turn the wagon around."

Eugene mumbled that he was thankful the road had been widened. It took some doing, but he finally got the mules and wagon turned around safely.

"Good day, sir." Rachel nodded her head to the guardsman as they passed. He tipped his hat to her and spit as Franklin passed by in the back of the wagon. Franklin just kept his eyes down and remained quiet.

When they were out of earshot, Eugene turned to Rachel and exclaimed, "War! What war?"

Eugene pulled the wagon up to the auction barn praying the owner would board Morceau for the night. It would solve at least one of their problems if the horse could be given a stall, but finding a place for their family to stay overnight was going to be a more difficult task.

The door was open to the auction office with a half a dozen or so men inside. Eugene stepped through the door and a rotund, balding gentleman leaning on the edge of the desk stood up. "Can I help ya, Son?"

Eugene stuck his hand out. "Sir, my name is Eugene Hawkins."

"Pleasure to meet ya, Eugene. Name's Dorsey, Willard Dorsey. What can I do for ya?"

"Pleasure to meet you too, Mr. Dorsey. Sir, I've got a horse for auction tomorrow, but I need a place to board him till morning. Would it be possible for me to rent one of your stalls for the night?"

"Well now, young man, I'm familiar with the horses from your farm. We've had some mighty fine animals come through here with the Hawkins name. Let me take a look at him." He followed Eugene to the wagon where Franklin had removed Morceau's blinders to help him adjust to his surroundings.

A long, shrill whistle emanated from Mr. Dorsey's mouth. "Whoa. He's a beauty." He walked up to Morceau and slapped him on the neck while Franklin held the rope taut and spoke soothing words to him.

As the owner of the auction barn, Willard Dorsey received a percentage from every animal sold here. No doubt, from his reaction, he was already calculating the profit in his head. "Young man, I'll not only allow you to keep this fine animal at the barn tonight, but I'll give you one of the choicest stalls and throw in a place for your colored to bunk too. How do ya like the sound of that?"

Eugene didn't like the sound of that last part one bit and was just about to say so when Rachel walked up with her hand extended to Mr. Dorsey. "That's a very generous offer, Mister . . .?"

"Dorsey ma'am, Willard Dorsey."

"I'm Rachel Hawkins and we gladly accept your offer with thanks."

"My pleasure, ma'am." He turned to Franklin. "Bring the horse and I'll show ya where to bunk."

All three followed Willard Dorsey to his row of private stalls. Morceau was led into a roomy stall with fresh hay, water, and feed in the bucket. Mr. Dorsey pointed to a cot at the other end of the barn. "You're welcome to sleep there for the night or pull it over and sleep near the stall. Your choice."

"Thank ya, sir." Franklin lowered his eyes with hat in hand.

Eugene asked, "Mr. Dorsey, how much do we owe you?"

"Young man, you don't owe me a thing. It's just a

privilege to have this fine animal in my barn. I'm looking forward to seeing how the bidding goes tomorrow. You can keep your mules in the paddock out back if you like." He extended his hand to Rachel and then to Eugene as he took his leave.

Franklin took one look at Eugene's face and said, "Now Eugene, don't you go startin' to apologize for nothin'. Me and Morceau are gonna have a real nice night."

Rachel wanted to reach out to her husband but knew she didn't dare risk it. "Eugene and I will go into town and find a hotel for the night. I think it's best for us to get all of our supplies tomorrow after the auction and head back to the farm."

"I agree with that, Rach."

Eugene stepped into the stall and rubbed his hands down Morceau's forelegs. For some reason, that had always calmed the horse when he was nervous.

Franklin stepped in behind him. "Son, he'll be in your hands in the mornin'."

Eugene stood slowly and turned to see a twinkle in Franklin's eye. "Are you sure?"

"I'm sure as I've ever been," Franklin replied.

Rachel and Eugene now walked through downtown Lexington looking for a hotel and desperately searching for a newspaper. Neither had wanted to leave Franklin at the barn, but they knew it was their only option. As they walked down Main Street, Eugene spotted a hotel at the corner of Broadway and Main. They crossed the street keeping a close eye on all the traffic.

The Stanford Hotel was a little fancier than they were expecting with a marble staircase and ornate fixtures hanging in the lobby. Rachel accepted the key to a room on the second floor, and they were headed for the stairs when she suddenly remembered the newspaper. Turning back to the desk she asked the clerk, "Excuse me, do you know where I might purchase a newspaper?"

"Ma'am, I've got one right here that I've already read. You're more than welcome to it."

Rachel smiled as he handed her the *Lexington Herald*.

"Thank you so much."

"My pleasure. Enjoy your stay."

Rachel and Eugene hurried up the stairs with their belongings and opened the door to the room. It was a nice sized room with two beds and a view of the street below. The baths were just down the hall.

Eugene was already looking at the newspaper in disbelief.

"Mama, says here the U.S. has been in a war with Germany since April."

"Oh Eugene, we've been in our own little world and had no idea what was going on outside the farm. We're going to have to find a way to get news of world events more often."

"They have a list of local men going into the third draft. It says, 'It is probable that a large majority of the men from the third call will have to go to war to fill this country's quota.'" Eugene looked up. "It says we have troops fighting in France. Germany must have invaded France." Together they scoured the newspaper for every bit of news on the war they could find.

For supper they went to the restaurant just off the hotel lobby. Eugene had never ordered from a menu before. He'd been to a couple of restaurants when he was younger, but he'd never done the ordering. If it hadn't been for leaving Papa at the auction barn and all the talk of war, he might have been able to enjoy the experience. Instead, Rachel and Eugene ate with very little conversation.

Finally, Rachel broke the silence. "Tomorrow's going to be a long day, I'm afraid. By the time we do all our shopping, I don't think we'll be able to get on the road until after 3:00."

Eugene agreed. "We'll get in late. It'll probably take more than six hours to get back to the farm in the dark."

Another silence fell between them while Eugene picked at his food. "I feel bad that we can't be with Papa tonight," he said. "We shouldn't be eating such a nice meal without him."

"Don't you worry about your papa; he'll be fine. Besides, he has plenty of food to eat from our wagon." Eugene could tell she was just trying to cheer him up. So far, it wasn't working very well.

"Mama, do you think that soldier was telling the truth about a race riot?"

Suddenly another voice broke into their conversation. "Oh, it's the truth all right." Eugene and Rachel looked up with a start to see their waiter standing at the table with a check in his hand. "It was one of the worst things that's ever happened in this town."

Eugene couldn't help but ask, "What happened?"

"Well, there was this Colored A&M Fair in Lexington last month, and hundreds of coloreds came to town. They mostly stayed over on the west side of the city, but some of the guardsmen came into town just to check it out. From what I've heard, it was three guardsmen who started pushing some of the coloreds around in front of one of their restaurants, and it got out of hand right quick. The other guardsmen came flooding into town when they heard what was happening, and it turned into a race riot. It was pretty ugly for several hours until the police finally took control. We even had to lock down the hotel until it was over." He handed Eugene the check and added, "Nobody was killed, but a lot of people ended up in the hospital."

Rachel looked like she was going to be ill. Eugene immediately rose from the table and paid the bill. He knew he needed to get his mama back to the room.

The night couldn't seem to go by fast enough for either one of them. By the time the sun was up, Rachel and Eugene were already walking into the auction barn. Franklin was with Morceau grooming him for the big day. He was whistling and looked like he'd had a good night's sleep.

"Papa!"

"Shhh, don't let no one hear ya say that." Franklin kept his voice low as he looked around to make sure they were alone.

"Sorry," Eugene replied. "How's Morceau?"

"He had hisself a peaceful night. He's good and ready to show off today."

Within an hour, the auction barn was bustling with activity. Dozens of horses were being led by their owners into stalls and rubbed down with oil to make their coats look extra shiny. No oils were needed for Morceau. He was magnificent just the way he was.

When Eugene led him into the arena later that morning, Rachel could hear the buzz all around her in the stands. She couldn't take her eyes off of the two of them. Together they made a striking pair and the bidding went wild. At one point the auctioneer stepped down from his platform and whispered something in Eugene's ear. Rachel wasn't sure what was happening, but she noticed Eugene nod his head in agreement. Out of the corner of her eye, she saw Willard Dorsey enter the arena carrying horse tack. Eugene quickly saddled Morceau and mounted him. The performance that followed was breathtaking, and the stands became hushed as everyone's attention was riveted on the young man and this extraordinary animal. Overwhelmed by a sudden, strong emotion, Rachel suddenly covered her mouth with her hands. She wasn't sure that Eugene and Morceau should ever be separated.

When the bidding was over, Eugene dismounted and whispered his thanks in the horse's ear. Mr. Dorsey was waiting for him at the other end of the arena and led him back to the private stall where Morceau had spent the night.

Willard Dorsey was acting as proud as if the horse was his own. He opened the stall for Eugene and said, "The new owner wants to meet you, Son. He said for you to wait for him back here."

"Yes, sir," Eugene responded. He led Morceau into his stall and removed the saddle and bridle. He was talking to him as if he was still a part of the herd when Eugene realized he was not alone. He turned around to find a young lady watching him.

"Hello. My name is Anne Harrison, but everyone calls me Annie."

Eugene guessed her to be about his age. She had strawberry blonde hair and blue eyes, and he suddenly felt shy. He'd never had any problem talking to the horses, but he wasn't quite sure what to say to this girl.

"Hello," was the only thing that would come out at the moment.

Annie giggled. "Aren't you going to tell me your name?"

"Oh yeah, Eugene. I'm Eugene Hawkins and everyone just calls me . . . uh, Eugene."

This time she didn't giggle, she laughed. Eugene quickly turned back to Morceau, blushing.

"He's the most beautiful horse I've ever seen. Do you think he'll let me come into the stall?"

"Open the gate slowly and just stand inside the door without moving. I'll tell you if he accepts you or not."

Annie slowly opened the gate and stood inside the threshold. Morceau showed no signs of nervousness, so Eugene told her to approach. He talked soothingly to the horse while Annie stroked his beautiful neck and head.

"What's his name?"

"*Morceau de ciel.* It's French for *piece of heaven.*" Suddenly, Eugene was no longer at a loss for words. He told Annie the entire story of Morceau's birth and how he had saved his life by helping him breathe. Annie continued to stroke the horse's neck throughout the story, but never once took her eyes off of Eugene.

"The horse is down here, Mr. Harrison." Willard Dorsey was on his way back to the stall with Morceau's new owner, Nathan Harrison.

Annie stepped out of the stall. "He's incredible, Daddy!"

"Indeed he is." Mr. Harrison moved into the open doorway of the stall. Instantly, Morceau threw his head into the air and started pawing the ground. Nathan remained still as he observed the boy rub the animal's forelegs and speak to him in a calming voice. "You have an amazing way with him, young man."

Eugene stood and offered his hand to Annie's father. "I'm Eugene, sir."

"Eugene, I'm Nathan Harrison. I see you've met my daughter." Annie gave Eugene a big grin and playfully raised her eyebrows. "I've got a lot of business to take care of here at the auction this morning, but I'd like for you to join me and my daughter for lunch. I want to know more about the way you've trained this horse."

"Yes sir, I'd be glad to."

"All right, it's settled then. We'll be back at noon to take you to lunch."

Annie moved toward the stall but kept her gaze on Eugene. "Daddy, I'd like to stay with the horse if that's all right with you."

Mr. Harrison was already halfway to the other end of the barn as he yelled over his shoulder, "That'll be fine, honey."

Eugene and Annie sat down on a bench outside of Morceau's stall and were in deep conversation when Rachel came briskly around the corner. Eugene jumped to his feet, embarrassed that he had completely forgotten about his folks.

Rachel smiled as she approached. "The paperwork has all been taken care of. It's time to go back to town." She turned her attention to the girl now standing beside Eugene. "I'm Rachel Hawkins, Eugene's mother."

Eugene cleared his throat and said, "Mama, this is Anne Harrison and her father is the one who bought Morceau."

She warmly received Rachel's hand and smiled, showing a slight dimple in her cheek. "You can call me Annie."

"Annie, it's a pleasure to meet you." Rachel now looked at Eugene. "Do you need some time with Morceau?"

"Just a couple of minutes." Eugene disappeared into the stall while Rachel and Annie moved to the other end of the barn.

"Mrs. Hawkins, my father and I would like for Eugene to join us at lunch today. We want to know more about Morceau and how to handle him properly."

"Will you be lunching in town?" Rachel inquired.

"Yes ma'am."

"I think that would be perfectly fine. Could he meet you

at a certain restaurant? We're trying to leave town by 3:00 and have a lot of purchases to make before then."

"Oh, I'd be glad to help with your purchases. I don't have anything else to do around here this morning."

At that moment, Eugene emerged from the stall, striding toward them. His heart was grieved at the loss of Morceau, but seeing Annie somehow made his loss easier to handle.

Rachel quietly asked, "Are you okay, Son?"

Eugene nodded, then looked at Annie with a smile and replied, "I think Morceau will be in good hands."

They turned to leave, but as Eugene walked out of the barn that morning, he had no way of knowing that he would look back on this day, for years to come, as the last carefree day of his life.

Chapter 12

Rachel pulled a shawl around her shoulders in the cool evening air. Barely two hours on the road, and it was starting to get dark. Franklin drove the wagon while Eugene lay on top of the feedbags as the sun slowly disappeared over the horizon. All three were contemplating the day's events with satisfaction.

Eugene had been drawn to Annie from the moment he saw her, but he had truly been impressed with her when she was introduced to Papa. They had come out of the barn that morning to find Franklin waiting with the wagon and mules. Eugene introduced him by his first name, and Annie extended her hand to him. Without knowing this was his papa, she had shown him more respect by shaking his hand than anyone had given him the whole time they'd been in Lexington.

Franklin had parked the wagon in an alley to keep it off the street. Automobiles were everywhere in the city, and he didn't want to spook the mules. He stayed with the wagon while the others split up to buy supplies. Rachel went to the fabric store, bookstore, and grocers while Eugene and Annie purchased horse feed, chicken feed, and kerosene. They would visit the butcher shop on the way out of town.

Eugene's lunch with Annie and her father had gone well, and he felt good about leaving Morceau in the Harrison's hands. He had been impressed to find out that Annie's home in Louisville had electricity just like the Stanford Hotel.

"Eugene?" Rachel turned in the seat to face her son.

"Uh huh." He was half asleep.

"Uh huh?"

"I mean, ma'am." He flashed her a big smile that she returned in kind.

"Papa and I want you to know that the farm will always be your home for as long as you want."

Eugene sat up to face Rachel. "I don't want to leave."

"I know you don't want to leave *now*, but someday you'll want to get married and have a place of your own. We just want you to know that it's all right; that's what we want you to do." Franklin was nodding his head in agreement.

Eugene lay back down and listened to the steady *clop*, *clop*, *clop* of the mule's hooves on the road. He couldn't imagine ever leaving the farm, but then again, he'd never imagined having a wife someday either . . . until today. Deep down he knew it would be a long time before he'd be ready to leave. He would've never survived without Rachel and Franklin. Right now he had an overwhelming feeling of gratitude for the two of them; they had been his salvation.

He looked back at his mama in the fading light. "Thank you." Rachel took in those two quiet words as if she was taking Eugene into her arms. She silently thanked God again for the night he led Eugene to their light.

Franklin had never before looked so worn out after one of their trips to Lexington. He could barely help unload the wagon in the hour just before midnight. Rachel tried to pick up the slack for her husband but was looking weary herself. Eugene insisted they both go on to bed. "I'll take care of the mules and the wagon. I want to check on the horses anyway and then I'll come to bed."

In the past he would've met up with some resistance, but not this time. Neither Franklin nor Rachel seemed to have the energy to argue with him.

Eugene felt like he was getting his second wind as he took care of the mules. They kicked up their heels when he released them from the harness. He'd always been amazed that none of the animals ever wandered away. Their loyalty to Franklin and now to him kept their hearts tied to this farm, kind of like an invisible fence.

When all the chores were done, Eugene sat down on the top step of the porch in the moonlight and leaned back against the post. He couldn't seem to get Annie off his mind. She had kissed him on the cheek when they said good-bye earlier that afternoon. He now put his hand to the corner of his mouth where her kiss had strayed a little from his cheek. Grinning, he wondered how far away Louisville was anyway.

The next morning, Eugene was awakened by the sound of crates and boxes being moved around. He allowed himself to lie in bed just a little longer until his conscience got the better of him. He was still buttoning his shirt when he came into the kitchen.

"Mornin' Mama."

"Morning Eugene." Rachel barely looked up as she continued emptying the box of flour and salt.

"Papa already in the pasture?"

Rachel stopped what she was doing long enough to tell Eugene that Papa wasn't feeling well this morning and was still in bed. She saw the worried look on Eugene's face.

"Don't you worry; he'll be fine. This trip was just extra hard on him, that's all. He's not as young as he thinks he is."

"I hear that, Mama." Franklin was still in bed, but he wasn't deaf. They could hear him chuckle in the other room, but it sounded raspy.

It was midday before Franklin finally got out of bed and came to the table. Rachel wanted to bring him something to eat in bed, but he insisted on getting up. She sat down beside him at the table, and laid a gentle hand on his face.

"You're burning up with fever. You get right back in that bed, and I'll bring you some soup and a wet cloth to cool you down."

Franklin looked at her through yellowish eyes, "I gotta admit I'm feelin' achy all over."

When he rose to his feet he started to sway, but Eugene quickly came to his side to steady him, and got him back into bed. Rachel worked the rest of the day and night trying to get Franklin's fever down, but nothing seemed to do the trick.

The following day was cloudy and Rachel felt the crisp breeze sweeping through the house. She announced to the men, "It's time to move downstairs."

This was Rachel's yearly declaration at the end of October. But this time she knew Franklin needed to be out of the unwelcoming air in the worst way. He was still feeling quite ill and dizzy when he sat up in the bed. It wasn't easy for Eugene and Rachel, but between the two of them, they were able to get him moved and comfortable in the bed downstairs.

Rachel went back upstairs to gather several items, and when she returned, she noticed Eugene's bed had been moved across the room next to Franklin's.

"What is this?"

"Mama, I want you to have your own bed next to Papa, so you can sleep at night but still be close to him in case he needs you. I'll make a pallet over there on the floor and be just fine."

"Oh Eugene, you don't need to do that."

"This is the way it's going to be until Papa gets well." Eugene wouldn't take no for an answer.

As it turned out, none of them could sleep that night with Franklin's horrible coughing. Rachel tried every remedy she knew, but nothing seemed to bring the fever down or help Franklin's hacking cough. There was a constant prayer in Rachel's heart on his behalf; she simply didn't know where else to turn.

By the end of the week, Franklin was struggling mightily to breathe. Eugene sat by his side trying to make him as comfortable as possible. He arranged several pillows behind Franklin, so he could sit up in the bed and breathe a little easier.

"Papa, what else can I do for you? Do you need some water or could I help you eat some soup?"

Franklin seemed to cough with every breath but managed to say, "No Son, I don't need anythin'."

Eugene rested his hand on his papa's arm, and Franklin reached with his other hand to cover Eugene's. Through a hoarse whisper Franklin said, "You're a good son, Eugene."

"And you're a good papa."

Franklin squeezed Eugene's hand with what energy he had left.

Rachel tenderly watched, as Eugene sat with Franklin until he drifted off to sleep. Every breath rattled in her husband's chest, and she wondered how he could possibly sleep. Eugene gently slipped his hand out from under Franklin's and stood to see Rachel staring at him with a troubled look. She motioned for Eugene to follow her upstairs; it was time for them to have a serious talk about Franklin's condition.

Eugene spoke as he joined Rachel by the fireplace. "Mama, he needs a doctor."

"Yes, he needs more than the remedies I've been using." She paused and prayed to God that she was making the right decision. "Dr. Randall used to practice in Winchester years ago. I don't know if he's still in town, but I know where his office is right off the square."

Eugene instantly replied, "I can saddle one of the mules and ride into town. I'll be back with the doctor as soon as I can find him."

Rachel's heart was about to beat out of her chest. The thought of Eugene going into Winchester scared her to death, but the thought of losing Franklin scared her even more.

"Eugene, please be careful. Just go straight to the square and you'll see his office across from the hardware store." She grabbed him and held him tight up against her. "I'm not worried about the doctor knowing how we live; I just want him to help your papa."

When she released him, Eugene kissed her cheek and ran out the door as he was putting on his jacket. A few minutes later, he galloped by the porch where Rachel was standing. Before he disappeared down the trail in the woods, she heard him yell, "I love you! Tell Papa to hang on."

Rachel pulled the shawl tighter around her shoulders. Letting out a deeply anguished sigh, she quietly replied, "I love you more."

Businesses were just opening for the day as Eugene raced into town. He left the mule tied to a post on the far end of the square and ran toward the hardware store. Just as he spotted the doctor's office across the street, a man came striding out of the hardware store and ran smack into Eugene, knocking him off his feet. Eugene was momentarily stunned as he heard the man let out a curse word. Jumping to his feet, Eugene apologized to the man without looking at him and started heading across the street. Before he could step off the curb, the man had him firmly by the arm.

"You're not going anywhere, Eugene." His name had been spit out of this man's mouth like venom. "I'd recognize you anywhere."

Eugene's heart beat hard and fast. He turned to meet Louis' eyes, not with fear this time but with anger. There was only one thing on his mind, and he was determined nothing would stop him from getting help for Papa. Not even this evil-minded man.

As Eugene struggled to get out of Louis' grasp, a small crowd of people stopped along the sidewalk to stare. Louis clearly had the upper hand now. He had both of Eugene's arms clasped tightly at the elbows behind his back. He had no choice but to go where Louis was guiding him.

The moment they reached the courthouse steps, the door swung open and the sheriff stepped out. "Well, well, well. What do we have here?"

Louis said, "I want this boy arrested. He ran away over five years ago and caused me a lot of pain and grief. I want him to pay for what he's done to me."

The sheriff slowly descended the stairs with a puzzled look on his face. "Well now, let's see here. I thought this boy was kidnapped."

Lying was second nature to Louis, and he didn't miss a beat. "Sheriff, he just admitted to me that he ran away."

Eugene started to speak, but the grip on his arms was painfully tightened to keep him silent. Louis was an expert at inflicting pain.

The sheriff pulled Eugene's hat off of his head to get a better look at him. Through narrowed eyes he said, "Boy, you cost us a lot of money and manpower around here. We thought we had us a kidnapping. You know what we do with boys like you? We send 'em off to the boy's state pen over in Paducah."

"Sir, please," Eugene was begging, "please let me go."

"Now boy, you know I can't do that." The sheriff was clearly enjoying himself as he watched Eugene squirm.

To Eugene's horror, he felt handcuffs being snapped on his wrists, and the sheriff roughly pushing him up the steps and into the courthouse. Just off the sheriff's office in the next room were two holding cells. The handcuffs were removed, and Eugene was shoved inside one of the cells.

"Please sir, I'll make it up to Louis I promise, but please just let me go for today. I swear I'll come back and pay for what I've done."

A bellowing laugh came out of the sheriff's mouth as he walked back into his office. Eugene could hear the sheriff and Louis talking in muffled voices in the next room. He felt like a caged animal with an intense desire to be set free back into the wild. How could this have happened? What are the chances of running into Louis at that exact moment in town? *Oh please God, make the sheriff listen to reason.*

After a while, Eugene could no longer hear voices in the next room. There was nothing but silence as the minutes ticked by.

"Sir?" Eugene's voice grew louder, "Sir please, I need to talk to you." No response. The sheriff and Louis were gone, and he was alone in his cell. He sat down on the edge of the bunk but couldn't relax or rid himself of the fear deep in his gut. Pacing was the only thing that was keeping him sane—pacing and praying.

God, please put your hand on Papa and heal him. You are the Great Physician, and you can do the healing if it's your will. Give Mama strength and peace right now. The words just kept coming and he knew he needed to have enough faith to believe that God was in control, but he was still struggling mightily within when the sheriff unlocked his cell.

"Let's go, boy."

"Am I free to go now?" Eugene's hopes began to soar.

The sheriff's laugh bellowed once again in his ears as he cuffed his hands in front this time. "Just keep your mouth shut and come with me." The sheriff led Eugene out the back door of the courthouse and loaded him into the back of a black automobile with *Clark County Sheriff* painted on the side. There was some kind of wire separating the front seat from the backseat, and when Eugene tried to lift the door handle in the backseat, it didn't budge.

"Where are you taking me?" The sheriff was pulling away from the courthouse now and Eugene caught a glimpse of Louis watching from the sidewalk. Just the sight of him made Eugene want to vomit.

"Boy, it's none of your business where I'm taking you so just shut your mouth and enjoy the ride."

They hadn't been on the road long before Eugene recognized where they were going. He didn't know if Lexington was his final destination but he knew that's where they were headed.

Pulling up behind the Fayette County courthouse Eugene was amazed that a six-hour trip by wagon was less than an hour's ride by automobile. *Maybe he and Papa should look into buying a farm truck.*

The sheriff got out of the car leaving Eugene alone for only a few minutes. When he returned he said nothing but pulled the automobile back onto the street for another couple of blocks. He pulled the vehicle up to a building that housed a clothier, a bakery, and an army recruiting office.

Eugene watched the sheriff open his door from the

outside. "Get out and do exactly what I tell you to." He unlocked the cuffs and threw them in the back seat before slamming the door. The sheriff's grip on his arm was so tight Eugene's desire to run was instantly squelched.

"Good afternoon." A middle-aged man sitting behind a large, wooden desk rose to his feet. He was wearing an army uniform.

"I'm Sheriff Boyd from Clark County, and I've got a young man who will be enlisting today." Eugene looked Sheriff Boyd in the eyes and realized this was no joking matter.

"How old are you, Son?"

Eugene looked back at the recruiter. "I'm sixt . . ."

"Eighteen, he just turned eighteen," the sheriff interrupted. His grip clamped down even tighter, which hardly seemed possible.

"You look a bit young for eighteen but then you wouldn't believe how young most of our recruits look these days. I'll need a copy of your birth certificate."

Oh good, that should keep me from being able to enlist. Eugene had a glimmer of hope that this little plan of the sheriff's wasn't going to work out.

Sheriff Boyd was as quick with a story as Louis. "Captain, uh?" He was straining to see the man's name badge.

"Actually, it's First Lieutenant Jones, sir."

"Lieutenant Jones, as you may be aware, birth certificates weren't issued in Clark County until '04 so he'll need to enlist without one. But I'm here to vouch for him."

First Lieutenant Jones took out two forms, put carbon paper between them, and loaded them into his typewriter.

"Name?"

Sheriff Boyd nudged him in the side. "Eugene, sir."

"Full name, please."

"Eugene Haw . . . I mean Wyatt, sir."

First Lieutenant Jones looked up. "You got a middle name?"

Eugene had to think about that one. He'd only heard his

mother use his middle name a handful of times in his life, usually when he'd been up to mischief. "Uh, Lloyd, sir."

"Wyatt, Eugene Lloyd. Age eighteen. Parents names?"

"James and Rachel Wyatt."

"Living or deceased?"

"Deceased."

Lieutenant Jones kept typing without looking up. "Nearest relative?"

"None sir, I have no living relatives that I know of." Eugene certainly wasn't going to give away Franklin and Rachel's identity. He would protect them with his life, if that's what it came down to.

The sheriff piped up, "Louis Tillman, that's his stepfather."

"All right. Education?"

"Yes, sir."

"Well?"

Eugene just stared at him. "Sir?"

"Did you graduate high school, go through the eighth grade, what's your education?"

"Um, well sir, I made it through the fifth grade in school."

"Not the makings of an officer, that's for sure," Lieutenant Jones quipped. Both men shared a laugh at Eugene's expense.

"All right, if you can pass the physical, it looks like you'll be in the army, Son. Just have a seat, and the doctor will see you as soon as he's done."

Eugene didn't have a chance to sit down before the door to the next room opened and a young recruit followed the doctor out to the desk. Lieutenant Jones opened the young man's folder and read out loud. "Rejected?"

"Poor eye sight and flat feet," the doctor grumbled. He was an older gentleman who looked none too thrilled with his job. "Go back home to your mama, boy, and forget about the army." He then trained his sites on Eugene and barked, "Next."

Eugene watched the other boy despondently walk out the door, secretly praying that he too had flat feet—whatever that meant.

"Let's go; we don't have all day," the doctor growled from his examination room.

Sheriff Boyd gave Eugene a shove and said, "I'll be right outside this door."

Twenty minutes later, Eugene followed the doctor back into the office. Lieutenant Jones took the folder and opened it. "Accepted. Congratulations!"

Eugene looked at him in shock. "What does that mean?"

The sheriff decided to answer that question. "It means you're in the army now. Lieutenant Jones, tell him what they do to deserters in the army."

"They execute 'em. But you're not official yet; just sign this paper and you will be." He pushed the paper across the desk toward Eugene.

Eugene didn't sign it. He just stood there staring at the document.

"Excuse us for a minute, gentlemen." Sheriff Boyd took Eugene by the arm and walked him across the room. In a hushed, but angry voice, he said, "I don't care whether you sign that document or not. If you don't go with the army, I'll take you straight to Paducah and have you thrown in the juvenile prison. Sign, and I'm done with you, don't sign, and we get to spend several more hours together—your choice."

Resigned to his fate, Eugene walked slowly back across the room and signed the paper.

Sheriff Boyd walked to the door. "He's all yours, fellas. I hope you don't have to execute him!"

Bellowing laughter followed him out the door, and he was gone.

Chapter 13

Eugene desperately pleaded for Lieutenant Jones to listen to reason. "I promise I'll be back by morning, please just let me go for the night."

"For the third time, NO!" The lieutenant's patience was now about as thin as a razor blade. "Sheriff Boyd told us you might be trouble. I can see why he wanted you as far away from Kentucky as possible."

"Where am I going?"

"You're headed out to Texas first thing in the morning. Camp Travis, outside of San Antonio." With a smirk on his face, he said, "It's all Texas and Oklahoma boys—you'll fit right in." His laughter was as annoying as the sheriff's.

Eugene was back on his feet again, pacing the floor of the office. It was driving him crazy to think about what his mama must be going through right now. She was depending on him to bring the doctor back, and he had let her down miserably.

Lieutenant Jones was on his feet in anger this time. He yelled, "Sit down now or I'll take you out and shoot you myself!"

Eugene obediently sat down in the chair. He leaned over with his elbows on his knees and rested his head in his hands. He had so many emotions running through him, and he didn't know how to handle any of them. He felt like he was stuck in a maze and couldn't find his way out. Eugene was still in that position half an hour later when the door to the office swung open and another man in uniform walked in.

"Now that was a good meal. You've got to try Edna's Café. She's got a chicken fried steak that'll melt in your mouth."

Eugene sat back in his chair to see a fairly young man,

maybe in his early 30s with buzzed hair and one more stripe on his uniform than First Lieutenant Jones. The man turned to face Eugene. "What have we got here, a new recruit?"

Lieutenant Jones said, "Yes, sir. Eugene Lloyd Wyatt ready to report for duty." He was so eager to get Eugene out of his hair.

"I'm Captain Barker, United States Army Reserves. Do you have your orders yet?"

Eugene quietly replied, "Camp Travis."

"Camp Travis?" Captain Barker turned to the lieutenant in surprise. "Why's he going to Texas? That's the T-O Unit, nearly everyone of 'em are Texans and Oklahomans." He turned to smile at Eugene. "I guess you're just gonna have to show 'em what a Kentucky boy can do." He clapped Eugene on the back. "Don't let us down."

If Captain Barker was expecting a resounding *Yes, sir,* he was sorely disappointed. Eugene just stood silently in front of him.

"What's a matter, you don't wanna go?"

"Sir, I was just wondering if I could . . ."

"Oh no you don't, Wyatt," Lieutenant Jones quickly interrupted. "Captain, he's been nothing but trouble since he signed that paper. I'm ready to get him out of here."

Captain Barker's brow was raised as he turned back to Eugene. "Wyatt, it's time for you to become a man. Let's go."

Eugene followed the captain through a back door and into an army truck. "Boy, I don't know what your story is, and to be honest I don't really wanna know, but I'm gonna warn you, once you signed that paper you belong to the United States government. Do you understand what I'm sayin' to you?"

Eugene nodded his head.

"You try to run and you'll be shot. Do you understand that?"

Eugene simply nodded his head again.

"And if you just nod your head to an officer without saying, 'Yes, sir' or 'No, sir' you'll be severely punished. Have I made myself perfectly clear?"

"Yes sir."

"Yes sir, what?"

Eugene sat up a little straighter. "Yes sir, I understand that I belong to the United States government and if I run, I'll be shot, and if an officer talks to me, I'll say 'yes sir' or 'no sir.'"

Captain Barker looked over at Eugene to see if he was being mocked. But there was no sign of such a thing. The kid was speaking to him with the utmost respect.

"Well, it's good to see you now have a perfect understanding of how things work around here."

The truck pulled into the Army National Guard camp, and Eugene recognized it from a week ago. Captain Barker walked him into a tent, and the guardsman behind the table stood and gave the officer a salute. The captain handed him Eugene's papers and told him to take care of him.

"He'll only be here for one night. He's on the train tomorrow morning at 7:15 headed west."

"Where's he headed, sir?"

"Camp Travis, San Antonio. Don't issue anything to Wyatt from our camp. The commanding General at Travis wants his recruits to come in with nothin' but the clothes on their backs." He looked over at Eugene. "Lucky for you, 'cause that's all you've got." Captain Barker turned on his heels and left the tent.

"Come on, I'll show you where you'll bunk tonight."

Eugene was led down several rows of tents until he came to one with the number 167 on the flap. "This is yours for the night. There's already five others staying here so just take the empty cot." Nothing more was said and the guardsman walked away.

Eugene lifted the flap and walked inside. No one else was in the tent, so he looked around for his cot. There was one that still had the blanket rolled up neatly at the end of the cot with a pillow on top. He slowly unrolled the gray wool blanket and laid the pillow at the head. He suddenly felt exhausted, so he took off his hat and stretched out on the cot. *Father, if you've got a plan, please don't let me mess it up.* With that semi-comforting thought, he drifted into a light sleep.

A bell was clanging somewhere in the distance and Eugene had it worked into his dream until he realized something was going on in the camp. He could hear the conversations of the men walking by his tent. He jumped to his feet and went outside. It was late afternoon, and everyone was on the move. Eugene just fell in step behind a group of guardsmen laughing and joking. Soon, it was clear that the men were heading for supper.

Eugene went through the chow line and was handed a metal dish with a boiled potato in it. Brown beans were slopped into the dish as he continued down the line and a piece of bread was thrown on top as he reached for a fork and a tin cup full of coffee. Not knowing any of the other soldiers, he moved off by himself and sat down by the river. As he ate his meal, he pictured himself jumping into the river and swimming away from the army. Suddenly, an image of him being shot in the back and his body floating down the river came into his mind. He shook his head trying to get rid of the image and resolved that it would be better for him to stay alive and just pray for a speedy end to the war.

It was a cold night, and Eugene only caught snatches of sleep here and there. The blanket didn't do much to keep him warm. When the morning bugle sounded, he rolled up his blanket and returned the pillow on top at the end of his cot. All of the men headed out into the open field and lined up in neat, long rows. One of the men from his tent pushed him into a spot and said, "Calisthenics."

Eugene hadn't done calisthenics since his primary school days in Winchester, and they'd definitely never done calisthenics this long. After thirty minutes of nonstop sit-ups, push-ups, jumping jacks, and running in place, the men fell out for breakfast, if you could call it that. Eugene wasn't quite sure what the mush was in his bowl, but he did recognize the toast and coffee. Just as he finished his last bite, an officer climbed a makeshift wooden stand and began to call the names of the men leaving on the train going west. There were only three names called and Eugene's was one of them.

Eugene quickly went down to the river and washed his face to prepare for the journey. When he was done, he walked up to the road with the other two guardsmen. A few minutes later, Captain Barker drove up with the truck and signaled for them to climb into the back. At the train station, the captain handed each of the men their orders, train schedule and ticket, and watched as they boarded the train.

This was Eugene's first time on a train and he had to admit he was feeling some excitement about that, but as it began to move down the tracks, his feeling of apprehension returned. He looked down at his train schedule. Lexington westbound to St. Louis with three stops in between, change trains in St. Louis heading south to Oklahoma City with two stops in between, and on to San Antonio with stops in Sherman, Ft. Worth, and Austin. He leaned his head back watching the countryside go by. *Papa, hang on. Don't you give up. Hang on.*

It took ten hours to get to St. Louis. Every time the train stopped, Eugene stepped off to get a drink of water and stretch his legs. It was 5:30 PM, and his stomach was letting him know how hungry he was, but he had no money.

In St. Louis the two guardsmen told Eugene they were at the end of the line and he'd be going south without them. He found a porter on the platform and told him he was looking for the train to Oklahoma City. The porter kindly showed him to the southbound train that was already in the station. For a split second, Eugene was tempted not to get on that train. But the porter gave him a little shove and said, "You better hurry and get aboard; it's just about to leave."

Just then the train lurched, so Eugene hopped aboard and found a seat in one of the less crowded cars. Not long after the train left St. Louis the sky began to grow dark and Eugene watched the lights of other people's houses pass by his window. *I wonder what's going on in those houses.* He would've dearly loved to stop in and see what they were having for supper.

Thirteen and a half hours later, the train pulled into Oklahoma City. It was now 6:45 in the morning, and Eugene had been without food for twenty-four hours. His head ached and he felt miserable. He decided to get off the train to stretch his legs but before he could make his way to the door, dozens of men started flooding the train cars. If he didn't get back to his seat quickly, he wouldn't have one at all.

A boy plopped down in the seat beside him, and two other boys dropped into the seats facing him. They were laughing and talking and seemed to be friends. As the locomotive barreled toward Texas, Eugene learned that all three boys were indeed high-school buddies ready for an adventure in the War to End All Wars. As soon as they had each turned eighteen, all three of them had dropped out of school and headed to their local recruiting office in Oklahoma City. Eugene couldn't help but catch a little of their excitement. If it hadn't been for Papa lying sick in his bed back in Kentucky, he might have felt as proud to be serving his country as these boys did.

Around noon the boys reached into their bags and pulled out food that their mothers had prepared for the trip. Eugene was so far past hungry, he didn't know if he could sit there and watch them eat.

"You want some?" The boy sitting next to him named Thomas held up a box of biscuits and chicken.

"Are you serious?" Eugene's eyes were the size of the biscuits he was eyeing.

Thomas laughed and shoved it in front of Eugene. "Take what you want. My ma cooked me such a big breakfast this morning, my belly's still about to bust."

Eugene tried not to act like a savage but he sure felt like one when he pounced on a chicken leg and biscuit. He was thankful for the nourishment, but hungry again by the time they reached San Antonio at 8:15 that night. All in all he'd been on a train for thirty-six hours straight, and he didn't care if he ever stepped foot on one again.

* * *

An officer from Camp Travis greeted the ragged recruits as they stepped off the train in San Antonio. His voice reminded Eugene of a rusty door hinge, but it was loud enough to get everyone's attention on the platform. "All recruits going to Camp Travis, either get yourself on a truck or a mule wagon. Anyone left at the station, will have to walk."

Suddenly, Thomas grabbed Eugene by the sleeve and yanked him through the dense crowd toward an army truck. "Come on, Wyatt. We don't wanna ride no mule wagon!"

They sat on the packed truck for so long, all the boys started complaining about empty stomachs. Finally, an officer came by and laughed when he heard their conversation. "You won't be seein' any food till mornin', boys. Mess was over four hours ago."

The officer jumped into the driver's seat of the truck and yelled over his shoulder, "Hang on back there. We don't wanna lose anyone before you get to fight those dirty Huns."

The way Eugene was feeling, he figured he'd probably starve to death before he had to face the Germans.

When the truck came to a screeching halt, Eugene and the other recruits jumped to the dusty ground. Camp Travis was nothing like the National Guard camp in Lexington. Even in the dark Eugene could see row after row of large, wooden barracks.

All the new recruits had to be processed as they came in, and the receiving officers were not in a very good mood when they had to take in recruits late at night. Eugene followed a long line of men into a warehouse-type building with a dozen or so tables. He handed one of the officers his papers and waited patiently for the officer to read them, check him in, and get him a uniform, bedroll, and hygiene pack. It was midnight when he walked into his barracks and found a bunk. There must have been fifty or more bunks in one room by Eugene's estimation.

A barrel-chested man, in a neat uniform strode into the barracks and cleared his throat. "All right, listen up, men. My

123

name is Sergeant Craig. Welcome to Camp Travis. Tomorrow each one of you will be assigned to your new battalion and regiment. Until then, you will answer to me. Is that understood?"

A meager "yes, sir" wafted through the open spaces of the barrack.

Sergeant Craig's voice raised another decibel or two as he boomed, "Boys, it is well-passed my bedtime, and I'm in no mood for your half-hearted response. So, let's try that again. Do you understand me?"

A resounding, "Yes, sir!" reached the ears of Sergeant Craig.

"Much better. Now pay attention." The Sergeant grabbed one of the recruit's bedrolls and said, "This is how you make your bed in the army."

After each bunk was properly made, all the recruits were led into the adjoining washhouse where Sergeant Craig spent the next half hour instructing them on proper hygiene.

Finally, during the early morning hours, Eugene stripped down to his underwear and climbed into his bunk. He lay awake for a long time staring up at the ceiling. He still couldn't figure out how all of this had happened. It had now been almost three days since he'd ridden into Winchester looking for the doctor. He couldn't bear to think of what his mama must be going through. He racked his brain trying to think of a way he could get a message to her, but he simply couldn't think of any possibilities. Resolved to leave it in God's hands for now, he drifted off to sleep, lonely and hungry.

Chapter 14

November 1917

At 5:00 AM in his new uniform and boots, Eugene was already on a large, sandy field doing calisthenics. Camp Travis had a much more rigorous training schedule than the National Guard camp in Kentucky. When an hour had passed, the men fell out for breakfast. Later that morning, Eugene and the other new recruits were instructed to report back to the mess hall to be assigned to their battalions and companies. Eugene, along with several dozen other recruits, was assigned to the 179th Brigade, 357th Infantry division and that night he moved his gear into their barracks. Most of the men in the regiment had been together since September and had been training for two full months.

As Eugene walked down the row of bunks, he noticed groups of men playing cards, some reading or writing letters, and others sitting around talking. Nearly all of them stopped what they were doing to watch the fresh recruits walk in. Eugene found an empty bunk and started making his bed the way he'd been instructed the night before.

"What part of Indian Territory do you hale from?"

Eugene turned around to face a tall, lanky private. "I'm from Kentucky."

To Eugene's surprise, the private yelled out, "Hey fellas, we got Daniel Boone in our regiment!" The barracks were suddenly hushed as everyone now stared at Eugene.

The soldier picked up Eugene's pillow and looked underneath. "Where is it?"

Bewildered, Eugene asked, "Where's what?"

"Where's your coon skin cap? I know you got one around here somewhere."

By this time, everyone was laughing, and Eugene felt like crawling under his bunk.

One of the men in the regiment put down his letter and started walking down the aisle toward them. "Hey Pratt. How about you give it a rest tonight." The soldier's hand was now resting on Pratt's shoulder.

"You know I'm just messin' around. Hey kid, I didn't mean you any harm. But Kentucky? Every last one of us in here is from Oklahoma."

The other soldier countered, "No, we've got a few from the Dakotas and Tennessee." Someone let out a whoop at the mention of Tennessee.

"Welcome to the 357th, I'm Corporal William Gano but you can call me Will." His hand was extended, and Eugene gladly made his acquaintance. Will was a little shorter than Eugene, a good two or three inches under six feet with a stockier build. He had sandy brown hair and gray eyes that showed warmth and concern. "Let me know if you need anything, kid."

"Thank you, sir."

Corporal Gano was already headed to his bunk. Without looking back he said, "Call me Will."

For the rest of November and the first three weeks of December, the men of the 179th Brigade spent eight hours a day in basic drills, bayonet exercises, minor tactics, and maneuvers. Nearly all the men in the regiment were recent recruits, so the officers pushed their soldiers hard, to prepare them for duty overseas. They were also fed extremely well to Eugene's delight.

Will Gano made it a habit of eating supper with the recruits. Oftentimes the twenty-two-year-old corporal sought out Eugene's company, and eventually a friendship was forged over the clanking of forks on metal plates.

"I think I've gained weight since I got here." Will grinned at Eugene across the table as they ate their supper one evening.

"The only thing I can't seem to get used to though, is how they sweeten the iced tea." He grimaced as he tipped his glass.

"It's a good thing we get so much exercise or we'd be fat," Eugene chuckled.

"Just what I was thinkin', kid. But we burn off just about everything we eat in exercises. You know, they're trying to make us physically perfect before we ship out."

Eugene had felt indebted to Corporal Gano since the first night he came to his defense in the barracks. Will always had an easy smile and a down-to-earth manner that Eugene admired, and he was thankful for the growing bond between them.

The rules were strict at Camp Travis, and Eugene was learning a lot about discipline. The officers stressed personal appearance, hygiene, and neat uniforms, and the barracks and grounds were constantly being policed. There wasn't a lot of free time until the weekends, but whenever Eugene got the chance, he found himself drawn to the stables. The army kept hundreds of horses and mules that would eventually be used in the war effort overseas. The pungent odor of horse sweat and manure instantly reminded him of the farm, and he wondered how his folks were getting along. He just prayed that Papa had recovered his health by now.

At Christmas, Eugene found himself missing home more than ever. The men were given a three-day holiday, which meant a break from training. However, none of the recruits were allowed to leave Camp Travis. Brigadier General O'Neil, the camp's commanding officer, made sure there was plenty of entertainment for his men though. The general had a fondness for athletics, so football, baseball, boxing, and running events were held throughout the holiday.

Instead of wallowing in self-pity, Eugene threw himself wholeheartedly into the sporting events. He steered clear of the boxing but felt pretty good about his chances in a foot race.

Eugene toed the line drawn in the parched earth, and focused his full attention on the finish line two hundred yards straightaway.

"Try not to choke on my dust, pal."

Eugene turned his head to see a confident soldier grinning at him. He knew the man as Corporal Alvin Haney, one of the fellows in his brigade. Everyone called him Al.

Just then, the whistle blew, and Eugene found himself a full step behind the gigantic stride of the cocky redhead. Eugene kept his arms relaxed, and let his legs do all the work. By the time the field of ten runners reached the halfway mark, Eugene had pulled even with Al and the other leader. When Al turned his head to check on the rest of the pack, Eugene seemed to punch into another gear altogether. He kept his eyes trained solely on the finish line, and soon not a runner remained in his peripheral vision. By the time he crossed the line to rousing cheers, Al was a distant second place.

Will was the first to greet him at the finish. "You can fly, kid! What do you say you join our baseball team this afternoon? We could use some of that speed in the outfield." It was clear at Camp Travis that a speedy outfield was necessary in order to be successful. If the ball ever got past the outfielders, the joke was, that it could roll for a week on the flat, barren Texas ground around the playing field.

Just then Al strode up, still carrying an air of self-importance, but willing to concede the victory to Eugene. "Good race, buddy. You'd better be ready next time, though." He roughed up Eugene's hair, then turned his attention to his good friend, Will. The two men had been together since the beginning of training camp last September. "We'd better get this kid in left field this afternoon." Al glanced at Eugene and asked, "How about it? You ever played baseball?"

Eugene had played stick ball with his friend, Robert, many times growing up, and felt confident he would be fine in the outfield. He replied, "Sure, I'll give it a shot. But I don't have a glove."

Will assured him as they watched the next race begin, "We've got you covered."

***

During the second week of January 1918, Eugene's regiment was assigned to Camp Bullis for two weeks of rifle training. Camp Bullis was on the northwest side of San Antonio and was only used for training exercises. A tent camp was set up to house the 357th while they trained with small arms and rifles.

Eugene didn't know where the time had gone. He was now seventeen, but hadn't told anyone about his birthday back on New Year's Day. Deep within, he still carried a fierce desire to protect Rachel and Franklin so he figured the less anyone knew about his life, the better.

Every day in rifle training, Eugene's marks were impressive. Corporal Gano's marksmanship was equally impressive and at the end of two weeks, Will asked him, "Where'd you learn to shoot like that, kid?"

"I did a lot of hunting back home in Kentucky." Eugene would've dearly loved to be hunting with his papa right now.

"What'd you hunt?"

"In the winter mostly rabbits and squirrels, and sometimes I'd take down an elk or deer. In the summer I did a little coon huntin' at night."

"But no coon skin cap, huh Boone?" Will clapped him on the shoulder, laughing as they walked back to the barracks.

Eugene laughed too, and said, "I must've lost it on the train from Kentucky."

Corporal Gano laughed even louder.

For the first two weeks of February, the 357th Infantry was scheduled for combat problems and maneuvers on the massive training grounds at Camp Bullis. Sunday morning, the day before the maneuvers, every soldier and officer in camp attended the weekly worship service in front of the bandstand. That afternoon, Eugene's regiment was playing a baseball game against the 359th Infantry made up primarily of Texans. Every time the Oklahomans played the Texans, there was a lot of good-natured name calling floating in the air. Today, the Texans had the upper hand, but the 357th threw down their challenge for the following Sunday afternoon before everyone dispersed.

Will and Eugene were gathering up the equipment together after the game. "Kid, I won't be going to Bullis tomorrow for maneuvers," Will said. Eugene was curious as to where he was going but waited for him to continue. "I signed up for Snipers and Scouts School here at Travis. It starts tomorrow afternoon." Will threw a glove at Eugene who caught it one-handed while dust filled the air. "Why don't you sign up? You're a good marksman, just what they're looking for."

"I've already signed up for the Saddlers and Cobblers," Eugene replied.

"I guess that's fine, but your talent's gonna be wasted."

"I worked with horses back in Kentucky. That's what I know best. But now that you mention it . . ." Eugene shook his head. "Oh well, it's probably too late to change now." Eugene simply hadn't given thought to joining the Scouts, but it sounded more appealing to him than saddling the horses and nailing horseshoes all day.

The next morning after Eugene finished his breakfast, he was met by a staff sergeant as he left the mess hall. "Wyatt, Eugene Lloyd?"

"Yes, sir."

"Change of orders." The staff sergeant handed him a paper and walked away. Unfolding the paper, Eugene read:

Memorandum:

The following is a schedule of instruction in Snipers and Scouts School, 179th Brigade:

Feb. 4th & 5th Concealment and color contrast Observation. 1:30 to 4:30 PM
Feb. 6th & 7th Lecture on Sniperscope, Rifle, and Rifle Rest. 1:30 to 4:30 PM

Feb. 8th & 9th Elementary map reading. 1:30 to 4:30 PM

Feb. 11th & 12th Sketching and reporting. 1:30 to 4:30 PM

Feb. 13th & 14th Scouting. 1:30 to 4:30 PM

Feb. 15th & 16th Night Patrols. 2 hours after supper each evening.

Students detailed to this school will report to 1st Lieut Yancey L. Culp, 358th Inf., N.A. 1:30 PM Monday, Feb. 4, 1918, at Band Stand, 358th Inf. Drill Grounds.

By command of Brig. General O'Neil

Eugene couldn't believe it. How did this happen?

At that moment, a hand clasped down on the back of his neck, and Corporal Gano started playfully shaking him around. "Whatcha got there, kid?"

"Orders to report to Snipers and Scouts School."

"Well, what do ya know! I wonder how that happened?" Will was grinning from ear to ear.

Eugene looked at him with a raised brow. "Yeah, I'm wonderin' the very same thing."

"Seriously kid, when I mentioned your range scores to Lieutenant Culp, he went after you himself. He didn't want you to be wastin' away with the cobblers." Someone from the regiment called Will's name, and he gave Eugene a friendly shove. "I'll see you this afternoon at 1:30. Don't be late, kid."

Eugene's sniper notebook was completely full of notes and drawings by the end of May. He had been training exclusively with the Scouts of the 357th for the past three and a half months.

Main points for sniper posts:

1. *Loop-holes should be 21/4" x 4", should avoid straight lines while making them and the slope of the ground should not be changed so as to cast shadows.*
2. *Good view—the sniper and observer should have a good view of the enemy's lines, if not he is of no use. A sniper never fires unless sure of his shot.*

   The posts are made large enough for observer and sniper and should be as comfortable as possible. The sniper does not look for the enemy but lets the observer locate the target.

There were pages and pages of how to set up a good sniper post, methods for spotting an enemy post, and map reading. He had been trained extensively as an observer, as well. The sniper's chief duties were observation, concealment, and shooting. His primary target as a sniper was to take out the enemy sniper. The observer's job was to keep a record of shots and their effect, examine the rifle and ammunition, and test the telescopic sights. Both sniper and observer were required to fill out an accurate report of their activity and send it in to the scout office at a fixed time every day.

Three afternoons a week were spent on the east side of Camp Travis across the railroad tracks in a complex of trenches and fortifications that the engineers had built. It was a particularly hot afternoon the first of June and Eugene was paired with Will for the first time that week. They made their post behind a low wall of dirt, higher than the enemy trenches. Their loop-hole was made, both men were concealed, and now they lay boiling in the hot Texas sun. Talking out loud was strictly forbidden, but today the two buddies conversed in whispers.

Will broke the silence first. "I'm thinking of a big glass of iced tea, even sweetened."

Eugene's mouth started watering. "I'm thinking of a huge dish of strawberry ice cream."

"Not fair, kid. What I wouldn't do to kick back, eat ice cream, and read letters from home right now."

"I've never seen anyone get as many letters as you, Will. You had four yesterday and three the day before. I swear you never miss a day without mail."

"Only when the mail don't run," Will joked. He had once received eight letters in one day. "That's 'cause I've got a big family, plus my girl writes every day."

"What's her name?"

"Mary. We'll be gettin' married as soon as I get back home. Already gave her the ring and everything. What about you? Got a girl in Kentucky?"

"Not really, wish I did though." He was thinking of Annie and wondered if she even remembered who he was.

"That's all right; you got plenty of time for that when you get home. What about your parents? Do they ever write?"

Eugene's heart skipped a beat and a sad, lonely feeling crowded into his chest. "Naw, they don't ever write."

"Well, you can write them you know. I'm sure they're anxious to hear from you." Corporal Gano was supposed to be watching the enemy trench for movement, but he was watching his buddy now.

"There's nowhere to send the letters." Eugene wasn't sure he wanted to have this conversation.

Will turned his attention back to the sites of his rifle. "Are your parents still alive?"

"Yeah, but there's no address on the farm, so I can't send 'em anything."

"Maybe you could send letters to a neighbor or somethin'." Will had kept in close contact with his family since his arrival at Camp Travis last summer. He wrote his parents and Mary at least twice a week.

Just then, Eugene spotted movement. A head popped up in the enemy trench. Will clicked his rifle and both men recorded the time of their *kill* on the record sheet. Nothing more was said about Eugene's family, but he carried a heavier burden around with him the rest of that day.

At the end of the week, the 179th Brigade received their marching orders. It was finally time to cross the Atlantic and join their brothers in action. By the time they sailed for England on June 20, Will had made sergeant, and Eugene was a private second class in the United States Army.

Eugene and Will stood on the ship's deck as they sailed out of New York harbor past the Statue of Liberty. It was an awe-inspiring sight for both country boys. Will had spent his entire life on the family wheat farm in Oklahoma, and Eugene had spent his last five years on a secluded horse farm in Kentucky. Most of the eleven hundred men aboard their ship had never seen Lady Liberty either. Everyone was vying for a prime viewing spot up on deck.

Eugene spent the first two days as sick as a dog from the ship's rolling and pitching. He couldn't eat a thing; it turned his stomach just to look at food. But on the third day, he started feeling a little better and with the exception of one other day of extremely rough seas, he didn't get sick again. After Eugene was finally able to hold everything down, he realized he hadn't been missing much where the food was concerned. There was a bit of grumbling among the troops on that account.

To pass time on the ship, most of the soldiers played poker until late into the night. Eugene was fascinated as he watched many friends in his regiment lose their entire month's pay before ever reaching the shores of England.

"I'm having fifteen dollars out of my pay sent home every month," Will said to Eugene as they walked the sunny upper deck on their eighth day at sea. "Hopefully I'll have enough money saved for me and Mary to buy a place of our own." He stopped at the railing and gazed longingly across the horizon. "Everyone at home is working the wheat harvest this month."

Eugene was thinking about his papa and mama too, and wondering what they were doing on the farm at that moment. What he wouldn't give to be sitting down for supper with the two of them. He missed them both so much. Not a day went by that they weren't in his thoughts and prayers.

On the eleventh day of their journey, the convoy of ships reached the harbor at Liverpool, England. The troops disembarked for the night but were right back on the ship early the next morning sailing for Southampton where they promptly left for the European continent.

When the ship arrived at its destination on the afternoon of July 2, Eugene and Will once again disembarked. They immediately assembled with their battalion and began a two-and-a-half-hour march on French soil to the train station. Once there, they were loaded onto boxcars until they reached their destination in Aigney-le-Duc, France. A massive tent camp was assembled by the troops, and for the next six weeks, the entire battalion was once again subject to basic drills, tactics, and maneuvers for eight hours a day.

Eugene had gotten to know the men in his company well. They were now his brothers, and in order to survive against the enemy, they would need to be tightly bound together. This was a proud battalion bearing the big red shoulder patch with a T-O emblem representing Texas and Oklahoma. Before even reaching the trenches, they were already referring to themselves as the "Tough-Ombres" and they were eager to live up to their self-made reputation.

Finally, by mid-August 1918, the 179th Brigade was on the move. France was a beautiful country, and Will wrote home to his family wishing they could see it for themselves under different circumstances.

Eugene couldn't get over the boldness of the French women. In every village his regiment passed through, the women came out of their houses hugging and kissing the men and bringing them food and wine. One particular afternoon, Eugene's company was treated to a meal underneath a large tree at the edge of one of the villages. Will was leaning up against the tree when an elderly local man approached and started talking to him.

"Vous sont debout sous un arbre, c'st de 1400 ans, jeune homme," the gentleman said proudly, as he patted the tree.

Eugene amusedly watched Will nod and pat the tree just like the old man. Will had no idea what the Frenchman was saying, but the old man continued to ramble.

Finally, Eugene decided to come to his rescue. "Your last name is French and you don't speak the language?" he joked.

"Not a lick. We even dropped the French spelling *Ganeau* a few generations back so we'd be completely American." Will looked imploringly at his buddy. "How about helping me out here, kid?"

Eugene started conversing with the gentleman in French and finally turned back to Will. "Sergeant, you happen to be leaning up against a fourteen-hundred-year-old tree. This gentleman says they keep a record on it in their village."

Will put his hand out to touch the trunk and muttered to himself, "It doesn't look that old to me."

Eugene continued to speak with the man as Will watched in fascination. When the conversation was over, Will asked him, "Where'd you learn to speak French?"

"My mama taught me French back home on the farm. I guess it's coming in handy now, huh?" This time Eugene clapped his sergeant on the back as they started down the road with their regiment.

So far, the 179th had been warmly welcomed into the beautiful country of France. But that was all about to change. Very soon, they would be undergoing a baptism by fire.

Chapter 15

August 1918

On August 16, the 357th received their first orders for battle and by a cruel twist of fate—Eugene was thrust headlong into the war against the Huns. After a three-day march, his regiment relieved the 16th Infantry in the trenches on the front line. That night they endured a harrowing welcome. The Germans greeted their division with a three-hour artillery barrage. As if that wasn't enough, a drenching rain commenced as soon as the German shells fell silent. The Americans were waterlogged and miserable in the trenches during the dark hours.

Eugene gained much of his confidence that night from Sergeant Gano, as did many other men in the trenches. With every German shell that hit nearby, Will exclaimed, "That's one less shell they have to fire, boys! Keep your heads down and pray." His sanguine smile was reassuring to the soldiers around him.

By morning, Eugene was freezing cold and covered in mud, but he was alive. As a matter of fact, not one man in the 357th lost his life that night. The T-O's proclaimed that to be a good omen indeed.

At daylight, regular trench duties and patrols were taken up. Eugene found himself on patrol with the scouts in no man's land, which was the land between the German and American trenches. When he got his first glimpse of the German's moving about in their trenches, he realized they were men just like the ones in his regiment. He was having a hard time hating them the way he thought he should if he was going to have to kill any of them. He dearly hoped he didn't have to.

On his second day of patrol, Eugene was assigned to the company of Sergeant Alvin Haney. Al and Eugene had a good relationship, despite Al's inability to beat him in a foot race. Sergeant Haney was an energetic officer, who was known throughout the regiment for his loud, boisterous behavior. He had a fiery disposition, which everyone attributed to his flaming hair. But he was also the best rifleman in the 357th. Al was one of the few men in the battalion from Tennessee, and Eugene had never failed to have his spirits lifted when he was in the company of Al and Will back at Camp Travis.

On this particular afternoon, Eugene was assigned as Sergeant Haney's observer. "I hope you know you're with a daredevil," Al said quietly as they inched their way across the ground in no man's land. "I wanna get as close to those Huns as we possibly can."

Eugene knew he didn't have much of a choice in the matter, so he put his trust in Al's judgment. By the time they set up their post behind an old stone wall that had once been a property barrier, Eugene was amazed that there were only sixty yards between them and the enemy. He checked his sniperscope twice just to make sure.

There were miles of enemy trenches, and the Germans had spent years building a maze of concrete dugouts and forts that were called pillboxes. From their post, they had a good view of the east end of one of the German trenches.

Sergeant Haney took down one German soldier that afternoon thanks to Eugene's observations. Eugene didn't feel so good about that, but Al was ecstatic. At four o'clock, both men crept away from the post and made their way back to their regiment. A report had to be filled out and in the hands of their commanding officer by five o'clock sharp.

"You did a good job today, Private." Al sat between Eugene and Will as they ate their chow in the trenches.

"Thanks," Eugene replied stiffly without looking up.

Sergeant Haney, misreading Eugene's response said, "Hey now, that kill was just as much yours as it was mine. If it hadn't been for your slick observation, I never would've taken him down."

And now that man won't be going home to his family. That one thought kept running through Eugene's mind over and over again. Somewhere on the other side of no man's land, a grave was being dug for the man he had personally pointed out to Sergeant Haney.

Eugene had barely eaten any of his chow, but what he had eaten now felt heavy in his stomach. He didn't think he could take another bite without being sick. Silently he stood up, walked to the other end of the trench, and slung the rest of his food over the top.

In the days to follow, Eugene found himself constantly paired with Will. Unknown to him was the fact that Sergeant Gano had gone to Colonel Hartmann, the regimental commander, and asked for Private Second Class Wyatt to be assigned as his permanent partner when they were on sniper duty. Eugene had never had a real brother, but he believed Will was the closest thing to a brother he would ever have. Their deep friendship was a continual source of encouragement that helped Eugene get through the arduous days.

During their second week on the front line, Will and Eugene had taken up a post in a shelled-out house less than 125 yards from the German trenches. They moved to the back wall of the house as far away from the window as possible so they couldn't be seen. They remained at their post from eight o'clock in the morning until four in the afternoon, charting enemy movements, and switching off as sniper and observer every two hours.

Will spoke to Eugene in a low voice on one of his two-hour shifts as observer. "How old are you really, Eugene? I'm pretty sure you didn't come in at eighteen."

Eugene didn't take his eyes off of the rifle sites and remained silent.

"Hey kid, this is just between you and me. I feel like there shouldn't be anything false between us."

Eugene slowly let out the breath he'd been holding, and said, "I came in at sixteen and turned seventeen last January."

There was a long silence between them. Eugene was reliving the dreadful events that had led up to his being forced into the army. He wanted to share the whole truth with Will, but he wasn't sure how to tell him. Besides, sitting in a sniper post was hardly the place for such a conversation. Instead he asked his own question. "Why did you join the army if you were engaged to be married?"

After a momentary pause, Will said, "I didn't sign up for the army in the beginning. My Christian beliefs were really in opposition to the war." Will's father, Ralph, had been one of the founders of the church in their little town in Oklahoma and had baptized his son in the pond behind their house at the age of thirteen. It was a day Will would never forget. They had to break the ice on the pond for the occasion.

Will kept an eye on the enemy trenches as he continued. "When I received my draft notice, I knew I had to put my personal beliefs aside and do my duty for the sake of our country."

There was another long comfortable silence between the two friends.

"Hey Will?"

"Yeah?"

"Do you hate the Huns?"

This time, Will paused and let out a long, slow breath. Very quietly, almost as if his voice was a part of the breeze, Eugene heard him whisper, "No."

Eugene caught wind of the rumors flying through the trenches of a coming offensive in their sector. When troops from the 359th started flooding to the front line, they knew an assault against the Germans was imminent. It was good to see their Texas buddies from Camp Travis again, wearing the red T-O emblem. A large number of the "Tough-Ombres" were back together, and it seemed to give everyone new courage and spirit.

Nearly two and a half kilometers separated the Americans from the Germans. In between was a godforsaken wasteland of wire entanglements, trenches, and pockmarked earth full of shell holes. It would be an incredibly difficult assault considering the number of machine guns in the German trenches.

During the early morning hours of September 12, 1918, the U.S. Army launched a four-hour artillery barrage against the enemy to prepare the way for the infantry. The regimental chaplain made his way through the trenches that night praying with the troops. Eugene and Will gained strength through the prayers of their brothers in the trenches.

At five in the morning, Will sat down beside Eugene where he reclined against the wall of the trench. "How ya holdin' up, kid?"

Eugene's voice was a little shaky, but he bravely replied, "I'm okay."

"You know what God says in the book of Hebrews? He says, 'I will never leave you or forsake you.'"

All of a sudden, Eugene felt so weak—both physically and spiritually. He lowered his head and leaned into his friend. Will put the crook of his arm around Eugene's neck and grabbed the front of his uniform, pulling him close. "So that we may boldly say, The Lord is my helper, and I will not fear what man shall do unto me." Will tightened his grip just for a second then turned him loose.

At five minutes before six in the morning Eugene's rifle, with bayonet attached, was firmly gripped in his hands. He faced the trench wall and the dank odor of black dirt filled his nostrils. His breath now came in quick, shallow puffs.

Finally, at 6:00 sharp, the excruciating wait was over. A loud whistle blew in the American trenches, and Eugene, with heart pounding wildly, went up and over the top. He ran with the men in his regiment across no man's land, working his way through the barbed wire and leaping over obstacles in his path.

Deafening German shells started falling among the troops, and Eugene could hear the machine guns begin to fire.

His mouth felt like it was stuffed with cotton balls—he couldn't even swallow.

Dozens of machine guns ripped through the T-O Brigade. Eugene could hear the *zip, zip* of bullets flying past his head, but he kept running with all his might. He hurdled over a fallen comrade he recognized as Thomas, the boy who had shared his meal on the train. In the deep recesses of his mind, that information was hastily stored away, and immediately forgotten.

Eugene could hear screaming all around him and still he ran blindly through the choking smoke and flying dirt. The Tough-Ombres continued their mad race between the trenches. When they finally reached the Huns, they landed in on them, unleashing their fury. Eugene had no idea where his wild rage was coming from, but he knew without it he would surely die. Ear-piercing weapons were now firing at close range, and bayonets were thrust by Germans and Americans alike. Soon, hand-to-hand fighting ensued in the trenches as both sides fought furiously for survival. The scene was bloody and brutal.

When the battle ended, Eugene was utterly exhausted and covered in blood. He found himself wondering whose blood it was, his or his enemy's. He moved farther along the trench, away from the bodies, and collapsed on the ground. His chest heaved uncontrollably, and he fought for every breath in the thick smoke. Slowly the rush of the battle began to wear off, and he was shocked by his own savage brutality. He never dreamed that he would have been capable of such violence. For a while he lay at the bottom of the trench staring at his bleeding knuckles, aware of every aching muscle. Gradually the smoke began to clear, and Eugene gratefully breathed in the pure oxygen that his lungs craved. He stared up into the blue sky, watching the milky clouds drift by. They seemed so incredibly peaceful. They reminded him of their Creator, and with that thought, Eugene's heart was overcome with guilt. His eyes had been stinging earlier from the smoke, but now they stung with genuine remorse. *Oh God, please forgive me.*

Though his ears were still ringing mercilessly, Eugene could hear the men of the T-O Brigade begin to move about the German trenches. This piece of land belonged to the Americans, and they would not be giving it back. They had taken out nearly two hundred enemy machine guns in the assault. Eugene joined in with the other soldiers as they started clearing the trenches of the dead Huns and lovingly carrying their fallen comrades back across what once was no man's land.

Will spotted Eugene first and called his name loudly from several yards out. Will's face was covered in dirt and blood, the same as his own. Eugene choked back tears as his comrade wrapped him in a big bear hug.

When he released him, Will slapped the T-O emblem on the side of Eugene's shoulder. "It's good to see a Kentucky boy can hold his own. You all right, kid?"

Recovering from his momentary bout with emotions, Eugene said, "I'm fine." Then with a slight grin, he added, "We ran 'em out of here, didn't we?"

"We sure did, kid!"

That night the Germans were determined to take back what they'd lost and launched several counterattacks. Again, hand-to-hand combat ensued but the rugged U.S. soldiers refused to give up even an inch of ground and repelled every attack. Four days later by September 16, the 357th had battered its way through everything the enemy had to offer. Still their regiment remained on the front lines.

On September 18, Will and Eugene situated themselves inside a gully at the base of a small hill, only a hundred yards from enemy trenches. They had spotted the gully the day before while on patrol and actually had to flip a coin with Sergeant Haney to win the post. After crawling across no man's land in the still, dark hours of the morning, the two country boys made themselves comfortable in the gully and waited for the sun to rise.

Will said quietly, "Hey kid, let me do the shootin' today. You don't need more on your conscience right now than you already have."

Eugene knew Will had a noble heart. He was the best of men, even under the worst of circumstances. He greatly appreciated Will's offer, and replied in a quiet voice, "That'd be fine. Thanks."

From the moment the light appeared they knew they were going to be able to pick off several of the enemy that day. Their location had a perfect view of one of the main trenches.

By noon, Will had taken down three of the Huns in their trenches but it appeared their location was compromised on the third shot. The problem, they soon realized, was that they were on the German side of the hill. If they retreated in daylight they would have to make a run for it over the hill and hope for the best. If they waited until dark, it would no doubt be too late. Even as they considered their next move, they could see the enemy focusing on their position.

Will said, "Eugene, I'll open fire on 'em while you run over the hill."

"No, I'm not leaving you here, Will."

"Yes, you are, and that's an order. You can't disobey a direct order from an officer."

Eugene dug his heels in and refused. "I don't care; I'm not leaving you here alone."

"Look kid, all you gotta do is run back to our lines. You can bring support and get me out of here."

Eugene knew in his heart it would be too late by then, and he stubbornly refused to leave Will's side.

Two long hours passed as the pair lay perfectly still side-by-side. If they so much as tried to pick off one more Hun, their location would be blown for sure and they would be overtaken.

Will stayed focused on the German trenches as he quietly breathed the first words from the twenty-third Psalm, and then fell silent. "The Lord is my shepherd; I shall not want."

When Eugene realized Will's intention, he picked up the next verse. "He maketh me to lie down in green pastures." What

Eugene wouldn't give right now to be lying down in the bluegrass pasture at home.

"He leadeth me beside the still waters." Will had the mental image of the pond behind his house on the farm. It was so peaceful sitting by the water in the evening contemplating life and faith.

"He restoreth my soul." *Lord, I need restoring.*

"He leadeth me in the paths of righteousness for his name's sake."

"Yea, though I walk," the two were in unison now, "through the valley of the shadow of death, I will fear no evil: for thou art with me."

Before they could finish the Psalm, a dozen or so Huns came up and over the trench headed for their location. Will and Eugene pushed back the fear that endeavored to put their faith to the test and readied their rifles. Just before Will could squeeze the trigger, shots rang out, and two of the enemy dropped on the spot. Bullets continued to rain down on the unsuspecting Germans as a voice bellowed out from behind the hill, "What are you boys waitin' for? An invitation?"

Will shoved Eugene as hard as he could to get him moving. They ran out the side of the gully and around the hill as fast as they could go. When they made it around the backside, a small company of men including Sergeant Haney was firing continuously to force the Huns back into their trenches.

Al was laughing as they all turned on their heels and ran for the forest. They covered the next kilometer in a few short minutes before stopping to take a breath.

With a huge grin on his face, Will grabbed his good buddy and gave him a big hug. "Al, if you weren't a man, I'd kiss you right now!"

"Willie, if you weren't a man, I'd let you."

The whole company erupted in laughter.

Eugene, still breathing hard, just had to ask, "How'd you know we were in trouble?"

Al hooked Eugene's neck in the crook of his elbow and

pulled him up against his chest. "I was just curious how you fellas were gettin' along in what should've been *my* post." Al let go of his hold so Eugene could pick up his helmet. "When I realized you were in a bit of a rough spot, I went back to get you some cover."

Will slapped Al on the red shoulder patch to honor his good friend. "We owe you one, buddy."

"Naw, that was fun."

If anything, this adventure had livened up what Sergeant Haney had thought was a dull afternoon.

That evening, Will and Eugene were back in their billet in an old barn. Eugene liked this billet a lot better than the last one, which had been a rundown chicken coop. The smell alone had made it hard to sleep at night. The roof was missing from the barn they were in now, but the loft was still standing to provide cover over their heads. The men had reinforced the structure and added sandbags around the outside. Now some forty troops from his company called it "home," at least for a day or two.

Will was just finishing a letter to his parents while Eugene lay back on his bedroll in the stale hay.

"Will?"

"Yeah?"

"Do you ever tell your folks about the bad stuff?"

"No. I don't want 'em to worry about me. I just tell 'em how pretty the countryside is and tell 'em some of the interesting things we've gotten to do over here." Will had written his parents about French Independence Day back in July when the troops celebrated with a nearby village. They had run races, played baseball, and been fed well by the villagers. He didn't think he'd ever get used to the cider and wine that the French people drank and he told his parents so.

Eugene didn't say anything else, so Will leaned back against one of the sturdy posts holding up the loft. "Hey kid, I was just thinkin' about what happened today and I was wonderin' if you'd do me a big favor."

Eugene rose up on one elbow. "Sure, whatever you want."

"I was hopin' that if anything should happen to me over here, you'd go visit with my folks and take 'em this letter."

Eugene sat up and Will handed him the letter he'd been working on. He wanted his dad to know how much he appreciated the way he'd raised him, and he wanted his mamma to know that every man should be blessed to have a mother so good. He also handed Eugene directions to their farm in Oklahoma.

Eugene took the letter and put it in his breast pocket, feeling honored just to carry it. Will continued to talk about his family, telling Eugene the names of his two brothers and five sisters, the two youngest ones still at home, and what life was like on the wheat farm. He talked about his church and how not a Sunday went by that he didn't wish he were worshipping with them.

Finally he said, "If you'll write a letter to your folks, I'll do the same for you."

Eugene thought about Will's offer for a few moments. He put his head down and exhaled slowly. When he finally raised his head, Will was looking straight at him.

"Talk to me, kid."

Slowly Eugene started revealing the details of his life, beginning with the death of his father when he was a baby and his mother's death at age ten. It wasn't easy talking about the yearlong abuse he'd endured at the hands of his stepfather, but when he started talking about how he ran away to Franklin and Rachel's farm, the floodgates suddenly opened.

Will sat riveted as Eugene explained what their farm was like in Kentucky—a house built over a cave, thoroughbred horses in the pasture, and no fence around the property. Eugene told him how they could sell one or two horses at auction every fall and live on the proceeds for the rest of the year. But what fascinated Will the most was how Eugene had ended up in the army. If he had revealed this information to him back at Camp Travis, Will may have been able to secure a discharge for him. But as it was, Eugene had kept everything bottled up inside, and now he had no choice but to engage in a war he was too young to fight.

When he was finished, Eugene felt so much lighter in his soul. If he'd known how much better he'd feel after sharing his story with Will, he would've done it a long time ago.

Will laid his hand on Eugene's shoulder and said, "Kid, I plan to protect you with my life, but if, God forbid, anything happens, I promise I'll find your folks."

Eugene spent the rest of that evening writing his letter and drew out a map with detailed instructions on how to find the farm in Kentucky. Will put it in his breast pocket and pat it with his right hand grinning. "Looks like I've got three brothers now." He lay back on his bedroll and pulled his blanket up around his chest. "G'night, kid."

"Goodnight, Will."

Eugene found it difficult to sleep that night. Sharing his past with Will had been a burden lifted, but a fleeting premonition had niggled into his mind just before he drifted off. From that moment on, sleep never came easily again.

Chapter 16

The next morning, Sergeant Haney dropped by while the men were having chow. "Looks like you'll be missin' me around here for a few days. I'm headin' over to the field hospital to get my arm checked out."

Will looked up with a mouthful of oatmeal. "I was wondering about that gash on your arm."

"Yeah, I cut it on the wire a few days back and it's infected. They think I may have blood poisoning. So it looks like you boys will be on patrol without your best man for a while."

Everyone in the company laughed as he added, "You better not have any more fun without me. Save all the good stuff for when I get back." He specifically pointed to Will and Eugene. "You two better stay outta trouble."

Will threw his good friend a mock salute. "Yes, sir!"

Al remained at the hospital for an entire week. When he finally returned to his regiment, he was greeted with news that sent him running to find someone who could give him more details. He found the captain of his company, Dewitt Neighbors, in his tent about a quarter of a mile behind the front line. They spoke for a very long time before Captain Neighbors handed him a letter that he had just drafted. Al took it slowly from his hands and read:

Dear Sir,

It is with the deepest regret that I write this letter informing you of the death of your son, Sergeant William B. Gano, who was killed on the afternoon of Sept. 22nd while leading a patrol across no man's land. His comrades made him a coffin out of the material at hand and laid him lovingly away in the soil he helped to win from the Huns.

In his death, the entire company feels the loss of a man whom we all admired for his quiet devotion to duty and his pleasing, congenial personality. The fearlessness and thoroughness with which his work was always accomplished won for him the admiration of the Battalion, and had he lived he would have two days later been commissioned a Lieutenant in our army.

I realize that the loss we feel is nothing as compared with the sorrow that comes from the vacant chair around his own fireside—but for those of you who have waited for him there—there is the consolation that his life was made to count much in the cause of human liberty—and that in the memory of us all—he will always be remembered as he really was—a sympathetic and efficient leader—a perfect gentleman—a true soldier.

With the sincerest sympathy for you and your family, I am sincerely yours,

Dewitt Neighbors
Capt. 357th Inf.

Al handed the letter back to his captain, stood at attention, and asked to be dismissed.

Captain Neighbors responded, "Dismissed." Then more quietly he added, "And Sergeant, I'm sorry about your friend."

"Thank you, sir."

That afternoon, Al waited anxiously for his company to return from patrol in no man's land. When they arrived in camp, he spotted Eugene instantly and put his arm around his shoulder.

Eugene choked back a sob.

"I need you to tell me how Will died. Can you do that?"

Eugene nodded his head, and the two moved away from their company and sat down on a fallen tree not far from their billet.

Eugene didn't quite know where to start, so Al prodded him a little. "You were on patrol when it happened, right?"

"Yeah, we'd been on patrol all morning and gathered the information we needed for our report. Will was leading the company, and we were almost back to the line. He stepped out of the woods just for a second to get a bearing on his compass when it happened." Eugene put his head down in his hands.

"Go on, kid."

"He was shot in the chest by a sniper." Eugene couldn't believe he had just said it out loud. He had thought that as long as he lived, he'd never be able to tell anyone what had happened that day. Just now he thought he was about to suffocate—his own chest felt so heavy.

Al gave Eugene a moment to compose himself, before he gently nudged him to keep going.

"He stumbled backwards and fell in my arms. I laid him on the ground and asked him where he was hit. All he said was, *I don't* . . . *before* . . ." Eugene's voice trailed off. He was marveling that Will had been smiling—even in death.

When his eyes fluttered shut, Eugene knew instantly that his best friend was gone. Two men from the company had stepped forward to carry their sergeant back to the line, but Eugene wouldn't allow it. He handed his rifle and pack to another soldier and lovingly carried Will on his shoulders all the way back. With every heartbreaking step, he silently vowed that he would deliver the letter in his pocket to Will's family in Oklahoma.

Al rose to his feet. "Come show me where you laid him."

Sergeant and Private slowly walked down the road into a beautiful valley near the village of St. Marie. Dozens of their comrades lay buried here in the French soil. Eugene pointed out the makeshift cross that belonged to Will, and both men stood silently before his grave in the sun's fading light.

Later that night, Eugene sat by the small fire near his billet, and stared at the letter in his hands—*Franklin and Rachel Hawkins, Winchester, Kentucky*. He had pulled it from Will's breast pocket, just before they laid him to rest. The lump in Eugene's throat told him he couldn't bear to look at it ever again, so he threw it into the beckoning flames. He watched it burn, until the hole in the corner with the dark brown stain, turned to ash.

During the first two weeks of October 1918, the 179th Brigade was on the move. Seldom did they billet in one place for more than a night. Eugene tried his best to shake the feeling that nothing seemed to matter anymore. There were times he felt so lost. Nevertheless, he carried out his duties faithfully, without complaining. Every night he took Will's letter out of his pocket and prayed for the Gano family just as he prayed for his own, but even that couldn't bring him the peace he longed for.

On October 21, the 357th moved in to relieve the 6th Infantry. They had orders to take the towns of Bourrut and Bentheville from the Germans. Despite their many casualties in the previous weeks due to combat and the flu, they were still a determined and hearty regiment.

As the Americans moved into the two towns, they met up with incredible resistance. The German machine guns seemed to be located everywhere in the towns. Many more casualties were inflicted on their brigade as they came under heavy artillery fire. After two days of bitter fighting, the 179th was ordered to hold its ground and wait for relief. Finally, with the help of the 180th Brigade, both towns were taken on October 26 due to the vigorous assault of the American soldiers.

The 179th Brigade, and particularly Eugene's regiment, was nearly completely exhausted from the constant bloody fighting and the high number of casualties. They were relieved on October 30 by the 180th Brigade in order for them to fall back and rest.

Several kilometers behind the front line now, Eugene lay in his billet completely depleted of all energy. He and several of the men in his company had chosen the ruins of a small house and had managed to put a roof over their heads with a piece of tin and a large piece of plywood. At chow, he could barely lift his fork. That night he fell asleep with his hand in his breast pocket. He hadn't enough energy to even pull out the letter or pray.

Early the next morning Captain Dewitt Neighbors stuck his head under the plywood in Eugene's billet. "Gentlemen, I'm looking for Private Wyatt."

Eugene wearily pushed himself up on his elbows and replied, "Right here, sir."

"Come outside for a while, and let's talk."

Eugene was surprised to see the captain already seated in a folding chair holding a mess tin full of chow. He pointed to an overturned bucket with another plate of food sitting on top. "Have a seat, Private, and join me for breakfast."

Eugene saw an aide standing nearby who must have helped set up their meal. He picked up his plate, and sat down on the bucket, facing the captain.

Unexpectedly, Captain Neighbors removed his cap and said grace for the two of them. When he put on his cap again, he looked Eugene squarely in the eyes. "Sergeant Gano was a fine officer, and a good man."

"Yes, sir," Eugene agreed.

"I happen to know he was always looking out for you, Private."

Eugene nodded, "Yes, sir. We were good friends."

Captain Neighbors started in on his chow and motioned for Eugene to do the same. The captain ate in silence for a few minutes, while Eugene pushed the food around on his plate.

After the captain took a swig of his coffee, he asked, "How are you holding up?"

"It's been pretty hard, sir."

"I know it's hard, Private. We're losing a lot of good men out here. Just don't give up."

"I won't, sir." Eugene rubbed the back of his neck in frustration.

"What is it, Private?"

Eugene looked away and said, "I don't know, sir. I just feel angry most of the time."

Captain Neighbors stopped eating and put his plate on the ground at his feet. "Look at me, Son. Anger's not such a bad thing. You just can't let it turn into bitterness. Do you understand the difference?"

"Yes, sir, I think I do."

"You'll find that a healthy dose of anger is what will get you through the day, but bitterness is what will keep you awake at night."

The captain stood and handed his plate and chair to the waiting aide. When Eugene stood, he motioned for him to stay and finish his breakfast. Before taking his leave, Captain Neighbors said to Eugene with conviction, "We're gonna win this war. You'll be back home before you know it." Then, through narrowed eyes, he added, "Stay angry, Son."

"No problem, sir." Eugene watched the captain stride away until he disappeared among the artillery guns. As he finished his chow, he thought about the anger he'd been harboring since Will's death. It was bitterness, plain and simple. The captain was right; it was eating him alive. Deep in his heart he knew Will would not want him to feel that way, but it had somehow made it easier the next time he had to pull the trigger.

By the following afternoon, Regimental Commander Colonel Hartmann, made his way around the camp sharing news with his men. The 180th Brigade was not able to hold the line, and the American Military Command was unwilling to give up any ground they had already won. The brave men of the 179th Brigade were being called on to pick up their arms once more. Colonel Hartmann was a powerful motivator to his men. By morning, they were marching with confidence to relieve the 180th and face the Huns again.

On the third day of November, relief was complete, but the resistance they were anticipating from the Germans never materialized. The enemy had made a hasty withdrawal from the region during the night. Eugene's regiment pressed forward without wasting any time, making it all the way to the Meuse River before their advance came to a halt. The Germans had destroyed the middle section of the bridge, making it impossible for an entire division to cross the river.

That night, Colonel Hartmann put together a small company of scouts to cross the river for reconnaissance. Sergeant Haney was chosen to lead the company, and Eugene was assigned as one of his scouts.

"Are you okay with this, kid?" Al had his hand on Eugene's shoulder.

"Yes sir, I wouldn't miss it."

Al let out a hearty laugh. "That's what I wanted to hear."

For the next hour, Sergeant Haney proceeded to go over the plan with his men. They would cross the river about half a kilometer north and work their way through the thick forest relying solely on their own night vision for reconnaissance. There would be no communication between the men except for hand signals.

So far, everything was going according to plan. All six men were lying on their bellies at the edge of the forest watching the German regiments just a few hundred yards away. Suddenly, they were caught off guard by the sound of German aircraft flying overhead. When the first bomb was dropped on their comrades across the river, Eugene turned his head sharply to look at Sergeant Haney. Al put his finger to his lips signaling for Eugene not to make a sound. All six men lay silently in anguish as the Germans bombed their regiment throughout the night.

Before dawn, Sergeant Haney led his band of men back across the river to their waiting commander. The night had been hellish for the Americans on the other side, once again suffering many precious losses from their battalion.

After turning in their reconnaissance report, Sergeant Haney and his men sat down for chow. Eugene was barely finished when the first German artillery shell made its way across the river. Quickly he and the other soldiers ran for cover out of range.

The next few days seemed to run together in one long blur. The Americans were being shelled by day and bombed by night. The regiment moved far enough from the river to stay out of the German's artillery fire, but at night the bombings were the hardest to endure. Eugene kept his head down and prayed fervently, trying to remember Will's reassuring smile in the midst of chaos. The worst he suffered during the bombings was a mild shrapnel wound to his left thigh. As painful as it was, his wound was nothing compared to the loss of life and suffering he witnessed among the men in his battalion.

Three times Colonel Hartmann sent small patrols from the 357th to cross the bridge over the Meuse River. On one of the attempts they tried to put a ladder across the gap in the bridge. But all three times, they were repelled by enemy machine gun fire.

Finally, on November 9, after a week of steady artillery fire, a reconnaissance patrol returned with information that the Germans were retreating. To cover their retreat, the Huns left two companies from each of their regiments with machine guns. The objective of the 357th was to immediately take the town of Baalon, which was heavily occupied by the Germans. On the night of the tenth, recognizing the power of the advancing American army, the Germans released poisonous gas on the nearby town of Mouzay. The Americans put forth a valiant effort to save the civilians.

Eugene strapped on his gas mask and entered the town. He banged his fist on the door of the first cottage he came to, but there was no answer. He lowered his shoulder and broke through the door with relative ease. Inside, Eugene found an elderly couple in their bed. The woman was lying motionless across her husband, and the man was gasping for every breath. Eugene felt for a pulse in the woman's neck—she was still alive.

The old man's eyes were filled with terror. "Veuillez ne pas tuer nous." Between each choking breath, he pleaded for Eugene not to kill them.

"Je suis américain. Je suis ici pour vous aider." Eugene told the man unabatedly that he was there to help them. He lifted the woman into his arms and ran with her to the nearest army medic just outside the town. When he was certain that she would be cared for, Eugene sprinted back to the cottage and pulled the man to his feet. When he reached the street, another soldier came to his aid, and together they brought the man to safety near his wife.

All night long Eugene carried women and children and elderly citizens outside the town to receive treatment from the waiting American army medics. There were countless civilian deaths that night from the poisonous gas. It was a gruesome scene—one memory among countless others that Eugene would struggle to forget in the years to come.

On the morning of November 11, 1918, patrols from the 357th entered the town of Baalon meeting with little resistance. Just past eleven o'clock in the morning, word reached the battalion that an armistice had been signed and the war was over. While Paris erupted in rapturous merrymaking, the men of Eugene's regiment quietly went about their duties, assisting the French people of Baalon and Mouzay.

All in all, the 357th Infantry had advanced further and had been in more engagements with the enemy than any other regiment in their division. They had never failed to attain their objective or fulfill their mission.

Eugene had now been away from his home for an entire year. With the war over, he had hoped to be able to return to Kentucky soon. His battalion was billeted in the town of Baalon, and their duties included taking care of the returning prisoners of war as well as hundreds of war refugees.

Eugene's ability to speak the language was a source of comfort to many of the French people with whom he came in contact. Rachel had taught him well. He recalled one evening on the farm conversing with her in French at the supper table. Papa had said, "If you're gonna speak them fancy words, I'm gonna take my meal outside and eat with the horses. At least I'm able to understand what they're sayin'." The three of them had shared a good laugh together, and from then on, Rachel and Eugene reserved their French conversations for after dinner.

"We won't be going home for a very long time, I'm afraid." Sergeant Haney was holding the other end of a medical stretcher from Eugene. They were carrying a wounded prisoner of war to the Red Cross wagon that was waiting to take him to a field hospital.

Eugene was trying to comprehend why it would take so long to leave France. "Once we get all of our men out of Germany, can't we just go home?"

Al laughed and said, "War's not that simple, kid. I've heard that our division will probably be headed into Germany for the occupation."

"What? You mean we're going in?" That thought was a bit unsettling to Eugene.

"More than likely. We won't have to fight anymore, but we'll be called on to keep peace until everything's under control."

Eugene was sorely disappointed and had hopes that the occupation would not last for long. As it turned out, his division was indeed one of nine American divisions to occupy Germany for the next six months.

Eugene was posted on guard duty for most of that time period, helping protect key points of the transportation system in Germany's interior. Discipline was extremely strict, and he was required to dress in full uniform and participate in daily training exercises. As set as Eugene had been on going home back in November, he now realized how much he had needed these six months to work through the horrors of war that he had experienced.

Eugene's division was the fifth of the Army Occupation to be withdrawn from Germany, and by the first of June 1919, he found himself back at Camp Travis. When he had first walked into this camp a year and a half ago, he had been a scared boy, but now he returned as a battle-scarred man. After his discharge, Eugene's only desire was to go home, yet his biggest fear was who would be there to greet him.

Chapter 17

June 1919

After spending the week at Camp Travis and receiving his discharge papers from the army, Eugene now walked down the streets of Lexington feeling no fear. His stepfather had caused him years of pain—both as a boy and as a man. But Louis would never again be allowed to rule any part of his life. Eugene felt certain he would never see his stepfather again, but even if he did, the man wielded no more power over him. That horrible chapter of his youth was dead and buried in the past. Now he was consumed with the mission of getting on with his life.

Eugene was in full army uniform, and everywhere he went, people slapped him on the back or shook his hand, thanking him for his service to the nation. One family was nice enough to buy his dinner as he sat in Edna's Café enjoying the country-fried steak.

"Sir, that's not necessary." Eugene was a little embarrassed about all the attention he was receiving. Besides, he had quite a lot of money of his own. He had never been one to gamble or spend money on drinks and women like some of his comrades. He did spend part of his pay on a beautiful mantle clock purchased in Germany that he had packed away carefully in his duffle bag. He couldn't wait to present it to his mama. Even more than that, he couldn't wait to be held in her arms.

The man in the café insisted, however, on buying Eugene's meal. "Young man, we're honored to be able to do this. My wife's brother, Charlie, served overseas and returned a couple of months back. It's admirable what you boys did over there."

"Thank you, sir. I'm much obliged."

After dinner, Eugene quickly made his way through the city and onto the road heading toward Winchester. It only took a few short minutes of thumbing before a man and his wife pulled over to give him a lift. They were heading into Winchester but were more than happy to drop him off a few miles south of town.

Waving to the couple as they pulled away, Eugene's heart pounded with excitement as he headed up the trail through the woods. It seemed a little overgrown, but the familiar surroundings brought such a feeling of elation Eugene was now at a full run. It was late afternoon and he was already picturing his papa sitting on the front porch while his mama prepared supper in the kitchen.

Bursting out of the woods, he stopped at the edge of the pasture to take in the familiar scene. For a few long minutes, Eugene was unable to move. His duffle bag slipped from his shoulder as he studied the site before him. Gone were the horse trails through the pasture—the grass was practically knee high. Papa wasn't sitting on the front porch and there was no smoke coming from the stovepipe outside the kitchen. No horses, no mules, no cow, no chickens and, worst of all, no people.

Eugene didn't bother to pick up his duffle bag. When he came to his senses, he took off running across the pasture and leapt onto the front porch, not bothering with the steps. He knew in his heart there would be no one home, but still he burst into the house calling, "Mama! Papa! I'm home!" The house rewarded him with a choking dust and bitter silence.

Slowly Eugene made his way through each room. The table in the kitchen stood alone with no chairs surrounding it. The bed was still in his folk's room, and he discovered his own bed as well. The trapdoor lay bare as did the reading room of all its furnishings save for the antlers hanging above the fireplace. Eugene lifted the trapdoor and was greeted by a familiar dank odor. It had always taken Rachel a few days to air out the room below. She would leave the trapdoor open and boil a pot of herbs and spices on the lower stove before she declared the room habitable. The faintest of smiles passed across Eugene's face as he was reminded of the sound of her voice.

Without a lantern it would do him no good to go downstairs, so Eugene decided to walk around to the far entrance of the cave. On his way, he stopped into the shed where he discovered some of the horse tack still hanging on the wall. For the first time since he'd left, he wondered what happened to the mule he'd ridden into town. Finally he entered the cave, and was thankful to discover that the lantern and matches were exactly where Papa always kept them. His disappointment, however, grew more and more intense the deeper he advanced through the passageway. By the time he reached the downstairs room, he felt a heavy weight settle onto his chest. All he had been able to think about for the past twenty months was coming home, and now home no longer existed.

Eugene barged through the trapdoor and rushed out of the house. He felt encumbered with anger and an overwhelming feeling of sadness. Sprinting into the middle of the pasture, he let out an anguished cry to God, "Where are they? Where—are—they?" And when his anger turned to confusion, he cried to the heavens, "Who am I?" He felt so lonely—even abandoned, just like the farm.

Eugene needed to find relief and, mercifully, he found it through a mournful lament. He dropped to his knees crying and sobbing loudly. Leaning back on his heels, he opened his arms, wailing toward heaven. When that didn't seem to be enough, he put his face to the ground and cried out in anguish. His fingers dug into the earth as he continued sobbing. He sobbed for the abuse he had suffered as a child, he sobbed for the horrors of war he had witnessed and been a part of, he mourned for Will the way he had needed to mourn for him months ago, and he cried in despair for his family. He allowed himself to continue the release of emotions, until his body and mind were utterly spent.

Finally, as he began to calm, Eugene put his face in his hands and quietly wept, "Oh God, I'm alone." A shudder pulsed through his body. "I'm all alone."

That night, Eugene lay on his bedroll under the stars in the middle of the pasture. He couldn't bear to enter the house again and somehow found comfort out in the open. Many a night in France, he had lain in the open, sometimes in fear of incoming artillery and sometimes in total exhaustion, but he'd never been alone. His buddies from the 357th had always been by his side in good times and bad. Now there was no one at his side—he had never truly felt forsaken until tonight.

Eugene had spent more hours on a train in the last year and a half than he cared to count. He could only bear to spend one night on the farm, and now he sat in his army uniform staring out the window as the countryside flew by. His destination was the train station in Enid, Oklahoma. How different this trip to Oklahoma was from his first one. This time he had enough money to eat in the dining car, so he wasn't going to be as hungry or thirsty as before. He was still anxious about finding his folks, but his attention was now turned to what he was going to say to Ralph and Susan Gano. He dearly wished Will would be at that train station to greet him. Instead, when he arrived on the Santa Fe at noon, he found himself standing on Independence Street in downtown Enid, wondering which direction to turn. Enid didn't look like a very big town, but it seemed to be bustling with activity. He decided to try his luck at the ticket window.

"Excuse me, sir, do you know which direction I should be heading to find Helena?"

The older gentleman behind the counter was more than glad to help an army veteran. "Helena's just thirty-three miles northwest of here. You got a ride, son?"

"No sir, I was hoping to catch one along the road."

"Hold on a minute." The man behind the glass pushed back his stool and came outside to meet Eugene on the platform. He offered his hand and introduced himself as Henry Stewart.

"Nice to meet you, sir. I'm Eugene Wyatt."

"My pleasure, young man, and I want to offer my thanks for your service to our country."

"Thank you, sir."

"All right, you say you're headed to Helena?" Mr. Stewart gestured with his hand down the street. "I'm thinking if you head over to the wheat elevator at the end of the street, you might find a farmer going north. The harvest is just getting started around here, and there are several folks from Helena that bring their wheat to Enid."

"I appreciate it, sir."

"Don't mention it, Son. If you don't find a ride, come back, and I'll take you myself when I get off at five o'clock."

Eugene threw his duffle bag over his shoulder and waved to Mr. Stewart as he headed down the busy street.

There wasn't a lot of activity at the grain elevator when Eugene arrived. He walked between the massive silos until he found one of the operators working on a lift handle. The operator told him they should have a few farmers coming in with a load soon.

"Can't start cuttin' wheat till the afternoon. Too wet in the mornin' so there won't be any loads brought in for an hour or so. You might find ya a ride then." The operator wiped his hands with a dirty rag he'd pulled from the back of his overalls. "You can hang around here till a load comes in."

Eugene looked around and noticed a barrel sitting next to the wall.

"Do you mind if I just sit over there?"

"Be my guest."

Within the hour, trucks started rolling into the elevator to dump their loads of wheat. By the sixth load, Eugene had found his ride north with an old wheat farmer from Alfalfa County. Just before three o'clock in the afternoon, he was dropped off in front of a cemetery and started walking down a dirt road headed for the Gano's farm.

The road was lined on either side with fields of rolling wheat. It made for a pretty sight and a peaceful walk. After a half a mile or so, Eugene spotted a neat white house sitting back away from the road with a stand of trees in the yard and a vegetable garden to the side. About a hundred yards or so from the house, he noticed the large, wooden barn standing guard over the fields of wheat. Eugene looked at the mailbox and read the name Gano on the side. His heart instantly started beating a hurried rhythm. *So this is where Will grew up.*

As Eugene stood in the road, two little girls came running out of the house with dolls in their hands giggling and chasing one another around the yard. Eugene walked up the short drive and into the yard. The two girls stopped playing and the older one asked, "Did you know Willie?"

Eugene was a bit taken back by the question until he realized she must have noticed his uniform. He smiled and answered, "Yes, he was my best friend." He walked over to where the girls had been playing.

"He was my best friend too," the older girl said, staring at Eugene with her hands on her hips.

"I bet your name is Blanche."

A sly smile came across the girl's face and she let her hands drop to her side.

"How did you know?"

"Because Will told me all about you. And this must be Ruth."

Six-year-old Ruth was very shy and hid behind her ten-year-old sister.

"Willie called us Blanchie and Ruthie. Do you wanna come in?" Blanche already had him by the sleeve dragging him toward the door.

"Are your folks at home?" Eugene asked.

"My mamma is, but my daddy's out in the field."

Eugene was led up the two steps of the front porch, and Blanche launched into the house calling her mamma. He didn't go inside, deciding it would be best to remain on the porch.

Susan Gano came to the door, and Eugene guessed her to be in her late forties. She had brown hair pinned into a swirl at the back of her neck and soft, gray eyes that began to moisten as she caught her first glimpse of Eugene standing there in his uniform.

Eugene searched for the words he'd rehearsed over and over again on the train, but the only thing he could think about at the moment, was how much she looked like Will.

After an awkward silence, he cleared his throat and began. "Mrs. Gano, I'm Eugene Wyatt. I served with your son in France, and I've come to deliver a letter to you and Mr. Gano." He felt a tremendous relief just getting those words out of his mouth.

Susan still hadn't spoken a word. Eugene noticed her lip begin to quiver as she opened the door wide, and softly said, "Please, come in."

Eugene followed her through the living room to the kitchen, and Susan motioned for him to have a seat at the table. She slowly took the chair across from him.

"Mrs. Gano, I just want you to know how sorry I am about what happened to Will. He was one of the finest men I've ever known."

A tear instantly escaped Susan's eye, and she quickly lowered her gaze to her lap. Eugene could only imagine how difficult this moment must be for her.

"Ma'am, your son spoke about you all the time. He was always talking about what a good family he had back home."

Susan took in a deep breath and looked up, but her gaze and her words were not directed toward Eugene. "Blanche, go get your daddy from the barn."

Blanche threw her doll on the couch in the living room and ran out the door while Susan rose to her feet and poured Eugene a glass of iced tea. He smiled as he took a sip. It wasn't sweetened.

A few moments later, Ralph Gano burst through the kitchen door, and Eugene rose to his feet. Ralph was considerably older than his wife with tanned skin and a large, white mustache. He extended his hand in welcome. "We're honored to have you here, soldier."

"Thank you, sir. I'm Eugene Wyatt, and it's a pleasure to meet you."

"I'm glad to meet you too, young man. Will told us about you in his letters. Let's go sit down in the living room where we can talk."

Eugene was directed to a comfortable chair while Ralph and Susan sat side by side on the couch. Ruth worked her way under her mother's arm, but Blanche sat down on the arm of Eugene's chair.

"Blanchie, get off the chair and give him some room," Ralph chided.

"Oh, it's okay, Mr. Gano. She's not bothering me any."

For the next hour, Ralph and Eugene exchanged stories about Will. Ralph sometimes referred to his son as Willie and held a picture of him in his uniform as they spoke. When there was a short silence between them, Eugene rose to his feet and handed Mr. Gano Will's letter, his Scouts notebook, and the picture he'd carried of Mary. Suddenly, both of Will's parents seemed to be struggling to keep their composure, so Eugene decided this was the time he should be on his way.

Ralph stood and shook Eugene's hand, and thanked him for coming, but Susan remained silent on the couch—almost in a daze. Eugene let himself out and quietly closed the door behind him. He lifted his duffle bag onto his shoulder and started walking back down the road. Somehow this was not how he had expected his visit to go.

By now it was late afternoon and he had no idea what he would do for the night. Maybe he could slip into someone's barn before he made his way back to the train station in Enid. He hadn't eaten since morning, so this would probably end up being a very long night.

As he walked down the road, he suddenly heard footsteps running behind him and a girl's voice yelling, "Eugene, hey Eugenie!"

"*Eugenie?* Who's that?" Eugene chuckled as Blanche approached him out of breath.

"You're Eugenie, who else?" she said with a capricious grin.

"Well, last time I checked Eugenie was a girl's name and I'm a boy."

Blanche slapped him on the arm, "I know that, silly. Mamma sent me to get you. We forgot to ask you to stay for supper and spend the night. She said to tell you she's sorry about that."

Eugene turned and looked into the little girl's blue eyes. "I'll only come back if you stop calling me a girl's name."

Blanche giggled as she took hold of his hand and started walking him back to the house. As he felt the small hand in his own and listened to Blanche's nonstop chatter, Eugene lifted his eyes to the sky above and smiled. All of a sudden, he didn't feel quite so alone.

Supper was as good a meal as Eugene could ever remember—pork chops, creamed corn, butter beans, fried potatoes, and biscuits. He didn't think he had room for even one more bite until he saw the bowl of peach cobbler Mrs. Gano set in front of him.

After the table was cleared, Ralph laid out a checkers board and asked Eugene if he played.

Eugene replied, "Yes sir, I sure do. But I've gotta tell you, I'm not very good. I think I only beat Will a couple of times."

"Join the crowd. I had a hard time beating him myself."

After the third game, Ralph threw his hands up in surrender, and Eugene noticed Susan smile as she dried the last supper dish.

"I must be out of practice. How about one more game so I can redeem myself?" Ralph asked.

"That's fine with me, sir. I'm enjoying it."

"I'm sure you are." Ralph laughed as he set his pieces in place.

Eugene wasn't sure if Mr. Gano was just being kind to his guest, but he was willing to play one more game to find out.

In the middle of the final game, a knock sounded at the kitchen door. Eugene could see three people standing on the back porch in the evening sun. He had seen Mary's picture many

167

times, and he was certain the young woman he now saw through the glass was she. Nervousness once again took hold, and Eugene stood as Alexander, Rosa, and Mary Rollmann were welcomed into the Gano's kitchen.

Ralph gave his good friend Alex a firm handshake, then turned and introduced him to Private Wyatt. Alex extended his weathered hand to Eugene, then introduced his wife as Mrs. Rollmann.

Mr. Gano added, "And this is Will's fiancée, Mary."

Mary took a deep breath and stepped forward to offer her hand to Eugene. He gently accepted her hand into his and said, "Miss Rollmann, I'm so glad to finally meet you. I only wish it were under different circumstances."

"As do I," she said quietly.

Once again, Eugene found himself sitting in the Gano's living room sharing stories about Will. Mary wanted to hear as much as possible about what Will's life had been like during his time in France. Eugene tried to share as many stories as possible without actually telling her how horrible it had really been.

Eventually Mary told a few stories of her own, and Eugene listened intently as she told the story of Will's proposal. When she had finished, Mary looked directly into Eugene's eyes and said, "Tell me how Will departed this life."

Eugene suddenly felt a wave of panic sweep over him and looked to Mr. Gano for help. How could he possibly tell any of them how Will had died? He had only told the full story one time, and that was to Sergeant Haney back in France.

Ralph put his arm around Susan and pulled her close to his side. He returned Eugene's gaze and said, "Maybe the two of you would like to take a walk before the sun goes down."

Eugene automatically rose to his feet when Mary stood, and he followed her through the front door out into the yard. There was a warm breeze blowing as they walked side by side in the evening shade. Eugene noticed they were walking toward the barn.

"Forgive me for asking," he began, "but are you sure you want to know the details of Will's death?"

Mary said, "I know it must sound odd, but I can't rest until I know what it was like for him in the end."

Eugene turned his face into the breeze and somehow felt it giving him the permission he needed to tell Mary the whole story about the man she loved. By the time they reached the barn, Eugene had told her every detail of Will's last moments. The gate into the barn was closed, so he put his hands on top of it trying to steady himself—for some reason he was shaking and couldn't stop.

Mary was a petite woman with a gentle manner and quiet voice. She rested her hand on Eugene's arm and said, "Thank you for telling me everything. I know it wasn't any easier for you to tell it than it was for me to hear it. But oddly enough, I finally feel at peace."

Eugene took a deep breath and felt his body relax as Mary went on. "Thank you for holding him for me in the end."

Eugene thought his heart was being ripped to shreds. It should have been Will standing here with Mary, not him. If only he could've taken the sniper's bullet instead.

Mary eased her arm through Eugene's, and they turned to walk back to the house. Neither one spoke again.

Mr. and Mrs. Rollmann were walking down the drive with Ralph and Susan when the two young people returned. Eugene and Mary followed them to the horse and buggy tethered near the road.

Mr. Rollmann turned toward Eugene and asked, "Will you be staying long?"

"No, sir. I plan to return to Kentucky in the morning."

"Well, if you decide to stay, we'll be glad to put you to work in the harvest." Alex extended his hand once more to Eugene and thanked him for coming such a long distance to keep his commitment to the Ganos.

Suddenly, Eugene remembered something he carried in his duffle bag and asked the Rollmanns to wait while he sprinted back to the house. When he returned, Mary was sitting in the buggy between her parents and reached out to accept the bundle of letters he handed her.

"These are all the letters you wrote to Will. He kept every one of them and read them over and over again. The one on top is the letter he was writing to *you* just before . . ." Eugene's voice trailed off.

Mary held the bundle tightly to her breast and quietly said, "Thank you."

As the buggy pulled away from the drive, she turned in her seat to face him and said, "You're a good man, Eugene Wyatt."

For the first time since they'd met, Eugene saw tears flowing down Mary's cheeks.

By nine o'clock, both girls were in bed and Susan showed Eugene to his room.

"This was Will's room until he went off to war. I hope you don't mind."

"Ma'am, I'd be honored. Thank you for everything."

Susan laid a gentle kiss on his cheek. "Thank you for coming."

Within a few minutes, Eugene was lying in bed with his hands locked behind his head on the pillow as he watched the breeze carry the light cotton curtains away from the windowsill. He thought he heard someone softly crying in the next room. Eugene's heart ached as he heard Ralph speaking in a low, soothing voice. Moments later he could no longer hear Ralph— the only sound that filled the house was Susan's mournful sobbing. By the time Eugene finally turned over to try and get some sleep he was surprised to find his own pillow was soaked.

At first light, Eugene dressed and sat underneath the window in his room penning a letter to Will's dear parents. He had thought about writing them many times while he was in Europe, but he could never seem to find the right words. This morning he had an unusual clarity of mind that compelled him to put his feelings into writing.

Dear Mr. and Mrs. Gano,

I deeply regret that fate has been such that I was in need of visiting your home. Only days before my beloved friend gallantly made the supreme sacrifice on the battlefield in France, he and I made an agreement that should either of us meet with disaster, we would visit the home of our fallen comrade. I have now fulfilled that promise.

To know Will was to love him, to be with him in battle when it seemed there was no chance, was to admire him. I regret that he was unable to return to his loved ones of whom he so often spoke, always speaking with that deep love that a worthy son should have for those who gave him life. I wish to extend to you my most sincere sympathy as well as the sympathy of those in his company. It will hopefully be a source of comfort for you to know that he is remembered by all who served with him as a true gentleman and a valiant soldier.

There will always be a vacancy in your home that can never be filled, but you should know that Will proved himself to be worthy of the love and admiration of all who knew him.

Please accept once again my sincere regrets, as well as those of his comrades, that he could not return home to you. He spoke of his faith often and the faith of his dear family. And so it is with faith that we hope to reunite with our beloved Will in the hereafter.

Thank you for your kind hospitality.

I am sincerely yours in grief,
Private Second Class Eugene L. Wyatt
Winchester, Kentucky

Eugene made his bed neatly and laid the letter on top of his pillow. After a hearty breakfast, Ralph pulled the truck out of the shed to give him a ride back to the train station in Enid. Susan met Eugene on the porch and handed him a bag filled with boiled eggs and biscuits.

"You'll be hungry on your long journey." She lovingly laid her hand on Eugene's chest, and searched his eyes as if she were searching for Will. Then she opened her arms and wrapped him in the kind of hug that only a mother could give. "God bless you, Son."

Blanche and Ruth were playing near the truck as Eugene threw his duffle bag in the back. "So when are you coming back?" Blanche had her hands on her hips again, no doubt expecting Eugene to give her the exact date of his return.

"Well, I don't really know. Maybe I'll just have to come back after you're all grown up." He pinched her cheek and she playfully slapped his hand away. "Bye Blanchie."

"Bye Eugenie!" She was already running toward her mother on the porch, giggling for all she was worth. Eugene stuck his arm out the window and waved as Ralph steered the truck onto the road.

"I want you to see something." Ralph had stopped the truck at the end of the road before turning south onto the highway. Eugene got out and followed curiously behind Mr. Gano as he walked into the Good Hope Cemetery.

"Eugene, this cemetery is part of Gano land. Someday Susan and I will be buried here." He had stopped in front of the piece of ground that had already been chosen.

"I staked this land back in '93 during the Cherokee Strip land run." He paused and looked out over his fields of wheat. "We were living in Kansas at the time, and I came down for a chance at free land. Will was our first child to be born here, in '95. God's been so good to us." His voice broke slightly, and Eugene looked out over the fields.

Ralph took off his hat and held it up against his chest. "I want to bring him home. I can't stand the thought of my boy lying in that field in France. I want to bring him home."

Eugene felt a lump forming in his throat but remained silent as Ralph started walking back toward the truck. Before opening the door, he pointed across the road. "That's the Rollmann place." Eugene could see the house and barn on the other side of the road where Mary lived.

Both men got back into the truck, and Ralph continued talking as they headed south toward Enid. "Mary's dad came for the land rush too. Alex and I didn't know each other at the time, but he staked his land on this prairie right next to mine. It's odd to think that Alex's father came over from Germany." He shook his head as if he was trying to clear his mind of the thought of Germans.

Ralph glanced at Eugene and smiled slightly as he continued his story. "Every Sunday our family passed by the Rollmann place in our wagon going to worship. Finally, Alex asked me one Sunday where we were going, and I told him we were going to church. The very next Sunday as we passed, he was waiting with his family in the wagon to follow us. One by one Alex's whole family came to the Lord." He slowed the truck as they passed a farmer with a wagonload of watermelons. Ralph took in a deep breath, then said, "I was never so proud than when Will asked Mary to be his wife."

After a few miles of silence, Ralph asked, "What about your life now, Eugene? Are you going back to your folks in Kentucky?"

"Sir, I'm not sure what I'll do now. My folks aren't around anymore." That last statement sent an unexpected pain through the middle of Eugene's chest. He would've told Mr. Gano about his life, but it somehow seemed easier just to let it rest.

"I'm sorry to hear that. Have you got any other family in Kentucky then?"

"No sir."

Ralph was curious and asked, "Then what are you planning to do?"

"The only thing I really know is horses. I'll just head

back to Lexington and see if I can get hired onto one of the horse farms."

"Eugene, if you have any trouble at all, I want you to know you're always welcome to come back here."

He could feel the sincerity in Mr. Gano's offer and replied, "Thank you, sir. I'll remember that."

When the truck pulled up to the train station, Ralph parked and went inside as Eugene bought his ticket. The Santa Fe station was a large two-story brick building with an attached freight house. The train master's offices were on the second floor while the first floor included the ticket office and two separate waiting rooms—one for the white folks and one for the colored folks. The train heading east wouldn't be in the station until noon.

With ticket in hand, Eugene approached Ralph and said, "Mr. Gano, I appreciate you bringing me to the station."

"I'll stay with you till the train pulls in," Ralph replied. Even though he had a full day ahead of him with the harvest, he felt compelled to stay with Eugene.

"You don't need to do that, sir. I'll be just fine."

"I know you will, but I'm going to see you onto that train if you don't mind."

Eugene nodded, and followed Ralph to a bench outside in the shade of the depot. The two men sat side by side in a comfortable silence. Ralph just wanted to sit beside this young soldier, and perhaps feel a sense of Will's presence.

The train pulled into the station just before noon and both men stood to face each other. Eugene extended his hand to Mr. Gano and said, "Sir, I just want you to know what a privilege it was to serve with Will. He was like a brother to me."

Ralph took Eugene's hand and pulled him into an embrace echoing his wife's earlier words. "God bless you, Son."

Ralph was still standing on the platform with hat in hand when the train finally pulled away from the station. He wondered if he would ever see Eugene again.

Chapter 18

Lexington

Deprived of sleep from yet another long journey, Eugene entered Mrs. Dixon's Boarding House on Baker Street at two o'clock in the afternoon. Luckily for him a boarder had moved out the day before and Lila Dixon had just finished preparing the room for a new tenant. Lila was a petite, snowy-haired bundle of energy with a twinkle in her eye. Everyone in the neighborhood loved her, and those who lived in her house loved her cooking even more. There were eight boarders, all men of various ages and Eugene would be the youngest.

"Just returned from the war, have you?" She was trying to size up Eugene and make sure he wouldn't cause any problems in her house.

"Yes ma'am."

"You look awfully young to me. How old are you anyway?"

"I'm eighteen—actually eighteen and a half."

Mrs. Dixon laughed. "Well now, eighteen and a half will get you the room." She liked Eugene from the moment she saw him. He was well built and handsome in his army uniform, but her instincts told her that this was also a good man. She could always judge people by looking into their eyes and had turned many away from her door by reading trouble there. When she looked in Eugene's eyes, she read a kind heart but a troubled soul.

"You'll like it around here. We're all kind of like a family. Breakfast and supper are served every day in here." She showed Eugene the large dining room just off the kitchen. There was a long, wooden table covered with a tablecloth and chairs all around. Beautiful pictures of landscapes hung on the walls and a walnut sideboard took up the entire length of one wall.

"You're on your own for lunch, but if you do a little extra work around here, I'll make sure you get a bagged lunch to take to work with you every day." There was that twinkle in her eye again. "You do have a job, don't you?"

Eugene blushed slightly. "Not yet, ma'am. I'm hoping to have one before the end of the week. But don't you worry; I can pay for my room."

"You'll pay me by the week and I'll have to have your first week's rent up front, which is $4.50." Lila started walking up the stairs. "But let me show you the room first before you decide." She unlocked a room at the end of the hall and swung the door wide.

Eugene stepped inside. He liked it instantly. It had a nice-sized bed, a bedside table and electric lamp, a desk, a chest of drawers, a wardrobe cabinet, and rectangular rug covering the floor.

Mrs. Dixon spoke up behind him. "One of the best things about this room is having a private door to the upstairs porch. Mind you, there aren't any stairs out there. You'll have to come and go through the front door just like everyone else."

"Thank you, Mrs. Dixon. I'll take it."

"Call me Miss Lila. I haven't been *Mrs.* Dixon for sixteen years now."

Eugene put down his duffle bag and paid Miss Lila for the first week. She put the money in her apron pocket and said, "Welcome to the family. We'll see you tonight at supper. Six o'clock sharp—same time every night."

She laid the key on the bedside table and closed the door behind her. Eugene opened the windows to let in a breeze, and then opened the door to the porch. There were several wicker chairs lining the porch, and he was looking forward to sitting outside in the evenings. But for now he needed a nap in the worst way. It was three o'clock in the afternoon, which would give him plenty of time before supper.

At five minutes past six, Eugene was awakened by a loud knock. He jumped off the bed and opened his door wondering who could be visiting him. A middle-aged man was standing in the hallway.

"Are you Mr. Wyatt?"

"Yes sir, Eugene Wyatt."

"Well, you better get yourself downstairs pronto or you'll have the devil to pay."

Eugene quickly put his shoes on and slipped his army jacket back on, buttoning it as he followed the stranger downstairs. He walked into the dining room and a hush fell over the room. All of the men had stopped talking and eating and were staring from Miss Lila to Eugene. Miss Lila rose from her chair at the head of the table to face him. "I don't know what kind of time you kept in the army, Mr. Wyatt, but in my boarding house you will be on time for every meal. Is that understood?"

Eugene thought his face must be the color of the sliced tomatoes sitting on the table. "Yes ma'am. My apologies."

Miss Lila pointed to Eugene's chair at the other end of the table. "We've already said grace, so you'll have to say yours in your heart."

"Yes ma'am." Eugene didn't dare disobey and instantly thanked God for his food. As soon as Miss Lila sat back down, the clinking of silverware on dishes and plates could once again be heard as all the men around the table continued to eat and reach for whatever food they wanted. Eugene timidly filled his plate and began eating.

"Gentlemen, as you can see we have a new member of the house. This is Eugene Wyatt and he's fresh out of the army. You all go around the table and introduce yourselves."

One by one, the men told Eugene their names and where they worked. It wasn't long before Eugene was drawn into their conversation and was answering numerous questions about the Great War.

After supper, Eugene followed Miss Lila into the kitchen carrying his dishes.

"Why honey, you're not supposed to do that. I've got all the help I need in the kitchen."

A young, black woman was standing nearby as Eugene put his dishes on the counter. He turned to face her. "My name is Eugene." He held out his hand but she didn't take it right away—not until Miss Lila nodded her head.

"I'm Cassie."

"Pleased to meet you."

Cassie shyly dropped his hand and moved into the dining room to clear the other dishes.

Miss Lila turned to Eugene and said, "Now you go on and get out of my kitchen. All the men are down the hall in the parlor. Shoo!"

With a grin on his face, Eugene started to leave but thought about one more thing. "Miss Lila, what time is . . .?"

Before he could finish his question, Miss Lila was already answering it. "Six o'clock sharp, just like supper. You've got less than twelve hours. Do you think you can make it on time?"

Eugene noticed the twinkle was back in her eyes as he answered, "Yes ma'am. I'll be on time for breakfast."

The first order of business after breakfast was to buy new clothes. Everything Eugene owned had been issued by the United States Army and he couldn't wait to wear regular clothes again. Carter's Clothing Store provided him with everything he needed. By noon he was headed outside of the city in search of a job.

Every day, for nearly a week, Eugene went from farm to farm seeking employment. Fortunately there were dozens of horse farms in the area, but he was beginning to think he would never find anyone willing to hire him. The economy was struggling because of the recent war, and no one seemed to want to take a chance on a young man fresh out of the army.

On the fourth day, Eugene walked to Mason Farms—much further out of town than any of the others he had tried. It took him a couple of hours on foot to finally reach the open gate and nearly another mile to walk the drive leading to the barns and the house. The scenery was beautiful and Eugene realized how much he had missed Kentucky in the last year and a half. He stopped a couple of times to admire the fine-looking thoroughbreds grazing in the bluegrass pastures behind the miles of white fence.

Finally coming over a hill, he caught sight of a huge white barn with green trim, settled down in a shallow valley. Two large stables and several sheds all painted white and green made up the complex. Higher up on the hill, above the barn, stood a three-story redbrick mansion with four white columns. The grounds around the house were immaculate, boasting well-trimmed shrubs and flower gardens. Eugene stood for a few minutes just trying to take it all in. He wasn't sure he belonged in such a place, but desperation compelled him to continue.

Eugene found a man coming out of the stables. "I'm looking for Mr. Mason, is he available?"

"Oh, you mean Mr. Collins, he owns the place. His wife was a Mason; her father is the one who owned the farm before he passed away." He motioned for Eugene to follow him into the barn. "He should be in his office around the corner on your left."

Eugene thanked the man and nervously rounded the corner. There was a horseshoe knocker on the door, but he decided to use his hand instead.

A deep voice answered, "Come in."

Eugene entered a well-furnished office that looked like it might have been a fancy office in downtown Lexington rather than in a barn. The man behind the desk was well tanned with brown hair that was graying around the temples. When he stood, Eugene was surprised by the man's height, and had to look up in order to make eye contact.

"Can I help you?"

"Sir, I'm sorry to bother you, but my name is Eugene Wyatt and I'm looking for a job."

"George Collins." The man gestured toward the chair. "Have a seat."

Eugene sat down in a nice leather chair facing Mr. Collin's huge desk.

"What kind of experience do you have?"

"Well sir, I trained thoroughbreds for five years, and I just spent the last year and a half in the army."

"Where'd you train horses?" Mr. Collins was leaning forward with his elbows on his desk.

"I grew up around Winchester, sir. My folks had a little horse farm just outside of town, and we sold several thoroughbreds at auction over in Lexington."

"Well, I'll just tell you up front Eugene, I'm not interested in hiring any horse trainers. I've got some of the best trainers this side of the Mississippi. So I'm afraid I can't help you." He stood as if their conversation was over.

"Sir, I don't mean any disrespect," Eugene had risen to his feet as well, "but I'm desperate for a job right now. I'd be willing to do any kind of work if you need another hand around here."

Mr. Collins thought about that for a minute, all the while sizing up the sturdy-looking young man standing in his office. After a short silence he seemed to come to a conclusion. "I'm sorry, Eugene, I'm not going to allow you anywhere near my thoroughbreds, but I think I could find something around here for a young army veteran. I'll tell you what; I've been meaning to hire another man on my maintenance crew. If you're willing to take care of the grounds, mend fences, and what not, I've probably got a place for you here."

Eugene reached for Mr. Collins' hand with a look of relief on his face. "Thank you, sir. I accept your offer."

Mr. Collins took his hand and said, "Where are you living?"

"Mrs. Dixon's Boarding House in town."

"Well, that won't do. You'll need to live here on the farm. Are you good with that?"

"Yes sir, I'm fine with whatever you need me to do."

"It's settled then; how about you start work on Monday

morning? That will give you time to get things squared away in town with Mrs. Dixon."

"That sounds great. Thank you so much, Mr. Collins. I really appreciate the work."

Mr. Collins gave Eugene the name of the man to report to on Monday and showed him where he'd be staying in the bunkhouse. There was even a cook for all the farm workers who lived in the bunkhouse.

Eugene thanked Mr. Collins at least three more times before he started back down the road to Lexington. It wasn't exactly the kind of job he was looking for, but at least it was a job for now.

There was a lot of time for thinking as he walked back to town. Since he had three days before his new job started, Eugene decided he would go into Winchester the next morning and search for his folks. He still remembered the names of the women Papa took money to every year. Maybe they would know where Franklin and Rachel had gone. That thought perked him up a bit, and by the time he got back to the boarding house, he was in a much better mood. Even more importantly, he was on time for supper.

Friday evening Eugene sat on the upper porch overlooking Miss Lila's backyard. It had not been a very good day, and he was in a melancholy mood.

Eugene had started the morning with enthusiasm, but it was now ending in bitter disappointment. He had thumbed a ride to Winchester without a problem that morning. Since his ride had dropped him off in the middle of town, he decided to find the doctor first. Perhaps his mama had been able to get help for Papa on her own.

Eugene had been relieved that Dr. Randall was still in practice. As they talked, he found out that the doctor was planning to retire next year after thirty-five years in Winchester. Dr. Randall explained that he had neither seen nor heard of a Franklin and Rachel Hawkins. He did, however, point Eugene in the direction of the part of town he was looking for.

Making his way through the colored part of town, Eugene had drawn more than a few curious looks. He knew better than most white folks about the bitter scourge of racism. He had seen too many hurtful things done to his papa over the years because of the color of his skin. He just kept remembering what Papa had said about people wearing blinders. Eugene examined his own heart as he walked through the town and hoped that he would never be guilty himself of wearing them.

Eugene found an elderly woman carrying a bucket of water down the road. He approached her and asked if he could carry the load for her. She looked at him as if he was a crazy man and kept walking. He then asked her if she knew where he could find Clara Eton or Anna Reed. Her response had been, "Well sonny, you just missed 'em both. Anna went on to meet her Maker last April, and Clara moved to Tennessee last Christmas to live with her son."

"What about Franklin and Rachel Hawkins? Have you seen them in town?"

That caused the woman to stop and put down her bucket.

"Sonny, I haven't thought of them two in more'n twenty-five years. What are you wantin' with all them folks anyway?"

"Is there anyone around here who might know where they are?" Eugene wasn't ready to give up yet.

She shaded her eyes and glared up at Eugene. "Sonny, I know everythin' that goes on 'round here and like I said, they ain't stepped foot in this town but once in a quarter century." The old woman reached down and picked up her bucket. "And that were an awful day."

Eugene just thanked her for her time and turned back toward town. He had been too late for supper by the time he got a ride back to the boarding house, but he didn't really care. He wasn't hungry after the news he'd received today.

There was a light knock on his door, and Eugene went back in his room to answer it. Miss Lila was standing in the hall with a tray in her hand.

"Honey, I don't know what's troubling you, but I know something's not right. I thought I'd bring you some leftovers from supper." Eugene accepted the tray from her with thanks. "I'll be glad to lend you an ear if you need one."

Eugene was thinking how nice it would be to have Miss Lila as his grandmother, but said, "I'll be fine. Thank you for your concern."

She put a loving hand on his arm as he stood there holding the tray. "I'm sure going to miss you around here. If that job of yours doesn't work out, you can come on back to your family here."

"That's just what I'll do, Miss Lila. You can count on it."

After church on Sunday, Eugene packed his belongings back in his army duffle bag. He looked at the mantle clock from Germany that was sitting on the chest of drawers and wondered if he should give it to Miss Lila. On second thought, he packed it securely in his bag once again. Leaving the clock here would mean he'd given up on finding his folks. Deep down, he realized there was a possibility that he may never see them again in this life, and that thought gave him an incredibly lonely feeling. He missed his folks tremendously. He missed being a part of a family.

The job Eugene was about to start at Mason Farms was nothing more than that—a job. It wasn't the kind of life he wanted to live—sleeping in a bunkhouse and working odd jobs on a farm that belonged to someone else. Eugene had to keep reminding himself that God had led him to Mason Farms and seen fit to give him that job. He needed to find a way to be grateful and live in a way that would honor the Lord for taking care of him thus far, especially during the war. But he was struggling under a load of guilt he couldn't seem to shed.

Eugene sat down in the chair in his room and leaned over to put his head in his hands. He felt incredibly guilty for leaving his mama all alone with Papa being so sick. It ripped his heart out to think of what she had gone through just waiting for him to return. As heavy as that burden was to bear, it wasn't nearly as heavy as the shame he carried within regarding the war. He had done things he wasn't proud of and had witnessed many gruesome scenes that he would never forget. Worst of all, he hadn't been able to save Will's life, and somehow, there was a disturbing notion that it should have been him lying in that field in France and not Will. What would it matter if he had died, there would be no one to mourn him. But Will had a precious, loving family waiting for him at home that would never see him again. Life just didn't seem to make sense.

That night, even his dreams were disturbing. He dreamt that he was riding Morceau de ciel. The horse was at top speed galloping through the Kentucky bluegrass, and Eugene was bent low over the powerful animal's neck. It was exhilarating for both horse and rider. Suddenly, Morceau leapt high into the air and hurdled a wide trench. Eugene could see German soldiers in the trench, and as Morceau galloped away, he could hear the bullets buzzing over his head. He felt something sting him in the back and knew he had been shot. Will was down in the trenches just ahead calling his name loudly and motioning for him to ride toward him. When Morceau came to a halt, Will pulled Eugene off the horse and told him everything would be fine. Franklin and Rachel were in the trenches too, taking turns holding him in their arms while he struggled to breathe. He knew he was shot, but no one seemed to be tending to his wound. As much as he was thrilled to see all three of them, he was frustrated that no one was acting like anything was wrong.

Eugene suddenly woke up gasping for air. No wonder— the pillow was over his face. *How did that happen?* He turned over on his back breathing deeply and thinking about the images that had been running through his mind. Slowly the realization dawned on him that he might never see his papa and mama again—they had both been with Will in his dream.

Chapter 19

For three long months, Eugene had been working for Mr. Collins on the farm. The best part of his week was going into town on Sunday morning to church. Not that his life was miserable on the farm, it's just that he wasn't being allowed to do what he did best—work with the horses.

Every Sunday morning he caught a ride into town with a family from his church that drove by the farm. He waited down by the road, and they picked him up on the way. Most of the time he spent the entire day in Lexington and either walked back to the farm that night or thumbed a ride along the road.

Miss Lila cooked up one of the best Sunday dinners in town, and she wouldn't allow Eugene to eat anywhere but with her. The first time he tried to pay her for the meal, she slapped his hand. He laughed and left the money on the hall table anyway. The next Sunday she told him that money went right to the collection plate at church, so he might as well put it in there himself. From then on, that's just what he did.

"Eugene, have you given any thought about courting?" Miss Lila had joined him on the upper porch in the wicker chairs.

Eugene looked over at her surprised by the question. "Well, Miss Lila, I don't have a lot of time to be courting and even if I did, I don't know of any girls to ask out." He didn't tell her that the only girl he'd ever been interested in lived in Louisville. Besides, he figured Annie had forgotten all about him and was probably married by now.

"Why there are plenty of girls at church who would be glad to go courting with you."

Eugene decided to humor her. "Is that so? Well, who did you have in mind?"

"Both of the Adams girls would . . ."

"Now hold on a minute, Miss Lila. For one thing, Amy is at least five years older than me, and Allison already has a beau."

"Well, how about the Tucker girl? She's just as sweet as she can be."

"But so shy she never speaks. I'd have to do all the talking if I took her out."

"All I'm saying is you should be keeping an eye out for a good Christian girl." Miss Lila reached over and patted him on the arm.

"I'll be sure and keep that in mind." Eugene gave her hand a little squeeze before he stood up. "I've got to start heading back. Thanks again for lunch. I'll see you next Sunday."

"Have a good week, Eugene. And you think about what I said."

"I will, Miss Lila."

Eugene decided to walk all the way back to the farm on this warm Sunday evening. It was the first of September, and he still had plenty of time to make it back before dark. He was looking forward to the solitude.

Miss Lila probably thought she hadn't been getting anywhere with her little conversation, but that was all Eugene could think about as he walked. He had to admit he was pretty lonely and wouldn't mind going out with a girl on occasion, but working six days a week on the farm didn't afford much of an opportunity for courting.

By the time Eugene started down the road to the bunkhouse, his spirits were in dire need of lifting. He walked over to the fence and leaned his elbows on the top rail. It was such a peaceful scene—dozens of thoroughbreds grazing in the pasture as the sun was sinking low.

He spoke out loud to the only One who could lift him up. "Oh Lord, I'm sure you've got a plan for my life." He took a long, slow breath and let it out just as slowly. "Is there any way you could reveal it to me soon? I know you're with me, but right now I feel so alone." He turned from the fence and whispered, "Amen." The strangest sensation came over Eugene that compelled him to stop and look back at the horses in the pasture, but whatever it had been, the feeling was gone.

It was Friday morning and for the last four days, Eugene had been repairing a section of fence on the far side of the farm. He was driving a truck down the back road of the farm remembering the first time he'd ever driven a vehicle other than a wagon pulled by mules.

At Camp Travis he'd been dragged along on an errand with Al and Will one Saturday morning. They were driving an army truck full of supplies over to Camp Bullis. Eugene was supposed to be scrubbing latrines, but Al had promised to keep him out of trouble if he'd join them. After dropping off all of the supplies, Al pulled the truck over to the side of the road on the way back to Travis and told Eugene to get behind the wheel. Eugene had been scared to death, but excited to give it a try. He could still remember Will's head nearly hitting the windshield when he first tried to change gears. Al was laughing so hard he could barely give Eugene instructions. None of them were laughing, however, when General O'Neil stopped to find out why their truck was in the ditch. Sergeant Haney was a smooth talker and true to his word, he'd kept Eugene out of trouble, but he and Will had never let him live it down. Will used to rib him all the time about driving that truck down into the ditch.

With all of the driving he had to do around Mason Farms, he'd gotten a lot better behind the wheel. He'd even applied for a driver's license and received it last month in the mail.

Eugene stopped the truck in the shade and started to work on the last section of fence that needed repairs. He was in a pretty good mood this morning after thinking about some of the fun times he'd had with Will and Al. There had never been a dull moment when the three of them were together.

Eugene went back to the truck whistling as he picked up

the bucket of paint and a brush. The section he had just repaired needed a good coat of white paint. He continued whistling the lively tune that Papa had always whistled. Today it didn't make him sad—for some reason, whistling Franklin's old tune seemed to boost his spirits.

After finishing the outside of the fence, Eugene crawled through and started painting the inside. He was squatted down painting the bottom rail still whistling when something unexpectedly nudged him in the middle of his back. When he turned around abruptly, the beautiful thoroughbred threw her head up into the air just as startled as Eugene was. He stood slowly to face the animal and recognition dawned on both of them at the exact same moment. Eugene knew this mare, and she knew him. He even knew where she liked to be scratched the most, right between her ears.

Eugene kept his voice low and calm as he scratched her favorite spot. "Oh girl, I've missed you so much. Tell me how you got here." She leaned her head into his chest and then nuzzled underneath his arm as if they had never been apart.

He must have stood with the mare for half an hour before he could pull himself away. Just being with her had taken him back home, and for the first time in nearly two years, he felt a sense of belonging flow through his veins.

Eugene was having difficulty breaking away from the mare, but he urgently needed to locate Mr. Collins to find out how she'd gotten here. He kissed her on the forehead and told her he'd be back. Placing his hands on the fence, he hurdled to the top and jumped over all in one motion. He left his tools and paint where they lay, and took off down the road leaving a trail of dust in his wake.

Luckily for Eugene, Mr. Collins was watching one of the trainers lunge his prize thoroughbred inside the indoor arena. He spotted his boss immediately as he ran into the barn.

Out of breath Eugene hurriedly said, "Excuse me, Mr. Collins, I was wondering where you got the mare in the north pasture."

"Slow down, Son, I've got a dozen mares up in the north pasture. Has something happened to one of them?"

"Yes sir, I mean no sir. It's just that I recognized the chestnut mare to be from my papa's farm, and I need to know how you got her."

"Eugene, I rarely buy a horse at auction in Lexington, so I'm not sure where I would've gotten one of your father's horses."

"Sir, I helped raise this mare and train her. We knew each other."

Mr. Collins moved away from the arena and said, "Go get the truck and I'll take a look at her with you."

Eugene ran as fast as he could to get the truck and pull it up to the barn. Mr. Collins climbed into the front seat beside him, and Eugene tried not to drive as wildly as his emotions were racing.

Back at the north pasture, both men got out of the truck, but there were no horses in sight. Eugene climbed through the fence and started whistling Franklin's tune. Within seconds, the mare appeared through the trees at the far end. George Collins was amazed by what he saw next. The mare spotted Eugene and broke into a fast-paced trot until she reached him. Eugene once again began to scratch between her ears, and she put her head down into his chest, working her way underneath his arm. George climbed through the fence trying to get a closer look.

"Eugene, I remember now where I got this mare. A woman came to me over a year ago with seven fine quality thoroughbreds she was selling. As I recall, she couldn't wait until the fall for the auction. There were two she wasn't willing to sell, this mare and a stud in the south pasture." Eugene had so many questions but waited patiently for Mr. Collins to finish.

"She didn't have anywhere to keep them, so we struck a deal. I bought the other five horses and she gave me the use of the stud as long as I would board him and this mare until she could return for them."

"Mr. Collins, what was the woman's name?"

"Well let's see, I don't recall off hand. But I've got papers from the sale back in my office."

"Do you mind if we go back and look?" Eugene was desperate to know.

"I don't mind a bit. Let's head back and I'll check for you."

Back at the barn, Mr. Collins closed his fancy wooden file cabinet and sat down at his desk. He was thumbing through his purchases when he came upon the papers.

"Here they are, April of last year. Oh yeah, now I remember." He opened the file wide and pushed it across the desk for Eugene to see. "A Mrs. Rachel Hawkins."

Eugene's hands were visibly shaking when he picked up the file. Mr. Collins noticed the color draining from his face. "Son, are you all right? Do you know Mrs. Hawkins?"

"Yes sir, I certainly do. Did she have anyone else with her—a man?"

"No, that's what was so surprising. She had every one of those horses tied to a mule wagon, and no one else was with her."

"Mr. Collins, do you know where she's living now? Is there a way for you to contact her?"

George reached to take back the file and said, "She sent a letter a few months back saying she was settled and would be coming for the horses as soon as she could. I didn't pay much attention to it. I figured when she was ready she'd come back. As long as I've got that fine animal in the south pasture, it doesn't matter to me how long she wants to leave him here." He continued to thumb through the file looking for the letter. "Here it is. The return address is in Louisville." Mr. Collins slid the letter across the desk to Eugene. "How do you know this woman?"

"Sir, she's my mother, not my real mother but she adopted me after my real mother passed away. I haven't been able to find her since the war ended."

Mr. Collins leaned back in his chair watching Eugene. "How long has it been since you've seen her?"

"Next month it'll be two years." Eugene almost couldn't believe it himself when he said it out loud.

Mr. Collins rose to his feet and replaced the file. When he turned back around, Eugene was reading the letter his mama had written. George Collins' heart went out to him so he asked, "Do you want to take a little time off and head over to Louisville?"

Eugene's face instantly lit up. "If you don't mind, sir. I'd appreciate it so much."

"I think we can spare you the time. You've worked hard for me all summer and I appreciate it." He took the letter back but handed Eugene the envelope with the return address.

"There's a 6:10 to Louisville every evening. How about I give you a lift to the train station this afternoon?"

Eugene could barely find the words to speak he was so excited. Finally he said, "Thank you, sir! You have no idea how much this means to me."

George laughed and said, "I think I do. I'll pull the car around at five o'clock."

Thanking Mr. Collins again, Eugene took off at a sprint to the bunkhouse and started excitedly packing his duffle bag. He laid out some of his nicest clothes to wear on his trip to Louisville and even bathed, so he wouldn't have the smell of horses on him. He tried not to get his hopes up too high just in case he wasn't able to find his mama. Even more importantly, he wouldn't allow himself to dwell on the fact that Rachel had been alone when she delivered the horses.

Chapter 20

Eugene stepped off the train in Louisville, conscious of his hammering pulse. His thoughts twirled between anxiety and excitement, but more than that, he was downright nervous. He had checked his reflection in the glare of the train window before disembarking. His dark hair was neatly combed, and his brown slacks and white dress shirt looked clean and crisp. Eugene wanted to make sure he looked his best for his folks. It was almost 9:00 PM and for a moment he considered looking for a hotel room, but he quickly swept that notion out of his head. If there was any way his mama was at the address he held in his hand, he needed to find her tonight.

An older gentleman was getting off the train directly behind him, so Eugene turned to him and asked, "Excuse me, sir. Are you by any chance from Louisville?"

The man looked at Eugene with a friendly smile. "Born and raised here."

"I was wondering if you happen to know this address." Eugene handed him Rachel's envelope.

The older gentleman thought for a moment. "I think I know which part of town it's in, but I'm not really familiar with that area." He handed the envelope back to Eugene. "You're welcome to share a taxi with me. I'm being dropped off about a mile from here, and the cabbie can take you to your address if you like."

"That would be great. Thanks for the offer."

Eugene made his acquaintance with Gerald Miller, and the two got into the taxi that had been waiting at the station. Conversation was polite and when Mr. Miller exited the car, Eugene handed the envelope to the driver who pulled out his map of Louisville city streets. In a couple of minutes they were on their way, and Eugene thought his heart would pound right out of his chest.

The taxi driver entered a neighborhood of small brick homes. Elm trees and sidewalks lined both sides of the street with steps leading up from the sidewalk to each of the homes. A few of the houses still had lights on, but many of them were already dark for the night. The taxi driver was creeping slowly along the street looking for house numbers when he finally came to a halt. "Hey, buddy, this is it. Do you need me to wait?"

Eugene hadn't thought about having him wait in case this wasn't Rachel's house. But after thinking about it he said, "No, I'll be fine." He paid the fare, grabbed his duffle bag, and stepped out onto the sidewalk as the taxi drove away.

Eugene swallowed hard; his mouth felt so dry. He stood in the dark for a little while, staring at the house. There was a single light on in the front room. It somehow made the house appear inviting, and Eugene sensed a feeling of déjà vu. He finally urged his feet to move forward. Every step he took brought back memories of a life gone by—a life that had molded him and made him into the man he now was. But it seemed like such a long time ago and he worried there might be nothing left of that precious life. Even though his confidence began to wane, he kept his eyes on the light and continued up the stairs of the wide front porch.

Eugene uttered a silent plea to God and opened the screen door. He knocked softly and let the door fall back into place. After a few moments, an electric porch light hummed overhead and the door slowly opened.

Eugene's breathing now came quick and shallow as his vision blurred with tears. "Mama?"

Rachel stood motionless for only a second. Recognition, joy, and anguish all pulsed through her body and painted themselves across her face.

"Eugene." She said his name with immeasurable love, and turned her eyes toward heaven. "Oh God, I never thought I'd see him again."

Eugene quickly grabbed the door handle, stepped inside, and pulled Rachel into his arms. Neither of them could speak. The only possible thing they could do was hold onto each other with all their might. Rachel began to sob in Eugene's arms, and he pulled her tighter as his own tears spilled down his cheeks.

Several minutes passed before Rachel put her hands on her son's shoulders, and held him at arm's length.

"You've grown," she said, laughing softly. "I have so many questions for you, young man. But right now, all I want to do is just look at you."

Eugene noticed the strands of silver running through Rachel's dark hair. Other than that, she hadn't changed much. As a matter of fact, he thought she looked more beautiful than ever.

"Mama, I'm so sorry I wasn't able to come back that day. I tried so hard." He couldn't help but pull her back into his arms.

Rachel laid her head on his chest and listened to the strong rhythm of his heart. "Eugene," she whispered, "where have you been?"

Words seemed so inadequate. How could he even begin to tell her what had happened to him in the last two years? It was almost unfathomable. Before he could begin his story, there was something of greater importance on his heart.

"First tell me about Papa."

Rachel moved out of Eugene's arms and took him by the hand. "Come sit down. I have a feeling we have a lot to say to each other."

It was in the wee hours of the morning when Rachel finally made up a bed for Eugene in the extra room. So much had happened in the last two years to both of them, they could've talked all night and still not been able to tell it all. They finally decided it would be better to go to bed and continue their heart-to-heart after a few hours of sleep. Rachel first showed Eugene through the house. At the age of sixty-one, it was the first place she had ever lived with electricity and indoor plumbing. When she finished making his bed, Rachel turned to see Eugene leaning against the doorframe of the bedroom.

"Thank you, Mama."

Rachel moved to him and touched his hair, much the same way she had when he was younger. "I missed you so much." She gently kissed him on the cheek then hugged him one more time.

As she held him, she heard Eugene whisper in her ear, "I'm sorry about Papa."

"I'm sorry too, darlin', but he's with the Lord now." She let her hand rest on his arm and thanked God again in her heart for sending her son home safely. "Sleep well."

"You too, Mama." Eugene gave her a sleepy grin and watched her disappear into the bedroom down the hall. He emptied his duffle bag, then quickly undressed and slipped underneath the sheet, turning out the lamp on the bedside table. He locked his hands behind his head on the pillow and stared at the ceiling calling to mind everything Rachel had just told him. She had answered his question first, about Papa, and they had cried together over the incredible loss they both felt.

To Eugene's amazement, Papa had recovered his health during that fateful November that he had been whisked into the army. Rachel had continued giving him round-the-clock care as she fervently prayed for him to recover and desperately pled for Eugene's return. At least one of her prayers had been answered, and Franklin thankfully returned to health by the end of the month. Together they had continued to search for Eugene and mourn his loss. Franklin had gone into Winchester at night looking for any signs of him, even finding Louis' house and watching him through a window. But he could find no trace of their son.

In March of that spring, Franklin took ill again. His lungs had already been weakened dramatically from the earlier sickness. This time, he didn't have the strength to fight it, and he passed away during the night with Rachel lying by his side. She had never felt so alone in all her life.

Eugene sighed deeply and shook his head as he lay in bed

recalling Rachel's account of Papa's last days. It crushed him that he hadn't been there for her, and he felt haunted by the fact that Papa had gone to his grave without knowing what had happened to him. If only he could go back and change the past.

Eugene was especially troubled by the thought of Rachel burying Franklin on the farm without any help. She had dug his grave right under the old oak tree in the pasture. Just contemplating what she had endured to put his papa into that grave caused Eugene's heart to ache. Had he walked over to the oak tree on his visit to the farm back in June, he would've seen the cross she had erected at the head of Franklin's grave. As it was, he had been so distraught and the grass had been so deep in the pasture, he had missed seeing the marker.

Now as he lay in bed, Eugene began to feel uneasy about Papa lying all alone in that pasture. He listened as sprinkles of rain began to tap an uneven pattern on the roof. For the first time, he understood fully why Mr. Gano had such a strong desire to bring his son home from France.

Utterly drained, physically and mentally, Eugene eventually drifted off to the music of a steady Kentucky rain.

The next morning, Eugene looked embarrassed when he walked into Rachel's living room after ten o'clock. The rain was still pouring outside, making it dark in the house, and Rachel was thankful that he had been able to sleep so long. She was sitting in a comfortable chair underneath a lamp and looked up from her sewing when he entered the room.

"I was beginning to wonder if I should check on you," she said teasingly, trying to put him at ease.

"I haven't slept that late since I don't know when."

"Come in the kitchen and let me get you something to eat." Rachel put her sewing aside and led him to the table.

She had gotten up early this morning, far too excited to sleep, and already had a vegetable stew simmering on the stove.

"What do you say to an early lunch?" She started filling two bowls of stew without waiting for Eugene's response. Along with the stew she produced slices of homemade bread and a fresh bowl of peaches. After sitting down at the table, Eugene reached for Rachel's hand and thanked God for bringing them back together, and then asked a blessing over the food.

This morning their conversation turned to the horses, and Rachel asked to hear the story about the mare in the pasture one more time. "I still can't get over how God used that mare to bring you back to me."

Eugene gladly recounted how the mare had nudged him on the back as he painted the fence in the pasture. "Mama, it was like we'd never been apart."

"I thought that chestnut was going to be the end of me," Rachel declared. "You have no idea how many times I had to stop for her. She was so spooked by everything along the road, I was afraid she was going to hurt herself." Rachel had given serious thought to removing the halter and letting her go. Thank the Lord He had given her just a little more patience to get that mare to Mason Farms.

After the meal, Eugene helped Rachel clean up the kitchen. In times past she would've fussed at him for being in her way, but today she didn't want to let him out of her sight. She wished it wasn't raining, so they could go for a walk and she could show him the neighborhood park and introduce him to her neighbors. But all of that would come in time. There were still so many things she wanted to know. Eugene had barely said a word about the war, and she longed to hear about his experiences in France.

Both of them made themselves comfortable again in the living room. Rachel had made it a cozy living space with a soft couch and chairs, two end tables, and a bookshelf lined with all the familiar books she had carried from the farm. The clock from Germany now sat proudly on the mantle over the fireplace.

From the time Eugene had come to the farm, there had been a special connection between the two of them, and now, one look at Eugene told Rachel that he was holding something back. She didn't want to push him to talk if he wasn't ready, so she started with what she thought was a benign query. "Eugene, tell me about France." Rachel purposely picked up her sewing again, hoping that her question wouldn't seem too intrusive.

When Eugene didn't respond, she looked up to see his demeanor had completely changed. He looked edgy and uncomfortable. She even noticed tiny beads of sweat had broken out on his forehead. He stood up so abruptly that Rachel dropped her sewing in her lap.

Rachel worried as she watched Eugene suddenly move toward the door. Maybe she shouldn't have mentioned anything about the war. It must've been too soon, but she had no way of taking back her words now.

He paused in the doorway for just a moment and Rachel detected the stricken look on his face. "Eugene?"

"I'm sorry," was all he said.

The door closed behind him, and Rachel sat in silence trying to quell the panic rising up within. She waited only a moment before stepping out on the porch to apologize, but to her dismay, he was already gone.

The rain continued to fall for the next two hours while Rachel paced the floor of her living room and prayed. Occasionally she stepped out onto the front porch glancing from one end of the street to the other, but there was no sign of Eugene.

Finally, Rachel sat down and tried to concentrate on her sewing, but she was failing miserably. Why had she pushed the matter of the war with him? She should have allowed him to talk about it when he was ready. But how could she have known what his reaction would be? A lot had happened since she'd last seen him, and he wasn't the same carefree boy he had been on the farm. She was overcome with a pang of sadness at the realization that nothing would ever be the same again.

Rachel was beating herself up over the matter fairly well when the sound of footsteps on the porch sent a wave of relief flooding over her. The door opened and without stepping inside Eugene quietly said, "Come sit on the porch with me."

Rachel grabbed a towel from the hall closet and joined her son on the porch. He was soaking wet from head to toe and gratefully accepted the towel as he sat down on the swing that hung near the end of the porch. Rachel took a seat in the rocking chair near the swing, and watched him rub the towel over his wet hair and then throw it across his shoulders.

"Eugene, I'm so sorry. I never should've . . ."

"No, please," he interrupted, slowly shaking his head. "It's not your fault and you don't need to apologize." He looked away from her trying to figure out how to explain the way things were. When he looked back, her brown eyes were swimming in tears, but he couldn't let that stop him from saying what he needed to say.

"Mama, there are things that happened that I'll never be able to talk about. It's not you. I just can't talk about it to anyone." Eugene felt certain if he attempted to tell her what he had done, it would somehow drive him into a dark place that he could never escape. He simply wasn't willing to take that chance.

"This is a burden that I have to carry alone. I know you can't understand that, but I promise I'll be fine." He raked his hands through his damp hair. "There are things I want you to know, people who meant a lot to me that I want to tell you about. But you just need to give me some time." He tried to give her a hint of a smile.

Rachel's eyes never left her son's. "Eugene, there is no shame in what you had to do to survive. But you need to remember that you've been washed by the blood of the Lamb— He's taken your shame and made it His own. You don't have to carry that burden all by yourself." She stood and went back inside to retrieve her Bible. When she returned, Eugene was leaning forward on the swing with his head in his hands.

Quietly she began reading from Hebrews: "Let us draw near with a true heart in full assurance of faith, having our hearts sprinkled from an evil conscience, and our bodies washed with pure water. Let us hold fast the profession of our faith without wavering; for he is faithful that promised."

Eugene's heart was instantly pricked. He had tried for so long to carry his burden of shame all alone. He had forgotten that he had a Savior who was willing to carry it for him. The only hope he could see now for his life and future was to repent of his pride and humble himself before the Lord.

Rachel didn't move from her chair until she saw Eugene's shoulders shaking. She crossed the porch, sat beside him on the swing, and gently pulled him into her arms. Eugene began praying through his tears, "Oh Father, forgive me for not trusting you enough. Thank you for your Son who took on the shame of the world. I give up my shame and guilt to Him now." His body shuddered through a deep sob, and Rachel pulled him closer as he continued his petition. "Forgive me for the terrible things I've done and help me to live the rest of my life as your faithful servant. In the name of Jesus, I beg for mercy. I'm so, so sorry."

When he fell silent, Rachel continued the prayer. She quietly asked God to bring Eugene the peace that surpasses all understanding and a healing for his soul. She invited the Spirit to take complete control of his life.

Eugene sat back in the swing with an immense feeling of relief. When he looked at Rachel, his face was stained with tears, but this time his smile reached all the way to his eyes. He had not known a moment's peace since Will had died in his arms nearly a year ago. Today he allowed the bone-crushing burden he'd carried to be lifted off of his shoulders, and boy did it feel good! Eugene grinned, and said, "Sorry I got you so wet."

"As I recall, it's not the first time," Rachel said with a laugh. "Why don't you go inside and get out of those wet clothes?"

For a moment he didn't move. The rain had stopped, and the sun gradually began to peek out of the clouds, reflecting his renewed spirit. He was determined that today he would start life over again. He already knew what it felt like to be given a second chance in life, and by God's grace Rachel had been there for him both times.

* * *

That evening the September air felt clean and crisp after a long day of rain. The sidewalk was still wet as Rachel and Eugene walked through the neighborhood. They greeted the neighbors who were sitting on their front porch or out on an evening stroll. Eugene was amazed that Rachel knew nearly everyone's name. Once she introduced him by saying, "I'd like you to meet my son, just home from the war." Eugene saw her glance at him with an apologetic look, but he let her know by his smile that he was completely comfortable with her introduction.

Walking together through the park at the end of the street, Eugene was curious about Rachel's new life. She'd spent nearly forty-five years on the farm near Winchester with almost no human contact other than him and Papa. Now here she was living in a new city, in a nice house, and an all-white neighborhood. These were not really *her people,* but she was obviously making the most of her new life.

"Mama, how'd you end up in Louisville?" There were still so many questions Eugene needed answered—just like when he'd first come to live with her and Papa on the farm.

"Tomorrow afternoon I'll explain everything to you." She slipped her hand through the crook of his arm as they watched a man and his son throw a baseball together in the park. "First, I want you to go to church with me." Rachel's eyes were gleaming as she added, "I've found a *morceau de ciel.*"

Eugene could almost imagine her saying *not now son, not now,* as she had done so many times when he was growing up. But for the moment, his curiosity was piqued as he tried to imagine what her *piece of heaven* might actually turn out to be.

Chapter 21

Eugene didn't own a suit, but he was dressed very neatly for church in his brown slacks and a tan button-down shirt with a tan and black striped tie. Rachel was wearing a lightweight navy dress that came down to mid-calf, a long wide-collared jacket, black low-heeled pumps, and a matching hat. Once again, Eugene was amazed at the transformation in the woman walking beside him.

The church was barely over a mile from Rachel's house, just outside of town. She was glad to walk the distance every Sunday unless the weather was bad. Today she could hardly contain her excitement with Eugene by her side. When the church building came into sight, Eugene saw another one directly across the road.

Noticing his glance Rachel said, "There used to be another congregation in that building, but six years ago the two churches came together. They felt like God wanted them to be united under one roof instead of divided by a highway."

Eugene could see why they had chosen the other building for worship. It was a larger bricked structure as opposed to the small wooden one across the road. There was also a large well-kept cemetery on the far side of the building.

Just before entering the door, Rachel uttered one solitary word. "Heaven!"

Eugene wasn't sure what to make of her enthusiasm for this congregation until he stepped inside. Immediately, he was greeted by a plump black woman standing just inside the lobby. She was apparently on a mission to hug every single person who stepped through the front door. After she released Eugene from her grip, Rachel introduced him to Miss Ruby. Miss Ruby's excitement over finding out that Rachel had a son caused her to exclaim loudly, "Child, where on earth have you been? I had no idee Rachel had her a son!"

"He's just come back from the army, Miss Ruby."

"Well, I declare. Ain't that somethin'." Miss Ruby was eyeing Eugene as if he was one of her prize pigs. Then without warning, she enveloped him in her ample arms again. "Welcome to the Lord's church!"

"Thank you, Miss Ruby. Nice to meet you."

Miss Ruby was already moving on to her next target and spoke over her shoulder. "Nice to meet you too, honey."

The sanctuary was nearly full as Eugene followed Rachel to a pew halfway down the center aisle on the right side. He was amazed to see white people and black people intermingled together on every pew. And they weren't just sitting quietly waiting for the service to begin—there was more hugging going on in that building than he'd ever seen in his life.

An older white gentleman with gray hair and a mustache ascended the steps of the platform and the crowd quickly hushed. He introduced himself as Brother Jim and welcomed everyone in the congregation, especially those who were visiting. He made a few announcements about some of the sick members of the congregation, and then asked them all to bow in prayer. Every soul in the building added their own *amen* at the conclusion, and Brother Jim stepped down from the platform. A young black man was already moving up the steps with his hymnal and stopped to shake Brother Jim's hand. He didn't introduce himself but called out the first number and started leading the congregation in spirited singing.

Eugene could see why Rachel had called this heaven. In an unsettling time of race riots and lynch mobs, this truly was a *morceau de ciel*. Surely this is what God had in mind for his children. If all races were going to be together in heaven, then they might as well start learning to love each other here on earth.

After the communion, two men—one white and one black—stepped to the podium and each brought a sermon to the congregation. One sermon built upon the other, making it obvious that these two men had collaborated during the week to bring their message together.

During the final hymn the congregation rose to their feet. Eugene just happened to look across the aisle about three rows up, and his heart skipped a beat. If he wasn't mistaken, he felt certain he had just recognized someone in the crowd. He leaned toward Rachel and whispered, "Is that Annie?"

Rachel nodded her head and continued singing. Eugene couldn't imagine why he hadn't been told about Annie attending this church.

When the service was over Eugene said, "I'm going over to see Annie." He didn't notice the look on Rachel's face as he turned to scan the crowd.

Annie was talking with two other women when Eugene walked up behind her, lightly touching her elbow. She turned around and looked up into his face. For a brief second she looked as if she would hug him but must have thought better of it. She just stood there staring at him.

Eugene had never known Annie to be speechless, but he realized he must have caught her off guard, so he simply said, "Hi, Annie."

"Eugene?" Her eyes darted nervously as if she were searching for someone else.

Eugene glanced over his shoulder then turned back a bit confused.

Finally Annie said, "Is Miss Rachel here?" She clearly was finding it difficult to speak to Eugene alone.

He didn't understand her uneasiness—not until he finally glanced down at her left hand. He couldn't miss the silver ring with a glittering solitary diamond. One look at that ring felt like a sucker punch to his chest.

Thankfully Rachel made her way over and rescued them both from the awkwardness of the situation.

"Annie, Eugene has come home!"

"Yes, I see." She couldn't seem to take her eyes off of him.

Rachel didn't mince her words when she told Eugene, "Annie's engaged to be married." Then she turned toward Annie and asked, "Have you set the date yet?"

"Uh, no ma'am. Not yet. Well, I mean it'll be sometime in the spring."

Rachel said, "I don't want to miss it, so please let me know when you've set your date."

"Oh I will, Miss Rachel. I will."

Finally, Eugene spoke his congratulations, hoping he sounded sincere. As he turned to leave, Rachel couldn't help but notice Annie watching him until he disappeared into the crowd.

"Why didn't you tell me about Annie?" Eugene kept his eyes straight ahead as he and Rachel walked home from church.

"You'd been through so much yesterday, I just couldn't seem to find a way to tell you." She paused, then added, "I didn't know if you still had feelings for her."

Eugene just nodded his head, keeping his gaze in front of him. How many times had he thought about seeing Annie again? It must have been in the hundreds. Somewhere in the back of his mind, he'd hoped that he'd end up with her one day. But he'd been jolted back to a stinging reality at the sight of the ring on her finger. It was silly for him to think she wouldn't have made a life of her own. It was also foolish to think some other man wouldn't want her. As a girl, Annie had been pretty, but as a woman she was gorgeous. Gone were the little freckles across her nose, and she had filled out quite nicely. Eugene had tried not to think about such things in the church sanctuary.

"Eugene, Annie's family is the biggest reason why I'm here in Louisville." Rachel had promised to tell him everything and he was anxious to hear it now.

"After your papa passed away, I knew I had to leave the farm. It took several days of hard work, but I finally loaded the wagon and secured the horses for the trip into Lexington. The drive took all day long, and by the time I made it to the auction barn, no one was there." She let Eugene know how utterly exhausted and frustrated she had been. She had no choice but to camp along the river for the night. She stayed far away from the National Guard camp but had been so fearful about being alone she didn't sleep a wink all night. Thankfully, the next morning, Willard Dorsey was in his office at the auction barn and had steered her toward Mason Farms. He felt certain Mr. Collins would want to take a look at her thoroughbreds.

"Mr. Collins was a lifesaver to me. I don't think I could've handled the horses even one more hour."

Curious, Eugene glanced over at Rachel for the first time, and asked, "Why didn't you sell him all seven horses?"

Rachel took hold of his arm then and they both stopped walking. She faced her son squarely, before she told him the purpose in her heart.

"I always hoped you'd come back." Tears welled up in her eyes. "Eugene, I never gave up on you. Those two horses are for you. I have everything I need, but you can start a brand new life with those two thoroughbreds."

Eugene couldn't believe what he was hearing. He had always known that God had given him a gift with the horses, but lately he feared he would never be given an opportunity to use it. All he wanted to do in life was be able to raise thoroughbreds the way Franklin had taught him.

Rachel turned and continued walking. Noticing they were almost to her neighborhood, Eugene prodded her to continue.

"I found a room to rent in Lexington. It was actually an apartment on the back of a large home belonging to an elderly couple. Mr. Dorsey kindly took the mule and wagon off my hands, and I stored our few belongings from the farm in a shed behind the apartment." It was hard to describe to Eugene how miserable she had been.

On a whim she had written a letter to Annie's family in Louisville telling them about Eugene's disappearance. She was hoping and praying that somehow Eugene had contacted Annie.

In return, the Harrison family had sent her a heartfelt letter along with an invitation to visit them in Louisville.

Rachel didn't have the heart now to tell Eugene how concerned Annie had been for him. But the two women had gained strength from one another as they shared their loss together during Rachel's visit to the Harrison's prosperous Louisville farm.

"Before I returned to Lexington, they took me to church with them on Sunday morning. That's when I knew I needed to move to Louisville. I never dreamed a church like this could exist."

Eugene agreed that it was indeed a special place. It had been an inspirational experience this morning.

"Since moving here over a year ago now, I've visited in the Harrison's home many times. Annie's mother, Claudia, has become a dear friend of mine. You remember Annie's father, Nathan?"

Eugene remembered him well from their lunch in Lexington after the sale of Morceau.

"He has generously offered to bring the two horses from Lexington onto their farm. I was beginning to make the arrangements for their transfer during the summer, but just kept putting it off." Eugene shuddered to think of it now. If she had moved those horses earlier in the summer, he most likely wouldn't be walking by her side right now.

Rachel glanced at him as they started up the steps of her porch. "I'm sure we can make the arrangements for their transfer while you're here." She paused for a moment. "You are staying, aren't you?"

It had crossed Eugene's mind to return to the farm near Winchester and start all over with the two thoroughbreds she had saved for him. But he couldn't imagine Rachel going back with him. She seemed suited for the life she now lived, and he wouldn't dream of taking her from her *morceau de ciel*. But he also couldn't imagine leaving his mama again, especially after being separated from her for so long.

"Yes, I'm staying." But he teasingly raised his brow and added, "As long as you make one of your chocolate cakes."

Relief flooded over Rachel's face as she playfully pinched him on the arm.

On Monday morning, Rachel wrote to George Collins, informing him that she would be transferring the two horses to Louisville during the following week. Eugene included a letter of his own, thanking Mr. Collins for so generously giving him a job and a place to live on his farm for the past three months. Eugene wanted him to know that he would be returning for the two horses but not for his job.

Rachel also penned a note to Nathan Harrison and his wife, Claudia, to set up a meeting concerning the horses' transfer to his farm. On Thursday she received a reply to her note from Nathan.

> *Our Dear Rachel,*
>
> *Claudia and I wish to invite you and Eugene to join us for the evening meal on this Saturday to discuss the transfer of your horses from Lexington. I will drive out to pick you up at 4:00 in the afternoon, as this will give me plenty of time to show Eugene around the farm and talk over the details before supper. Claudia is looking forward to an evening with her dear friend as I am looking forward to seeing Eugene once again.*
>
> *Sincerely yours,*
> *Nathan A. Harrison*

Early that Saturday afternoon Eugene came into the house to get cleaned up and put on a fresh set of clothes. He'd been working outside trimming the shrubs around the house and organizing the garage shed on the other side of the porch. Many neighbors on Rachel's street now had their own automobile parked inside their garages, but Rachel felt certain she would never have the need for such a thing. Eugene had other ideas on the matter, but it would be a while before he could think about that kind of purchase.

At three o'clock, Eugene joined Rachel on the porch and decided now would be a good time to speak to her about something that had been on his heart all week.

"Mama, I need to ask you something, and if you don't think it's a good idea, then I won't pursue it." He leaned on the porch railing in front of her, as she sat in one of the rocking chairs.

"I think we need to bring Papa here."

Rachel's rocking chair stilled and she glanced down at her hands in her lap. Eugene continued, "I've given it a lot of thought, Mama. We could buy a casket in Lexington, and I can do what needs to be done to bring him back. If we had him buried in the cemetery by the church, you could visit his grave whenever you wanted."

Rachel wasn't looking at him and Eugene began to worry about having made such a suggestion. Maybe it *was* better to leave Papa under his big oak tree on the farm.

Rachel rose to her feet and stood beside him at the railing, looking out toward the street. He didn't move, patiently waiting for her response, whatever it might be.

Taking in a deep breath, Rachel turned to face him with a look of resolution on her face. She laid an affectionate hand on his arm and simply said, "Yes."

"Yes?" Eugene raised his brow.

"Yes. We need to bring Papa here with us."

The next hour passed quickly as they made plans for not only bringing the two horses back to Louisville but bringing their trainer home as well.

Nathan Harrison was the kind of man who seemed to have life firmly grasped by the tail. Eugene had forgotten the amazing amount of energy this man had. He'd offered Eugene his firm handshake after pulling up in Rachel's driveway at four o'clock and apologized for not seeing him last Sunday at church.

The ride out to the Harrison farm was an interesting one as Nathan filled Eugene in on who owned each piece of property they passed. Outside of town they drove through beautiful rolling hills, and as they turned off of the main highway onto a smooth gravel road, Eugene was impressed with the beautiful farm laid out on either side. White fencing, much like Mason Farms, lined the road, and Eugene noticed cattle grazing on one side of the road and horses grazing on the other. Soon they entered a tunnel of large trees, and at the end of the tree line, Eugene could see the house. It was not the kind of house that made a statement like the one Mr. Collins and his family lived in. This was a modest but handsome two-story white farmhouse with a large wraparound porch on the lower level.

Nathan pulled the car to a stop in front of the house and walked around to open Rachel's door. Eugene followed the two of them onto the front porch as Nathan opened a beautifully etched glass door trimmed in shiny oak.

"Rachel, I'll let you find Claudia in the kitchen. I'm going to take Eugene down to the barn and show him around. Tell Claudia we'll be back before supper's on the table."

Rachel gave the two men a wave and headed toward the kitchen at the back of the house. She was looking forward to spending time with her dear friend.

Eugene walked beside Mr. Harrison as he led him past the house toward a large, red barn trimmed in pristine white. Nathan explained that his stables took up the front half of the barn, and the back half of the barn was an indoor arena. He also pointed out other structures around the farm used for storage of equipment as well as a small bunkhouse for the three full-time farm hands living on the property. Claudia cooked for the three men as if they were family and welcomed them into her kitchen for every meal.

Just outside the front of the barn was a rectangular outdoor arena, and from a distance, Eugene recognized Annie riding one of the horses. Nathan stopped at an outer fence to watch his daughter before moving down to the arena. She was riding his top mare named Lady Gwenevere. Annie always referred to her as Lady G.

Nathan put one foot up on the lowest railing and leaned his elbows on top of the fence. "She's beautiful, isn't she?"

"Yes sir. She is *that*."

Nathan had been talking about the mare, but Eugene's thoughts were somewhere else entirely.

Mr. Harrison smiled and slapped Eugene on the shoulder. "Come on, let's go down and watch Annie put her through her paces."

Moving closer to the arena, Eugene realized what an excellent rider Annie was. She was wearing English riding pants and boots and a white blouse. Her thick hair was pulled back into a ponytail. It was a little darker than the strawberry blonde he remembered from a few years ago, but it matched perfectly with the caramel coloring of Lady G. Together, they made a stunning pair.

Mr. Harrison began going over the particulars for transferring the two horses from Mason Farms. It took every bit of concentration Eugene could muster just to listen to the details. He was far too distracted by who he was watching, but tried his best to be polite.

Eventually, Nathan clapped Eugene on the shoulder again and said, "Let me show you around the stables."

Eugene reluctantly stepped away from the fence and followed Mr. Harrison into the barn. For the next half hour, the two men discussed Nathan's proposal for moving the horses and how they would be cared for on his farm. He offered Eugene the opportunity to live in the bunkhouse a few days a week and have the use of one of his vehicles on the days that he stayed in town.

Eugene responded with genuine surprise. Mr. Harrison smiled and said, "I want you to be able to get a good start in the horse business. Rachel told me what a fine trainer you are, and I'd like to see you in action."

Suddenly, Eugene remembered Morceau and inquired if he were still here on the farm.

"He most certainly is, and he's still a wild spirit. He's sired some mighty fine stock though. When we get your two horses settled, I'll make sure you and Morceau get reacquainted." Mr. Harrison rose to his feet from the bench where they had been sitting. "But for now, we'd better get back to the house, so we won't get scolded for being late to supper."

Eugene noticed that Annie was no longer riding in the arena as he and Mr. Harrison walked back to the house. He wondered if she would be joining them for dinner.

Back inside the house Claudia and Rachel were already setting the meal on the dining room table. Claudia looked up as the men walked in. "Wash up you two, we're just about ready to eat."

When Eugene came back from washing his hands, Mrs. Harrison greeted him with a friendly smile and told him what a pleasure it was to finally meet him. She, too, apologized for not having the opportunity to meet him at church last Sunday morning.

A large roast was laid out on the dining room table along with mashed potatoes, corn, green beans, and soft rolls. Eugene noticed five place settings at the table, but so far Annie had not come into the room.

Claudia let out a sigh. "That girl. We can't seem to get her away from her horses. Everyone go ahead and have a seat."

Just as the four of them sat down around the table, Eugene and Nathan hastily rose back to their feet as Annie whisked into the room. She had changed clothes and was now wearing a simple dress and flats. Her hair had been brushed out and was twisted at the back of her neck and tied loosely with a blue satin ribbon.

"I see I'm just in time!" She had a smile on her face warmly welcoming Rachel and Eugene to their table. Annie exuded energy just like her father, but she also had a natural joy about her that made Eugene want to laugh every time he was around her. She quickly took the seat beside Eugene and reached for his right hand. He wasn't quite sure what to make of that until Claudia reached for his left hand and everyone bowed their heads for Mr. Harrison to bless the food.

Eugene was ashamed of himself for not hearing a single word of the blessing. He had one eye open, staring at Annie's left hand in his.

When Mr. Harrison said amen, Eugene looked directly into Annie's eyes. He felt his face flush as she held his gaze unflinchingly. There was a challenge in her eyes, almost as if she was daring him to ask her where the engagement ring was. All Eugene knew was that she was no longer wearing it and he was certainly not about to discuss it in front of their folks.

As dinner progressed, Eugene knew he was eating much faster than Rachel would've liked. He glanced at her only once, and she had a puzzled look on her face. He didn't want to embarrass her, so he slowed the pace a bit. When he glanced at Mrs. Harrison, she appeared exasperated, but her look wasn't directed at him. He could tell she was trying to will her daughter to slow down and join the conversation. Annie didn't seem to pay her a bit of attention.

Both of them finished eating at almost the exact same time, and when Annie rose to her feet, so did Eugene.

Claudia was nonplussed. "I haven't even brought out the dessert," she said, looking from Annie to Eugene.

"Mother, the meal was wonderful. Maybe Eugene and I will have dessert later."

"Uh, thank you so much for supper, Mrs. Harrison. It was very good."

"You're quite welcome. I'm glad you enjoyed it. Strawberry cake will be waiting for you when you're ready."

Eugene thanked her again and excused himself as he followed Annie through the house and onto the front porch. The sun was sinking low, leaving a warm glow to the evening.

Annie sat down on one end of the porch swing and watched Eugene without saying a word. All he could do was stand there and stare at her.

"There's room for two of us you know." She giggled and moved over, leaving him only a little more space than before.

Eugene still didn't move. He somehow needed to know

CHAPTER 21

what was going on before he put himself in such close proximity to her.

"Annie, I don't know . . ." What was wrong with him? He couldn't even make a complete sentence.

Annie's demeanor suddenly changed and Eugene noticed the serious look on her face. She stood and walked to the porch railing at the far end of the house overlooking the horse pasture. She didn't look at Eugene when she said, "You should know that I never got over you."

When she finally turned around, Eugene had moved close enough to touch her. That's all he really wanted to do at the moment, but he wasn't quite sure what she was about to tell him.

Annie looked into his eyes and he sensed she needed him to say something, but for the life of him, he couldn't get the right words to form. Suddenly, she moved away from him, and sat down in one of the porch chairs. She indicated for him to take the one facing hers.

"I'm no longer engaged, Eugene. I gave back the ring and broke it off last Sunday night."

"Why?"

Annie laughed then. "A man of many words."

Eugene smiled but waited for her to go on.

"You're not making this very easy, you know."

Eugene didn't take his eyes off of hers and leaned forward in his chair. "Tell me why."

Annie closed her eyes and took in a deep breath. When she opened her eyes again she softly said, "Because I'm in love with someone else. I'm in love with *you*."

That's all Eugene needed to hear. He rose to his feet and took her by the hands, pulling her into his arms. He had thought about her so many times over the past two years but had never dreamed he'd be able to share a moment like this with her. He brought his hands to her face and gently kissed her. When he felt Annie's sweet passion, he knew he needed to step back and get control of his own emotions. He took her left hand and brought it to his lips, purposely kissing the barren ring finger, then led her across the porch to the swing. Annie leaned into him, and he put his arm around her and held her close as the swing gently rocked back and forth, and one by one the stars broke out in the night sky.

Chapter 22

Annie giggled every time Eugene had to shift the truck; after all, she was straddling the gearshift. With a benign smile, Rachel finally reached over from her seat by the window and pulled Annie's legs up tight against her own. Looking over at his mama, Eugene started laughing and Annie's hand shot up to cover her own mouth.

"You just watch the road, Son, and concentrate on your driving."

Eugene let out another laugh, and this time Annie couldn't hold back. She laid her head on Rachel's shoulder and tried to apologize through her laughter. Rachel wanted to laugh too, but decided this was probably not a proper thing to be laughing about. Instead, she looked out the window to keep them from detecting her amusement. The truth was, she felt a little younger just being around the two of them. Watching their love for each other grow by the day, brought back memories of her own sweet romance.

It had been a month since Annie told Eugene about her broken engagement, and since that time, the two of them had found a way to be together nearly every day. Of course, that was a lot easier to do now that Eugene was living on the farm most of the time. Mr. Harrison had helped him move his two thoroughbreds from Mason Farms and had given him a job as a trainer.

Now they were on their way to the farm near Winchester. Rachel had chosen a modest casket for Franklin in Lexington, and it was in the bed of the farm truck that Annie's father had allowed them to use. Rachel felt certain Eugene wasn't looking forward to what he would have to do, but he had assured her that he was up to the task. He had seen much worse in the fields of France.

Rachel now looked at Annie, nestled up close to her side. A few days ago she and Eugene had shared hers and Franklin's story with Annie. They wanted her to know that Franklin had been Eugene's papa and that he had been Rachel's husband for forty-five years. Annie's tenderhearted response had brought tears to her eyes and had engendered a close relationship between the two women.

Eugene was driving slowly now, trying not to miss the road leading up to the farm.

"There it is!" Rachel pointed to the barely visible trail through the trees.

"All right," Eugene said as he downshifted. "Hang on; this is gonna take a while." He turned the truck off the road and they inched their way up the overgrown path through the woods.

Rachel felt herself become increasingly anxious the farther they went up the trail, and it wasn't from the rough going. She was apprehensive about being on the farm again after all this time. Seeing the empty house would remind her of how empty she had felt when Franklin passed away. She had been devastatingly heartbroken over the loss of Franklin and Eugene, both within a few short months of one another. Now she was praying that God would give her the strength to face the pain she had endured on this farm.

When the truck finally came to a halt at the edge of the pasture, Rachel let out a deep sigh. Annie reached over and covered Rachel's hand with her own. All three sat silently in the truck for several minutes before Rachel glanced over at Eugene. "I'm ready." She gave Annie's hand a squeeze and opened the door of the truck.

Rachel had only one thing on her mind—she had to go to Franklin. As the three of them walked across the pasture toward the oak tree, Eugene asked, "Mama, do you want to be alone?"

Rachel stopped then, breathing in the familiar scent of the farm. Looking over at Franklin's tree, she could still picture him sitting against the trunk whistling and whittling as he waited for the herd to gather around. This had been his domain. If she could ever feel Franklin's presence again, it would be underneath the oak.

With a slight nod of her head, Rachel replied, "Why don't you show Annie around the farm. I need to spend some time with Papa."

Eugene and Annie both looked as if they would hug her, but Rachel turned and started walking through the tall grass toward the tree.

Not much vegetation could grow in the shade of the massive oak branches, but weeds had sprung up on top of Franklin's grave. Rachel instantly dropped to her knees and worked until his resting place was completely clear. She remained on her knees and reached out with her right hand, gently laying it on top of the barren earth. Franklin had been the love of her life. He had never wavered in his love and devotion for her, even when it became apparent she would never be able to bear him a child. She remembered how he had held her in his arms saying, "You're all I need, Rach." He had been such a strong man with an equally tender soul.

Rachel's throat tightened as tears threatened to sting her eyes. Without conscious thought, she stretched her body across Franklin's grave and gently laid her face against the earth. An incredibly tranquil feeling flooded Rachel's soul as God's Spirit covered her in a blanket of peace. It was the peace that surpasses all understanding. The Lord had seen fit to grant her such peace many times throughout her life and she gratefully acknowledged His presence now.

Rachel didn't know how long she'd been with Franklin when she finally made her way across the pasture toward the house. Eugene had primed the pump on the well and Annie was trying to get a drink without completely soaking herself. Rachel realized she must look a mess, with dirt stains on her face and blouse, but neither of them made a comment.

"I've cleaned out the stove pipe, and Annie cleaned up the stove and the counters in the kitchen. We should be able to use it tonight to warm up our supper."

Rachel noticed that Eugene and Annie had already brought their supplies from the truck and had them neatly stacked on the porch. She thanked them both and started cleaning herself up at the pump as she watched the two of them walk back across the pasture to the truck.

Annie helped Eugene carry the empty casket from the truck to Franklin's grave. When Eugene returned from the truck again with a shovel, Annie took it from his hand and laid it on the ground. She couldn't imagine what he must be feeling considering the responsibility that lay ahead of him. She gently kissed him on the lips and told him she loved him. He watched her walk all the way across the pasture before he turned back to Papa's grave. He would need to take his time since Franklin had been laid beneath the earth simply wrapped in Rachel's favorite quilt.

Eugene could hear the women's voices drifting from the kitchen as he washed himself at the pump. They were warming up a simple supper of beans and canned meat that would be served along with the cornbread Rachel had made the day before. With the most difficult undertaking of the day behind him, Eugene now looked forward to a relaxing supper and a night spent under the October sky.

Annie had spread a quilt on the front porch, so the three of them could eat their supper picnic-style. Neither of the women spoke as Eugene entered the kitchen. Both seemed surprised when he exclaimed loudly, "What's taking so long? I'm starving!"

"Eugene Lloyd Wyatt Hawkins, you just go right back outside and wait for your supper." Rachel had turned from the stove with her hands on her hips.

Eugene gave her a soldier's salute but had no intention of leaving the kitchen. He sat down on the edge of the table to watch his two favorite women prepare the food.

When Annie turned around to look at him, he gave her a big grin, and she responded by raising one eyebrow. He would've liked to grab her around the waist and pull her over to the table, but he knew Rachel would probably slap his hand with her blazing hot spatula. Instead, he crossed his arms and let out a low chuckle that sounded amazingly like Franklin's.

Conversation was quite spirited during supper on the quilt. Eventually, Rachel reached into the food basket and brought out a surprise. She'd baked sugar cookies—Eugene's favorite.

Rachel offered Annie a cookie and innocently asked, "Do you enjoy cooking?"

Annie looked as if she was afraid that little question would pop up sooner or later. Biting her bottom lip she replied, "Well, Mother did the best she could with me."

Crumbs of sugar cookie came spewing out of Eugene's mouth, and Annie raised her voice so she could be heard over his raucous laughter. "She was giving me cooking lessons when I was *engaged to be married.*" Annie's emphasis on the last four words was no doubt designed to take a jab at Eugene, but it didn't seem to be working at the moment.

Annie looked resigned to the fact that there would be no saving face where cooking was concerned. She lightly slapped Eugene on the arm and declared, "You can stop laughing now."

With a grin on his face, Eugene reached for another sugar cookie, but Rachel pulled them out of his range. "Not if you're going to waste them."

He knew he'd have to sincerely apologize if he wanted another cookie. It would be impossible for him if Rachel and Annie teamed up against him, even if they were half teasing.

"I'm sorry, Annie. Can you ever forgive me?" So much for a sincere apology! Annie teasingly stuck her tongue out at him, but thankfully, he was rewarded with another sugar cookie.

By mid-morning the following day, the three were on the road back to Louisville with their precious cargo in the back. The women had washed at the pump and put on fresh skirts and blouses while Eugene made his way through the woods and washed in the stream. They would be driving directly to Oak Hill Cemetery near the church building, anticipating an early afternoon arrival.

Rachel and Eugene had made prior arrangements for Franklin to be buried under the largest oak tree in the cemetery and the gravediggers would be standing by to help them with his burial.

Nearly a hundred miles lay between Winchester and Louisville. White, billowy clouds occasionally covered the sun and cast a long shadow, which seemed to mirror the trio's somber mood. By the time they pulled into the cemetery, all three were ready to get out of the truck and stretch their legs. It seemed like a much longer drive coming back than the trip had been the day before.

Eugene spotted two men dressed in overalls sitting down against the giant oak, and he stopped the truck on the road as close as possible to the gravesite. One of the men walked up to the back of the truck and asked, "Is this Franklin Hawkins?"

Eugene closed the truck door and joined him at the back. "Yes sir."

The other man walked up laying his hand on the coffin. "We'll take care of everything."

Eugene wasn't sure if Rachel would want to watch, so he asked her and Annie if they'd like to go for a walk to give the men some time to do their job.

"Yes, I think a nice walk would do us all some good," Rachel replied.

Eugene reached into his pocket and pulled out a dollar bill for each of the men and thanked them for waiting for their arrival. Each one tipped his hat to Eugene before unloading Franklin's casket from the truck.

The cemetery was one of the older ones in the Louisville area with graves dating back to the late 1700s. Any other time Rachel would've been fascinated to read some of the inscriptions, but today everything seemed so surreal.

Down a small hill at the very back of the cemetery, they came to a stop at an old, broken-down rock wall. On the other side was another cemetery, but this one had no headstones marking the graves. The only markers in this section were large rocks or sticks tied together forming crosses. Most of the graves were overgrown with weeds and no trees shaded any part of the cemetery.

Rachel spoke softly. "This is where my people are buried."

Eugene felt a disturbing wave rush over him. He turned from the Negro cemetery and looked back up the hill to where Papa was being buried. Didn't everyone deserve such a proper burial?

Annie wanted to protest against what she was seeing, but there simply were no words to express the shocking difference between the two sides of the wall.

Rachel suddenly felt very tired, and was thankful that Eugene offered her his arm. She gladly accepted it as they walked back up the hill. By the time they arrived under the oak tree, the two men had finished their task and were no longer in sight.

Still clinging to Eugene's arm, Rachel stood in the shade of the tree beside Franklin's grave. Soon a headstone would be added to honor the man who lay beneath, but for now, they would honor his memory with their presence alone.

Rachel noticed Annie standing behind them and reached for her hand. She wanted Annie to know that she was not intruding on the moment. Rachel had already said her good-byes to Franklin on the farm, on two separate occasions.

Eugene was the first to speak. "If only they knew who was buried here."

Rachel let out a soft laugh. She was astounded that the two churches had been united, but their dead remained determinedly separated. Her gaze wandered across the cemetery as she thought about those who had gone on before. "I suppose there's no difference between any of them now," she said. Oh how she longed for the day when all would be made right.

***

Eugene stood for a long time contemplating the countless lessons Franklin had taught him. Because of Papa, he was a better man, no doubt. Finally, he put his arm around Rachel and reached out to take Annie's hand in his. As the three of them turned to walk away from the giant oak, there was one thing for which Eugene was eternally grateful—God did not wear blinders.

Epilogue

June 30, 1922

Four flower girls in white, flowing dresses slowly walked ahead of the young army veterans down the shaded path. Each girl carried a beautiful wreath of summer blossoms as the soldiers carried their comrade to his final resting place. With reverence and measured step, Eugene helped lower the flag-draped coffin to the platform beside the open grave and stood at attention. At least four of the six men had had a bit of trouble buttoning the uniform they had worn during the Great War. Eugene's had been slightly snug as well, but Rachel had made a few alterations so that it would fit comfortably.

Eugene listened to the words being spoken by the preacher and marveled at such a vast crowd. Automobiles lined the road as far as he could see while hundreds of people stood shoulder to shoulder inside the cemetery. William Benjamin Gano had finally come home from France.

"The Lord is my shepherd, I shall not want." The passage floated through Eugene's mind, along with the memory of Will reciting those same words, while lying by his side on the battlefield in France.

"Would you care for more tea, Mrs. Wyatt?" Susan Gano held a pitcher of iced tea in her hand as she approached the long table underneath the trees.

"Oh yes, thank you. And please call me Annie."

Annie adjusted the baby in her lap, so she could hold up her glass to Mrs. Gano. Susan filled the glass and put the pitcher in the middle of the table. As she turned back to Annie she held out her arms and asked, "May I?"

Annie happily put her five-month-old baby in Susan's arms and watched the older woman hug him to her breast. William Franklin Wyatt rewarded her with a content cooing sound that brought a smile to Susan's face. What had started out as a difficult afternoon had now turned into a sweet remembrance of her dear son, Will.

Sergeant Gano now lay peacefully in the Good Hope Cemetery. For the first time in four years, his parents could rest at night knowing that their son was back from the war.

Now all of Will's brothers and sisters sat around the table talking and keeping an eye on their own children. Annie turned to look for Rachel and saw her standing in the shade of an elm tree talking with Rosa Rollmann. A small group had made their way back out to Will's grave and were standing quietly talking. Mr. Gano, along with Mary and her father, Alex Rollmann, and Eugene stood listening to Al Haney talk about his trip to France. Fourteen-year-old Blanche sat beside her brother's grave, attentive to their conversation.

Sergeant Haney said to Eugene in particular, "I couldn't believe how beautiful the countryside was." Al and Eugene stood in full army dress as they discussed the sergeant's recent journey to Europe. "No more barbed wire in the fields, and most of the villages have rebuilt from the ruins. It really was amazing to see."

"What about the trenches?" Eugene was curious if they were still visible.

"Most of them have been filled in and all of the garbage of war buried inside of them. I almost didn't recognize the place." Al went on to tell them how careful the French farmers had to be as they plowed their fields. Many had been injured by the unexploded shells lying just beneath the surface on their farms.

Mr. Gano looked up at Sergeant Haney and thanked him again for helping him make the arrangements with the United States Army. "My wife and I are indebted to you for bringing Will home."

"Mr. Gano, he was our brother. Eugene and I wouldn't have left him there."

"Thank you both," Ralph said sincerely.

"Yes, thank you." Everyone turned to see Mrs. Gano walk to her husband's side still holding little Will. Annie followed close behind and reached for Eugene's hand. Eugene gave it a squeeze, then let go and put his arm around Annie's waist.

"Mr. and Mrs. Gano, Annie and I were wondering if you have a picture of Will that we could take home with us. We want to be able to show our son his namesake someday."

Ralph and Susan exchanged a look that neither Eugene nor Annie could read. He hoped he hadn't asked for too much and added, "Of course I understand if you don't want to part with any of his pictures."

"Oh no, it's not that," Susan replied. "We already have something we want to give you when we go back to the house."

An hour later, the Gano's house was packed full of family members. There was not a place to sit and hardly room to stand with so many relatives inside. Most of the children decided it was better to play outside in the yard with their cousins. Some would be staying overnight while others were heading back to their homes in the surrounding communities. Eugene and his family planned on driving to Enid for the night and then spending the next three days leisurely driving back to Louisville. Ralph and Susan joined them on the front porch, apologizing for such a full house.

Susan handed Eugene a letter and rested her hand on top of his. "We've been reading all of Will's letters again and wanted you to have this one. There's also a photo inside."

Eugene gratefully accepted the letter and said, "I'm honored. Thank you so much."

Susan pulled him into a hug and held him tight. "*We're honored* that you were here for Will's homecoming."

Ralph and Susan followed Eugene and his family out to their automobile and both of them kissed the baby on his cheek.

"Please stay in touch," Ralph said as he offered his hand to Eugene. "We want to hear all about little Will as he grows up."

With a smile he added, "Hopefully he'll become a fine horse trainer like his father."

Susan embraced Rachel, then took Annie into her arms and kissed her cheek. "We're so thankful you made this trip with Eugene. You're welcome in our home any time."

Annie thanked her then turned to hand Will to Rachel who was already situated in the back seat of their car. Annie's father had helped them buy their first automobile right after the baby was born. As the car pulled away, Rachel lifted her grandson up in the back window for the Ganos to see one last time.

At the end of the road, Eugene stopped the car and walked alone into the cemetery to say a final goodbye to Will. The grave was piled as high as Eugene's waist with wreaths and flowers. Will was a hero to his community and rightly so.

The sun drifted slowly toward the horizon, leaving an orange glow across the fields and cemetery. Eugene reached into his pocket and pulled out the letter Will had written to his folks. It was dated June 4, 1918, just two weeks before they left Camp Travis for France. Eugene read the letter, remembering Will's fluid voice.

Dear Parents and All,

Well, I'm doing fine. I got three letters today, two from Mary and one from you. One of Mary's letters was held up, so I got them both at the same time. I don't know what the mail will be like when we get overseas. We're shipping out soon. I'll try to write as often as I can but if you don't hear from me, I'm okay.

I've become good friends with a boy named Eugene Wyatt. He's like a little brother to me. I say boy because that's what he seems to me—maybe too young to be here, but he's a fine soldier. Hopefully this war will end soon and you'll have the chance to meet him. Until then, I'm sending a picture of the two of us.

Mamma, you don't need to worry; I know how much you think of me. If only every man had as good a mother. Tell Blanchie and Ruthie I'll send them both a postcard from France. I hope the harvest is a good one this year. I wish I could be there to help out.

With love,
your son Will

Eugene held the picture in his hand remembering the day it was taken. They had just played a baseball game, and Will stood holding a bat over one shoulder with his other arm around Eugene. Both of them were smiling as they stood in the dust of the ball field at Camp Travis. Eugene turned the picture over in his hand and read the solitary word written on the back—*Brothers.*

Carefully Eugene unpinned the Victory medal from his chest and knelt beside Will's grave. Clearing a small space, he laid the medal lovingly on the dirt.

"Thank you for your sacrifice, Brother. You've won the victory and I'll see you again someday."

Eugene stood at attention beside the grave and honored Will with a final salute. As he turned to walk back to his precious family, the sun's last rays dipped below the horizon, and the cry of his son drifted sweetly on the breeze.

Author's Note

For most of my life I have dreamed of writing a book, so I guess it is only fitting that the story you have just read came to me in a dream in July of 2009. It was such a vivid dream, unlike any other I had ever experienced. The images and story fascinated me—I literally could not stop dwelling on it or talking about it for days. I remember one Sunday morning, while driving home from church, I brought it up again to my husband. I think he had heard all he wanted to hear about it, so he said, "Why don't you write the book?" Inspired, I sat down at the computer and began doing the research that very afternoon. A few hours later, I had named my characters, chosen the location and time period for the story, and written a rough draft of the first chapter. It could have so easily ended there, as school started the very next day and I began teaching and coaching the varsity volleyball team for the three months that followed. Patiently I waited until Thanksgiving break to begin again.

I have to caution you at this point—if you are reading this note before reading the book, you will find a spoiler. So please stop here and return after you've read the story.

Several characters in this novel are loosely based on true-life members of my family. Will Gano was my paternal grand-mother's brother, who sacrificed his life in France in WWI. He trained as a scout and sniper at Fort Travis in Texas then spent four months in France, one month of which was on the front lines, before being shot by an enemy sniper. This entire section of the novel was pieced together in part by reading Will's correspondence with his family, and the letters of his close friend,

Sergeant A. H. Haney. The letter from Captain Dewitt Neighbors to Ralph Gano in chapter 16 is authentic. Will and Sergeant Haney actually made a pact to visit the other's family if disaster should befall either one during the war. Sadly, there is no one still alive in my family to verify a visit to the Gano family by Sgt. Haney. My grandmother, Blanche Gano, Will's ten-year-old sister in the novel, married Henry Rollmann, Mary's brother, whose family lived across the road. Both the Ganos and Rollmanns staked their farms in the Oklahoma land rush in 1893. Will's body was brought home from France in June of 1921. He was buried with honor in the Good Hope Cemetery where my great-grandparents and grandparents now lie.

I have always enjoyed history, family folklore, and adventure. The combination of these three gave me an incredible amount of joy as I wrote this, my first novel. However, there were a few nights when I could not find rest in the wake of researching some of the darker moments in our country's history. The Lexington Race Riot of September 1, 1917, led me to other stories of cruel lynch mobs and race riots across our nation. I am grateful to my parents for raising me to never judge a person by the color of their skin. I have to say that I experienced some gut-wrenching moments during the writing of this book. But I am confident that someday Jesus Christ will come again and all will be made right.

> *And they all sang a new song to the Lamb: "You are worthy to take the scroll and to open its seals, because you were killed, and with the blood of your death you bought people for God from every tribe, language, people, and nation" Revelation 5:9 (NCV).*

I pray that your life has been blessed by reading this story. All for Him,

Kristy Shelton, a.k.a Coachy

Check out these titles by Innovo author Jason Creech:

Rich or poor, popular or unnoticed, we're all looking for the same thing—new life. But if young people don't get things right on the inside, they will never be the happy, successful people they were created to be. Happiness and success are an inside job. This is a book about "S-Words"—the "don't go there" words—those topics that get Sunday school teachers replaced and youth pastors fired: **self-esteem, significance, sex, secrets,** and **suicide.** Dive deeply into the topics we've all wrestled with and discover what God says about life's toughest issues.

Dealing with the S-Words
by Jason Creech and Sandra Saylor

Available Spring 2011 in paperback, MP3 audiobook, Amazon Kindle™, Apple iPad™, and Barnes & Noble Nook™ editions.

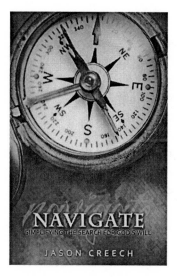

These books will be available Summer 2011 in paperback, Amazon Kindle™, Apple iPad™, and Barnes & Noble Nook™ editions.

New.U by Jason Creech
Are you just getting started as a new Christian? Then you probably have a lot of questions. In this four-week devotional, you'll discover a boat-load of answers. Learn the simplicity of the Christian life. Welcome to freedom. Welcome to the new u.

Navigate by Jason Creech
For most of our Christian journey we search for God's will. But what if we have it all wrong? What if we don't have to search for God's will? What if God's will searches for us?

ABOUT INNOVO PUBLISHING LLC

Innovo Publishing LLC is a full-service Christian publishing company serving the Christian and wholesome markets. Innovo creates, distributes, and markets quality books, eBooks, audiobooks, music, and videos through traditional and innovative publishing models and services. Innovo provides distribution, marketing, and automated order fulfillment through a network of thousands of physical and online wholesalers, retailers, bookstores, music stores, schools, and libraries worldwide. Innovo provides a unique combination of traditional publishing, co-publishing, and independent (self) publishing arrangements that allow authors, artists, and organizations to accomplish their personal, organizational, and philanthropic publishing goals. Visit Innovo Publishing's web site at www.innovopublishing.com or email Innovo at info@innovopublishing.com.

CPSIA information can be obtained
at www.ICGtesting.com
Printed in the USA
FFOW05n0059040414